*To the team at Wardini Books, the best local bookshop
a writer could wish for.*

Catherine Robertson writes smart, spicy romantic comedies, full of real-life emotions and witty banter, while surrounded by cats, dogs, chickens, friends and family in the beautiful wine country of Hawke's Bay, New Zealand.

Sign up for Catherine's newsletter
for bonus extras and first dibs on special deals!
www.catherinejrobertson.com

instagram.com/catherinerobertson11
facebook.com/catherinejrobertson.author

Also by Catherine Robertson

You're So Vine

Corkscrew You

KISS MY GLASS
Flora Valley

CATHERINE ROBERTSON

One More Chapter
a division of HarperCollins*Publishers* Ltd
1 London Bridge Street
London SE1 9GF
www.harpercollins.co.uk
HarperCollins*Publishers*
Macken House, 39/40 Mayor Street Upper,
Dublin 1, D01 C9W8, Ireland

This paperback edition 2024

1

First published in Great Britain in ebook format
by HarperCollins*Publishers* 2024
Copyright © Catherine Robertson 2024
Catherine Robertson asserts the moral right to be identified
as the author of this work

A catalogue record of this book is available from the British Library

ISBN: 978-0-00-865805-2

This novel is entirely a work of fiction. The names, characters and incidents portrayed in it are the work of the author's imagination. Any resemblance to actual persons, living or dead, events or localities is entirely coincidental.

Printed and bound in the UK using 100% Renewable Electricity
by CPI Group (UK) Ltd

All rights reserved. No part of this publication may be reproduced, stored in a retrieval system, or transmitted, in any form or by any means, electronic, mechanical, photocopying, recording or otherwise, without the prior permission of the publishers.

Chapter One

FRANKIE

I'm a practical gal, but there's one hill of superstition that I will die on. And that is: never challenge Worse.

You know what I mean. Shit happens and you say, "Well, at least things can't get worse." Big mistake. Huge. Because Worse is always listening.

Case in point: my day. This morning, I got into my car to go to work, and the battery was dead. My fault. Last night, I dropped a Snickers bar into the void under the driver's seat and switched on the interior light so I could see better. Found the candy. Forgot to switch off the light. My neighbor has jumper leads but she was at the dog park with Murray. (Yes, Murray is the name of her dog; she also has a cat called Phillip.) Was therefore forced to Uber and pay an extortionate surge pricing fee.

Got to work and was greeted by my manager with her "this will hurt me more than it'll hurt you" face on. I'll spare you the details but in short, I work for a big multi-state divorce and family law firm, and they want to shift me to an office in another state. And not just any state! Minnesota! I have nothing against Minnesota, except that I currently live in San Diego, California, lowest temperature around 50°F. Okay, so I grew up in a part of Northern California where it can get a bit chilly in winter, but it does *not* get so cold that your eyeballs freeze. I don't do winter sports. I play pickleball, and I go dancing – indoors. The only ice I'm fond of is in my beer cooler.

Technically, I can decline the offer, but law firms are big on hierarchy and working your way up the ladder. I've just been made an Associate Attorney. One step up from a Junior Associate Attorney, and approximately a million parsecs away from the top level of Partner. I chose family law not because I'm ambitious but because I wanted to make a difference. I want cases I can get my teeth into, and if I refuse to shift to Frozen Eyeball, Minnesota, I'll be handed the files no one wants to touch.

I have a week to think about it.

So that was my working day. I hemorrhaged more money on an Uber home and had just eased the cap off a cold beer when I heard a sound like a champagne cork popping, followed by an ominous gurgling. I own a two-bedroom cottage, and my home-brew set-up is in the laundry. I peered around the door to see my five-gallon carboy (for those who aren't into this stuff, it's the container that holds the beer) shooting a geyser of amber liquid up so high it was splashing off the ceiling. My guess is that the blow-off tube got something stuck in it and the pressure built until the stopper couldn't handle it. Nothing I could do but watch until it finally stopped gushing. My laundry was awash in beer, but I decided the clean-up could wait until after I'd eaten. I mean, it was hardly going to get any worse between now and then, was it?

Never. Challenge. Worse.

Thirty minutes later, I've got dinner in front of me, but I've barely stuck a fork in my mac 'n' cheese when my phone rings. Screen says "Shelby". My older sister by three years, who still lives in the Armstrong family home and manages our family vineyard in Flora Valley. Whereas I moved away to go to law school and stayed away. I never wanted to see a grape again in my life.

My sister and I are very different people. I'm direct, no nonsense, and I inherited our late father's pale blond hair and, let's say, full-bodied physique. Shelby's more like our mom to look at, a slender strawberry-blonde, full of bouncy perky optimism mixed (and I say this with affection) with a streak of super random weirdness. Occasionally reminds me of Dee Dee in *Dexter's Laboratory*, except that Shelby doesn't have a malicious bone in her body. Last year, my sis married Nate Durant, a Harvard boy who's basically been forced to become less uptight because there's no such option living with Shelby. I went to their wedding last November. Met Nate's four siblings, who seem pretty cool. Except for one brother. *He* is a sexist arrogant douche.

I set down my fork and pick up the call.

"Shel, what's up?"

"Frankeeeeee!"

Uh oh. Wailing is never good.

"I'm PREGNANT!"

"Wow."

That's ... good, I guess? I'm only twenty-six, so I haven't spent much time thinking about it.

"I'm due in AUGUST!"

Quick math tells me it probably happened on the wedding night. Fair enough.

"Okay, so—"

"That's the CRUSH!"

Right. The famous Flora Valley Wines crush. When the grapes are foot-stomped in big bins and the whole community is invited to help out. It's a big event, full of party spirit, and the only fond memory I have of the family wine business.

"I'm sure you can bow out," I say. "I mean, no one would want your waters breaking in the grape bin."

"Bacteria can't survive fermentation." Shelby flips suddenly into professional wine-maker mode, and then right out again. "But that's not the PROBLEM!!!!"

"What *is* the problem, Shel?"

All I can hear is a muffled damp sound. As I said, I haven't spent any time researching pregnancy and childbirth, so I'm not about to take a guess. But if Shelby's crying, it must be bad. She's a weirdo but she doesn't lack courage.

"I've got pre-eclampsia," Shelby finally hiccups. "I just got a diagnosis today."

Amazingly, I *do* know all about that because our mom had it when she was pregnant with me. Her blood pressure got so high, there was a risk I'd be starved of oxygen and nutrients in the womb. She had to be hospitalized during the last month, and I had to be delivered prematurely or we both might have died. I spent my first three weeks of my life in a neonatal unit incubator.

"Shel, I'm so sorry," I say. And then I utter the fateful words, the ones Worse has been waiting for since I got up this morning. "How can I help?"

"Come and stay with us!" Shelby implores. "Help us out and keep me company! I'm going to have to sit on my patootie for the foreseeable, and Nate will wreck himself looking after me *and* the vineyard, poor lamb."

Yes, my sister says "patootie". Like those people can't roll their tongues, she's genetically incapable of swearing.

"Why me? Why not ask Mom? Oh, right…" I remember now. Our hippy mother is about to go to Europe to do some woo-woo walking tour along an ancient pilgrimage path.

"Don't tell her!" Shelby pleads. "She knows I'm pregnant but thinks everything is fine, so she's coming back two weeks before my due date. If she knows I'm not well, she'll cancel her whole trip and I'll feel terrible."

"And none of your friends can help?"

"They have jobs," says Shelby.

"Shel, *I* have a job," I protest. "And before you say it, no, I *can't* work remotely. I deal with real people, who need me there in person."

"*I* need you," says Shelby. "And I thought you said you weren't that happy at work…?"

My sister doesn't quite wheedle but it's close.

Thing is, she's not wrong. Even before the threat to send me to Corpsicle, Minnesota, I'd not been loving my workplace. Too many people, *so* many processes. Cases get accepted for how they can boost the firm's reputation, not on how much the people need our services. I may have moaned about this on one of our irregular Armstrong family zooms.

But it's poor form for my sister to use it against me as emotional blackmail.

"I don't hate it enough to quit. But I suppose I could always ask for some compassionate leave…"

Too late, I realize that my sister will take this as an iron-clad commitment.

"Thank you!!" says Shelby. "Come for July and however much of August before the baby is born! It's those last weeks that are the riskiest for me. And that's when it's full on in the vineyard, as you know."

Oh, yeah. I know. I spent eighteen years as unpaid labor until I left home for good. Okay, more like thirteen years; Dad waited until we'd passed toddlerhood at least. All four of us Armstrong kids worked to help Dad make wine, because our profit margins were so low, it was the only way he could keep food on the table. I understand why he did it, but it would have been nice to have a choice. Three of us kids left as soon as we could – me, and my two big brothers. Scattered like quail. Only Shelby stayed. Only Shelby cared enough to try to save the business after Dad died, and Mom didn't want it. Shelby managed to find one investor who didn't laugh her out of town, and that guy brought in her future husband, Nate. Between them, with Nate as manager and Shelby as winemaker, they clawed Flora Valley Wines back from the brink and fell in love in the process. I'm glad it worked out for them. And yes, I feel guilty that we abandoned Shelby. But do I feel guilty *enough* to spend as long as six weeks in the place I couldn't wait to leave?

"Shel, I have a laundry room that's become a beer pond, and a dead car. Can I think about this and call you back?"

"You can have your old bedroom," says my sister. "And you can set up your home-brew in one of the sheds. The pigs will be super stoked to see you."

"I'll call you in the morning," I say. "Goodbye!"

I sit in silence and realize that Worse has won. My sister's personally asked for my help and that means more than I ever expected it to. Right now, I need a mop and bucket, my neighbor's jumper cables, and an order to commit me into a lunatic asylum for willingly making my life ridiculously complicated. So help me, it looks like I'm going home.

Chapter Two

DANNY

PSA: Don't match with an online date when you're pretty sure they're seeing someone else. Someone you're acquainted with. Distantly, but still – no excuse.

Of course, I say all this now in hindsight. Or half hindsight because I'm having trouble seeing out of one eye.

"Jesus, Danny! Who gave you the shiner?"

My older brother, Nate, has decided to FaceTime me instead of call. He only does that when he has something heavy to tell me. Can't wait to find out what it is.

"A guy who objected to me having a drink with his girlfriend the night before," I say.

"Did you know it was his girlfriend?" A typical Nate question.

"I assumed they'd recently broken up, but didn't actually check beforehand…"

Nate has his tight judge-y face on. He's a paragon of duty and upstanding behavior. It comes with the territory for the first born, but Nate takes it to extremes. I'm smack bang in the middle of us five Durant siblings. The only one not to go to college. I've built a great business trading in classic cars, but it's not exactly one of the top-drawer careers our father had planned for us all.

"Don't start," I warn Nate. "*I* wasn't the one putting myself out there when I wasn't available."

"True," said Nate. "But you should have checked."

"I got slugged in the kisser," I say, snippily. "Is that enough punishment for you, or should I go order a hair shirt from Penitents 'R' Us?"

Nate grins. "I've got a subscription to their newsletter, *Flagellation Monthly*."

He puts his serious face back on. By which I mean his usual face.

"Danny, Shelby's pregnant."

I'm confused. This should be cause for congratulations, but he looks like someone died.

"Was that not in the plan?" I ask. Shelby, my sister-in-law, is a little loose when it comes to organization, to put it mildly, but Nate plans everything.

"A little in advance of schedule," he admits. "By about three years."

"But you're happy, right? This is a *good* thing." I have a sudden thought. "I'm going to be an uncle!"

"I'm happy," says Nate. "We're both thrilled. But there's a complication: Shel's just been diagnosed with pre-eclampsia."

"I have no idea what that is. If it involves needles, don't enlighten me."

I can cope with many terrifying things, but when it comes to injections, I'm a gigantic weenie.

"It's a condition that puts both mother and baby at serious risk," says Nate. "Basically, Shelby's blood pressure is way too high, and she'll have to be monitored regularly and given medication. And the baby might have to be delivered early."

"Shit, Nate, I'm sorry," I say. "I thought we were all done with the medical crises."

Last year, our dad, Mitch, nearly died from a heart condition because he refused to acknowledge that goji berries and willpower wouldn't cure him. And hard on the heels of that, our sister, Ava, underwent tests for all sorts of alarming ailments. Luckily, the final diagnosis was burnout, which is debilitating but curable. Ava's now chilling and looking after horses for a riding therapy charity. Well, as much as any of us Durants knows how to chill.

"Yeah, well, let's hope shitty luck *does* come in threes because now we're done," says Nate. "Thing is, Shel's on medical orders to do as little as possible so as not to raise her blood pressure any further. I'll need to do the physical parts of her job as well as mine. So, uh…"

A weirdly sheepish look crosses his face. My big brother is not normally on the back foot. He likes to be in control at all times.

"Look," he says, rapidly. "I wouldn't ask if there was any other way I could manage this. But money's still tight at the winery, and I was wondering … could you come up for a month or so in July/August and take some of the admin load off my shoulders?"

"You want *me* to help *you*? At Flora Valley Wines?"

I just need to be clear here. Nate *never* asks for help. He'd sooner sink beneath quicksand than grab an offered rope. He was only half-joking when he said he subscribed to *Flagellation Monthly*. Nate's like Atlas, born to carry the biggest burden he can shoulder.

"I know it's not ideal, asking you to leave L.A.," says Nate. A flicker of a grin. "Unless the guy who gave you the shiner isn't done yet?"

"Ha, ha," I reply. "He ambushed me, threw the punch, and ran. I think he's done."

"So—?" Nate's looking sheepish again. "Do you think you can help out?"

Mentally, I review the business commitments I have coming up. I travel a lot anyway, and there's nothing that absolutely requires me to be in L.A. I live alone. No dogs or cats, or the weird kind of pets that people in this town like to own. Bactrian camel, anyone? Until last year when Dad almost died, I'd been a little slack about coming home for visits. Dad can be a pain, but Mom is great. It'd be nice to see more of her.

That said, I don't know about actually *living* with my parents for any length of time. One stretch of eighteen years was enough.

Nate's read my mind. "You can stay in the workshop accommodation. Cam's moved his barrel-making gear to his new place, so you won't be bothered. You'll just have to be okay about sleeping alone in the middle of a dark forest."

"Who says I'll be sleeping alone?" A typical me quip.

"I'll need to rely on you, Danny." Nate's back to being judge-y.

That stings. I might give the impression of a stereotypical car dealer, all slick showmanship and shiny teeth, but I'm not in the habit of letting people down.

"You *can* rely on me. But I will need time to keep my own business going," I tell Nate. "You know I've been approached by a film production company who want to make a reality TV show about buying classic cars? We've made a demo tape and they're hoping to pitch it to Netflix."

"I did not know that," says Nate. "Congratulations."

I'd half expected him to pour cold water on the idea. But I guess he needs me more than I need him right now. And even though we do butt heads, I'm fond of my big bro. Plus, who knows what kind of hidden vehicle gems are under tarpaulins in barns around Flora Valley. You'd be amazed what people hang on to when they've no idea how much it's worth.

"I'll sort things out here, and come up mid July," I say. "And I appreciate that you reached out. I know you had a choice of airline today, so thanks for flying with Dan-Air."

"You're a dick" is my beloved brother's parting shot. "But I'm grateful. And I owe you."

It's possible he might live to regret those words.

Chapter Three

FRANKIE

Seems Worse isn't done with me.

I thought it had backed off, because when I went to quit my job, my bosses had a sudden change of heart about shipping me off to Icepick, Minnesota. Apparently, I'm super valuable to the firm – one of their rising stars – and they'd hate to lose me. I explained the situation with my sister and, lo and behold, they offered me six weeks' special leave. Without pay, of course. They're lawyers, not humanitarian aid workers. I checked the fine print of their offer because I am also a lawyer, then signed it. I worked the weeks of my notice period, asked my neighbor to keep an eye on the house, and patted Murray and Phillip goodbye. Last night, I packed up my car with a small suitcase, a large amount of home brew gear, my pickleball paddles and wiffle ball, and at dawn this morning, I hit the road.

Nine hours later, driving through Verity, the closest small town to the family winery, I'd started to think that maybe this wasn't such a bad decision. Verity is ridiculously picturesque, with one main street that looks like it's been pickled in early 1900s aspic. I drove past The Silver Saddle, the locals' preferred drinking establishment that I intend to enthusiastically patronize. Past the world's worst pizza joint. Past the Cracker Café, owned by Iris, who's proud of her Florida roots and possibly killed by hand the stuffed alligator that adorns one wall. Past Bartons Hotel, which was bought a few years' back by a rich, posh British guy named Ted. On the outside, Bartons has echoes of the old watering hole it used to be, but on the inside it's like a velvet-lined, jewel-studded Birkin bag, pure luxury that's not for mere mortals. I was introduced to Ted at Shelby and Nate's wedding. My impression was surprisingly favorable, but I won't be drinking at a place that serves cocktails made with pine pollen and butterfly pea flower tea. Nate said he had one with octopus milk in it. I'm barely okay with adding a hint of citrus to my homebrew.

I might have also been sucked in by the summer beauty of the place. The lushness of the foliage, the pops of orange and yellow wildflowers, the homemade signs selling free-range eggs, freshly picked strawberries, and organic leafy greens. Not that I eat leafy greens, but it's nice to know there's plenty for others. It's July and by mid-August the grapes will be hanging heavy on the vines. At Flora Valley Wines, we grow organically, we harvest by hand, and we stomp by foot to break the skins to release the grapes' color and flavor. It's the oldest and most demanding way to make wine but Dad wouldn't hear of doing anything with machinery. "Rollers crush the stems and seeds," he'd say. "And all their harsh tannins come right out into your wine. Make it taste like shit." Unlike my sister, Dad swore like a trooper. He wanted his epitaph to read *Hey, cancer! Fuck you!* but Mom rightly vetoed that. Despite making constant jokes about having cancer, Dad fought it hard right to the end. I think all us kids couldn't quite believe it'd get him, but it did. I came back home for the funeral and left again pretty quickly afterwards. My excuse was a new job, but the truth was I couldn't handle being around that much collective grief. I was forced to be independent from a young age and I still like to handle things in my own way. And on my own.

My independent nature might be why I'm still single at twenty-six. More likely, it's because most single men my age are immature, self-centered jerks. Every so often I dip a toe online only to find it's still sewer water. Being what my high school PT teacher so delightfully once termed "a bigger girl", I make sure I'm open about that. Show a full-length photo and list all my vital statistics so there's no surprises when we meet in person. Yet somehow, men continue to be surprised. The last one came out with this gem: "I guess I was so focused on your pretty face, I forgot to check out the rest of you." My face *is* pretty, but it's also capable of expressions that can make a speeding locomotive back up and take a dirt road. The guy left the bar in such a hurry he forgot to take his knock-off Gucci sunglasses with him. I'm wearing them now.

And I'm glad of it, because as soon as I take the turn up the gravel driveway that leads to Flora Valley Wines and the old family homestead, my summer-mellowed mood vanishes, and I can feel my eyebrows slant downwards like an Angry Bird. I didn't have a terrible childhood, certainly not compared to some of the kids I come across through my work, but it was tough being the youngest of four. Especially as I wasn't loud and jokey like my oldest brother, Jackson, calm and patient like my next brother down, Tyler, or Dad's favorite, which was my sister, Shelby.

I suppose, to be fair, I was a tricky kid. I have a tendency towards defiance and some pickiness around food. Dad was loving towards us all, but when the vineyard got busy, he drove us like we were building pyramids in Egypt. No rest, no excuses. No summer camps. No hanging out with friends, wiling away the long, hot days. And Mom – well, let's just say that she had a lot on her plate. Four kids, and a husband who refused to do anything the easy way. Which meant a huge amount of effort for a chickenshit amount of money. If Mom hadn't been an artsy hippy who loved to grow herbs and vegetables, we might have been regulars at the soup kitchen.

In short, in case you hadn't gathered by now, coming home makes me tense. I think the word some people use is "triggered". Even though I have a job that pays well, a decent balance in my savings account, and thanks to an unexpected inheritance from an aunt, my own home, as soon as I'm back in Flora Valley, I feel unsettled, unstable, like everything is suddenly precarious. I know it's irrational, but knowing only makes it worse.

There it is again. Worse. Haunting me.

I motor carefully up the gravel driveway. My car is a 1967 VW Karmann Ghia two-seater convertible. It's baby blue, and deeply impractical. I would not part with it for the world. I park it in the shadow of the new Flora Valley Wines pick-up, a sedate replacement for Dad's ancient rattling Dodge. I remove the sunglasses and check my reflection in the rearview mirror. Eyebrows still angry. I push them up with a finger, but they snap right back down again. Might as well give in and, like the scorpion in the parable, accept what's in my nature.

"Frankeeeeeee!"

Shelby's outside the front door, waving both hands above her head like a lunatic. It's hard to miss the pregnancy bump stretching her T-shirt but in all other respects she looks exactly the same: petite, strawberry-blonde, and dressed in her standard summer uniform of faded cotton tee, denim cut-offs low-riding under the bump, and ratty sneakers. I'm in *my* standard summer uniform of fifties-style sundress, this one in yellow and white gingham, cropped cardigan, and strappy sandals. I have a yellow chiffon scarf holding back my hair. I'm the poster girl for retro cute, and I love the false impression it gives about my personality. People expect demure and sweet. They get me.

Shelby is also grinning like a lunatic. She's so pleased to see me, and I can't help but be pleased to see her. My sister is a genuinely nice person, open hearted and unfailingly positive. It's impossible not to feel happier in her presence. My eyebrows respond accordingly. It's safe to take off my sunglasses.

"You look *adorable!*" Shelby gives me the best hug she can with a bump in the way. "How can you possibly look so fresh after such a long drive? I'd be a crumpled, stinky mess!"

"I spritz," I tell her. "And I use men's deodorant."

"*That's* why you smell so sexy." Shelby releases me from the hug and grabs my arm. "Come on inside. We got some beer in specially, and Nate's made cheesy dinner food."

"Wait." I pull back, and Shel looks at me, worried.

"Are you okay?" I ask her. "Truthfully now."

My sister takes a deep breath. "I'm a little scared. I'm very bored and restless, and I've got six weeks of this to go. It sucks."

"But you and the baby are doing all right? Medically?"

"So far." Shelby rubs her bump. "Baby's fine and kicking up a storm at night. If it happens when you're around, I'll let you feel – it's wild!"

"Sure." I hope I'm never, ever around. It'd be like *Alien*.

"And I get monitored every week," adds Shelby, glumly. "I'm on tablets, and Nate's bought a blood pressure cuff so we can check at home. He may also be thinking about shutting me away in a nunnery for the final month so he can be sure I'll take it easy. Nuns are fierce, you know."

"I know. I've seen *The Blues Brothers*."

"Ooh, we can binge watch silly movies together!" says Shelby. "Nate refuses to see *Ghostbusters* for a tenth time, and he never liked *Wayne's World*."

"And you still married him?"

"He has so many other good points."

I swear Shelby's face turns into that love-hearts-for-eyes emoji. Ugh.

"Come on," she pulls me by the arm again, "Nate can't wait to see you, either."

I think that's overstating my brother-in-law's fondness for me. But he'll be relieved Shelby now has company, and reliable company at that. He knows I take no shit.

"She made it!" Shelby announces, as we enter the kitchen.

Nate steps away from the counter, where I see he's plating up quesadillas. Good man.

"Frankie," he says, kissing my cheek. "Really appreciate this. Thank you."

Nate can be overly intense and earnest but he's always sincere. I like him.

Then he gestures towards someone sitting at the table. "You know my brother, Danny, don't you? He's come to lend a hand here, too."

And there he is. The sexist arrogant jerk I had the misfortune of being seated next to at Shelby and Nate's wedding. Smiling at me with those too-perfect teeth and that fake sheen of inflated ego. Handsome and trades on it. Can't be trusted for a second. Danny Durant. Come to lend a hand at Flora Valley for who knows how long.

Hey, Worse! Fuck you!

Chapter Four

DANNY

Uh oh. Incoming. And thanks, Nate, for only letting me know five minutes ago that Shelby's little sister, Frankie, would be part of the home help team, too. She and I met at Shelby and Nate's wedding last year, and I'm still not sure what I did to piss her off. Judging by her expression, she's still pissed about whatever it was. Fun times ahead, it seems.

Thing is, despite the fact she's trying to turn me into a toad with her angry eyes, I'm blown away by how gorgeous she is. I was struck by her at the wedding, and I'm doubly struck now. That heart-shaped face, with ridiculously perfect luminous skin. Those huge blue eyes, and the mouth, wide and generous, with like a cupid's bow in the middle. I'm no poet, so I've probably made her sound like some weird identikit picture. Frankie Armstrong is gorgeous, let's leave it at that.

And she hates me. For some misdeed I guarantee she believes I ought to apologize for. If I knew what it was, I might.

"Danny," she says. The minimum viable acknowledgment.

"Frankie." Two can play at that game.

Nate, ever alert, spots the ice crystals in the air between us. Glares at *me*, as if it's *my* fault. I resist giving him the middle finger.

"Is there something Shelby and I should know?" he demands.

Shelby, who's getting beer out of the fridge, stares at us, wide-eyed. "What? What do we need to know? Is it bad? Please don't let it be bad. These days, I burst into tears when I can't solve Wordle."

Now, it's Frankie giving me a look, an accusatory arch of her perfect eyebrow. Right, okay then – everyone blame Danny. Durant family dropout. Least serious. Least reliable. I should be used to it by now, but it still rankles.

"I don't know." I don't bother to disguise my irritation, not even to spare Shelby. "Frankie here has taken against me for some reason."

"For *some* reason?" says Frankie. "You mean, there could be so many reasons, you're finding it hard to choose?"

"Here we go," I hear Nate mutter under his breath.

"I seriously have no idea! All I was doing was shooting the shit with the other wedding guests at our table," I say. "We were all slightly drunk and telling funny stories. You got huffy and stormed off."

"Wow," said Frankie. "Just – wow." She looks at Nate. "Has he always had his head stuck this far up his own asshole?"

Nate holds up his hands in the "leave me out of this" gesture.

"Frankie!" Shelby steps in. "You never told me you got angry with Danny at the wedding. Why didn't you say something?"

If you weren't concentrating, you'd have missed the flicker of discomfort cross Frankie's face. I see it, and I store it up as interesting intel.

"I was hardly going to bitch and moan on your wedding day," she says. "And besides, I'd forgotten about it until I saw him again."

"Sure," I say. "Obvious. Absolutely *no* grudge held all this time."

"Well, can we please resolve it now, so I don't have a complete meltdown?" Shelby says.

"I second that," Nate says. "Let's get this sorted. And quickly, before the quesadillas congeal into one solid mass and I drink more beer than is good for me. Frankie, you seem to have the better memory." Another barb in my direction. "You give us your version of events."

Frankie raises her gaze to the ceiling as if petitioning the divine for patience.

"He was telling everyone at the table about an older woman who'd tried to pick him up at a bar, and he described her as a 'cougar'," she says. "I objected to the term as sexist. Said it was a hypocritical double standard that society approved of older men dating younger women but saw the opposite as predatory and pathetic. He laughed and replied that he had no problem with dating older women – as long as they weren't an 1860."

"An 1860?" Nate asks.

He's trying to catch my eye but it's me who's now staring at the ceiling. It's all coming back to me. *Slightly* drunk might have been understating it.

"Oh, you've not heard that term, either?" says Frankie,

with pointed glee. "Your brother was happy to translate for everyone present. It's when a woman's so fit she looks eighteen from the back, but when she turns round, you get a nasty surprise, because she's actually—"

"Got it," says Nate, grimly.

"That's so sexist!" says Shelby. "And ageist! Danny, how *could* you?"

"It was a joke!" Let's face it, I have no other defense. "Not a great one, I admit, but—"

"And I did not storm off in a huff," says Frankie, who will clearly need to have the last word in every argument. "I left before I committed an act of violence that would make me lose my job."

"Did it involve an ornamental pumpkin?' Nate asks. Their wedding had a Fall theme.

"Cocktail skewer," Frankie replies.

"Those wedding cocktails were outrageous," says Shelby. "I got squiffy just from the smell."

I consider pleading overindulgence in cocktails as an excuse, but Nate gets in first. He's got his judge-y face on again.

"Okay, so now we've aired that unfortunate incident," he says, "let's wrap it up. Danny, Frankie's a hundred percent correct – that was a gross and sexist comment."

"Jesus. All right, I apologize. Mea culpa for being an insensitive pig."

"Ungracious but acceptable," says Nate. "Frankie, it's been months. Can you let it go and move on?"

"I guess," says Frankie, grudgingly.

"And can you promise me that you'll do your very best to

get along?" says Shelby. "My blood pressure won't cope if you're constantly sniping at each other like you're in some 1940s screwcap comedy."

There's a pause. Frankie gives me a cool stare with, if I'm not mistaken, a hint of humor.

"Screwcap comedy, huh?" she says.

"The cork comedies are staging a protest," I reply. "Claim they were there first."

"Are you making wine bottle jokes?" says Nate. "Because if so, I may have to slap you both."

Shelby's grabbed the platter of quesadillas and now she plonks it down on the kitchen table.

"Eat!" she orders. "Stuff your faces so I don't have to hear another stressful word!"

Nate hands Frankie a glass and a bottle of beer. She assesses the label in a manner that's familiar to me. I look at classic cars that way. Wanting to love each one but knowing that only a few will live up to expectations.

"It's a new local craft place," says Nate. "Hope it's not undrinkable."

Frankie pops the cap like a pro. Pours it into the glass slowly and holds it up to the light. Smells it as if it was a fine wine. Takes a mouthful.

"Decent," is her verdict. "Pine and citrus on the nose. Pineapple, mangoes, and melon in the taste. Some hoppiness. I generally prefer more bitter than sweet, but this is pretty good."

Nate grins at Shelby. "Runs in the family, I see."

"Frankie makes her *own* beer," Shelby says to me, then

turns to her sister. "I've cleared a space in one of the sheds. Did you bring your laboratory?"

"For creating Frankenbeer?" I suggest. "Drunk, of course, out of Franken steins."

I haven't had the best run with jokes, but that one, at least, was inoffensive. I hope.

Amazing. Her mouth lifts into half a smile. "Could be my label if I decide to go commercial."

Nate hands Shelby a glass of water, which she accepts glumly. He cracks two more beers, and hands me one. Raises his to me and Frankie in a toast.

"To you two. You answered the call and earned our undying thanks."

"Yes, thank you." Shelby is sniffling into her quesadilla. "Being sick and pregnant sucks. It's so good to have family around me. I love you."

My chest suddenly constricts, and I'm not sure why. Maybe it's because the Durants aren't big on saying "I love you". We prefer to express our fondness for each other through banter and insults. Our childhoods were packed full of competitive sport and academic pressure, so we never had time to just hang out. And soon as we became adults, we all moved away. We do our best to come home for Thanksgiving, and Christmas, but that's only a few days each year. Hard to feel like you even *have* a family when you spend more time apart than together.

Nate and Shelby are locked in a soft, murmured conversation. Despite being complete opposites, the love and respect they have for each other shine like a light. This house is their home, and I doubt they'll ever leave it. They're about to have a child. First of several, I imagine.

I make the mistake of glancing from them towards Frankie. I expect her to turn away, but she regards me with an expression that's more curious than aloof. As if she's wondering what I'm thinking. Fortunately, for me, all the Durant siblings have a masterful poker face. A necessary skill when you grow up highly competitive and can't afford to show weakness.

Frankie lifts up the platter and offers it to me. A truce? Maybe. Guess I'll take it. Along with another quesadilla.

"Thanks," I say.

She nods once, curtly, and replaces the platter. Picks up a quesadilla for herself, off which dangles strings of melted cheese. I watch, mildly hypnotized, as she catches the strings with one finger, then directs said finger into her mouth, and slowly removes all the cheese with her full, glossy, peach-colored lips.

Fuck. I have a semi. From watching someone eat cheese. From watching Frankie Armstrong eat cheese. The woman who, given that she can hold a grudge for months, probably still hates my guts.

At least when I'm out in the cabin in the dark woods, no one will interrupt me doing the five-knuckle shuffle. And yes, that's another shocker, but this time, I'm not saying it out loud.

Chapter Five

FRANKIE

I don't know what's worse. Sleeping in my childhood bed, or *not* sleeping in my childhood bed because I can't stop thinking about a guy I despise.

My old bedroom is an instant flashback. Shelby hasn't changed the décor in here one bit. Same crocheted blanket on my bed. Same faded wallpaper with oak leaves and acorns on it that's peeling in places (I may have helped it along when I was little). Same desk with Powerpuff girl stickers on it. Same posters of Pink, and Warhol's multi-colored Marilyn Monroe on the wall.

Mom and Dad bought this house along with the vineyard the year they got married. It was built by the previous owner, who favored a folksy arts and crafts style, all exposed timber and shaker tiles, wagon wheels in the garden, that kind of thing. The house wasn't renovated once in the whole of my eighteen years at home, because we had zero money. If Mom hadn't been arty, the place would have been a crusty dump. But she had the ability to brighten even the shabbiest corner, with arrangements of flowers and leaves, painted stones, and candles. She covered the walls with our kiddie daubs, family photos, and the very occasional painting she had time to make. She wasn't ashamed to scour the thrift stores for old furniture, and colorful throws and cushions to cover the holes. She used mismatched crockery before it became cool.

The one thing she never skimped on was new clothes and shoes for the four of us. We didn't have extensive wardrobes by any means but everything we wore was of good quality. I'm not sure if it was a front, to make the world believe that Flora Valley Wines was doing well, or if Mom refused to let us be singled out and shamed by the wealthier kids at school. Funny now that Shelby looks like she picked out her clothes from Goodwill's reject pile, and I'm the vintage thrift queen. Okay, I do have two quality suits for work but one's blush pink and the other's primrose yellow. I like to ensure my opposition underestimates me. It's fun to watch their faces when they suddenly realize they're being eaten alive by the young lady who looks sweet as candy.

I should turn out the bedside lamp, but I know I'll only lie awake in the dark. I stare at the Warhol Monroe print. It's the version with an orange face on a fuchsia background, lemon yellow mouth, and neon pink eyelids. I chose it because it's the most unsettling combination, the most unlike the real Marilyn. People, and not just guys, often call me "Monroe-esque". They think it's a compliment, but they're basically saying I should be grateful that I resemble her because I don't fit today's ideal of beauty. That's why I have the Warhol poster, to remind me that image is fleeting, and that character is everything.

Character. Integrity. Honesty. That's what I value. And

that's what Danny Durant lacks. He is a values-free void. A black hole of assholery. So why can't I stop thinking about him? And why is my body reacting to these thoughts? Was there something other than a hint of tropical fruit in that craft beer? Crushed up Spanish fly, for example?

Okay, let's do what I do best: assess the facts. Danny Durant is handsome, no doubt about that, if you like the preppy look: blond hair, neatly trimmed but with a wave on top as if he's casually pushed it over with his fingers, tanned skin, straight nose like the statue of David, and a firm chin. Great cheekbones like his older brother, and the same eyes, but where Nate's are a striking topaz blue, Danny's are softer, like denim. His mouth is softer, too, and mobile, like he smiles a lot. The kind of mouth you just *know* will be terrific to kiss…

Speculation, Ms Armstrong! Stick to the facts. Of course, he smiles a lot; he's in love with his own boorish, sexist wit. And don't call it a smile – it's a *smirk*!

The quip about the cork comedies wasn't bad, though. He was quick, I'll give him that. And he did apologize. Reluctantly, true, but I've grown to be skilled at judging body language, because it's super useful in court, and I can tell the difference between someone squirming because they've been caught out, and someone feeling genuine shame. Danny was in between, but definitely leaning towards the side of shame.

And I was watching him when Shelby said she loved us, loved having her family around. He flinched – actually flinched. Just for a second but I caught it. I'm not sure what it means, yet. He's allergic to expressions of affection? I can identify with that. Maybe he feels like he doesn't deserve love? That's getting into deeper psychological territory than I care to tread, but it's not out of the bounds of possibility. Some people are born with an iron-clad sense of self-worth – my dad was one of them. Most of us have to fight a little harder to feel like we matter.

Danny's staying in the tiny house attached to the workshop, built by our Flora Valley Wines handyman and barrel-maker, Cam Hollander. Cam's another who's had a hard road to self-respect. Dad and Mom rescued him over a decade ago, when Cam was a homeless army-vet hanging on to life by a thread. Now, Cam's shacked up with yet another Durant sibling, Ava, in a cute bungalow, surrounded by fruit trees. They took the cantankerous winery goose, Dylan, with them. Mrs Dylan died, and seeing as geese mate for life, Cam and Ava are the only family Dylan's got. Nate was relieved; he was convinced, accurately, that Dylan hated him. Shelby was a little sad, but her house and yard are full of cats and dogs. So many, I've long since given up trying to count or identify them. There are also two Vietnamese pot-bellied pigs, Ham Solo and Luke Skyporker, but they're kept in a pen. Ham and Luke were the only pets I really bonded with. I'll go visit them tomorrow morning, take some food scraps, see if they recognize me.

I start thinking about Danny again. A natural segue from pigs, obviously. The workshop and tiny house are about twenty minutes' walk cross country, through vines and trees. Four minutes' drive by road, but I didn't see a vehicle except the pick-up, so I assume Danny got settled in, then came over on foot. I know he trades in classic cars, and I'd be interested to see what he drove up from L.A in. I wonder if he'll give my baby blue Karmann Ghia the seal of approval or dismiss it as a faddish piece of crap? Maybe I *want* him to hate it, so I can keep on hating *him*?

Do I hate him, though? Or do I hate what he represents? The privilege that good looks and good breeding automatically unlocks. The Durants are wealthy, like super rich. Shelby says they live in a mansion with five hundred rooms. Okay, she might have been exaggerating in her usual feverish fashion, but unlike us, the Durant kids grew up with money. They went to the best private schools, the best colleges. The youngest two, twins Izzy and Max, are at MIT and Juilliard School of Music, for crying out loud! I got my law degree through a community college, and I had to work my ass off to get my foot in the door of a decent legal firm. Danny Durant has had everything handed to him on a plate, and he may as well have a badge of entitlement embroidered on his preppy shirt instead of that stupid dude on a polo pony.

Right, job done. I've worked myself up to a low boil of loathing. Not so much that I'll lie awake churning with rage. Just enough to ensure any thoughts I have of Danny Durant stay up in my brain and don't slide downwards to parts that are easily swayed by soft blue eyes and a kissable mouth.

Of course, I can't guarantee what might happen in my dreams.

Chapter Six

DANNY

This accommodation is getting a bad review on Tripadvisor. For one, it's so small, I keep banging into things. And all those things are made of wood, so I'm amassing a sweet collection of bruises. It's two floors, bedroom up, but bathroom down, and the stairs are narrow, so you want to reduce your liquid intake well before hitting the hay or risk a broken femur from a nighttime fall. There's no closet at all, only drawers built into the bed base. I've had to hang my jackets and shirts on the only two hooks available, which are downstairs, naturally, on the inside of the front door. The kitchen at least has been stocked with granola, milk, fresh fruit, and a bag of coffee grounds – *but there's no goddam coffee maker*!

Okay, I found the coffee maker. Next door in the workshop. It's no Wega, but it does the job. I've had my espresso now. Hulk Danny has retreated, and sane, calm Danny is back in charge, and very grateful to my brother and sister-in-law for the supplies, and for letting me stay here and not at my parents' place. I take a (wooden) chair out front and sit, listening to the birds, watching a few clouds scud across the patch of sky that's visible through the trees. It's barely seven o'clock and the sun is already warming my skin. It gets hot round here, but not like an L.A. summer, where it can feel like you're breathing through a greasy washcloth. The air here will stay fresh and dry, and the sky will stay blue. I grew up an hour's drive away and spent many a summer's day sweating on a soccer field, wishing I was fruit picking, or corn pollinating, or fighting off rabid sugar-hyped children while dressed as a Chuck E. Cheese mascot. Anything except running up and down scorched turf in a pair of tight nylon sport shorts.

I wasn't the only Durant kid suffering. Nate and Ava competed in track, and Ava, because she's the major overachiever of our family, also did a horsey thing. Eventing! (Thank you for recharging my brain, espresso.) The twins, Izzy and Max, played tennis because they could do it together. I chose soccer mainly because it was the one sport Dad knew nothing about. He was more interested in individual achievement than team sports, anyway. I got my driver's license soon as I turned sixteen and didn't need my folks to take me to matches. Soon as I turned eighteen, I left home. I can happily say I've never again worn tight nylon sport shorts.

Nate and Shelby asked me over for breakfast. I'll walk. I'm getting the hang of the path, though last night, I was grateful when Shelby handed me a torch. I could have driven, but I knew I'd have a few drinks and the cops round here are vigilant and pitiless. If I lose my license because of a DUI, I lose my business. And I'm hardly qualified to do anything else. Not even being a mascot at Chuck E. Cheese.

As I come out of the trees at the end of the path, I spy Frankie Armstrong exiting the house. She's in a fitted short-sleeved pink shirt and faded rolled up jeans, and a tingle of appreciation for her sensational figure zings straight to my guy down south. But any primal instincts are swiftly stifled by my conscience. Last night, I admit, I indulged in some hand-held hijinks, but it doesn't seem right to have sexy thoughts about a woman who's real and less than twenty feet away. All right, so we've established that I can be a meat-brained chauvinist with a couple too many strong cocktails in me, but on the whole, I do try to be respectful. I didn't sleep with my online date after I'd confirmed she was spoken for. I thought about it but that's not the same thing.

Now that my brain is in charge again, it becomes curious about where Frankie is headed. I realize the only way to find out is to follow her. So, that's what I do.

I haven't spent much time exploring the Flora Valley Wines property. Nate and Shelby's wedding was in the big barn, but there are a lot of other outbuildings, some filled with what I assume is wine-making equipment, some with barrels, and others with sacks of … stuff. There's a garden with herbs, vegetables, and flowers planted between the spokes of an old wagon wheel. There's a rustic bench on which a scarecrow in a flannel shirt is seated. I feel like I should be wearing overalls and chewing on a stalk of hay. And I've lost sight of Frankie.

Spotted her. Over by… Are those *pigs*? I always thought pigs were pinkish white and cute, like in *Babe*, but these two look like VW Beetles covered in black bristly hair.

I hesitate. Frankie's talking to the pigs. The tone of her voice sounds gentle, affectionate, and I'm not sure she'd want me to know she has another side to her than her usual full frontal attack mode.

Too late. She turns her head and sees me. Lurking. Spying. I see her mouth rise in that ominous half-smile and brace myself for the above attack.

"Do you want to help me feed them?" she calls over.

No, I absolutely do not. They look like they should have muzzles on, like pit bulls or Hannibal Lecter. But I know a challenge when I hear one and a Durant never shies away from a challenge. Us kids, especially me, Nate and Ava, would enter into mortal combat over anything: comparative size of meal portions, who gets the last banana, who deals the cards out for a wholesome game of *Go Fish*. I know most people think *Monopoly* can be a homewrecker, but you've not seen the Durant family play *Go Fish*.

"Sure," I respond, and casually saunter over.

Jesus, the pigs are even more intimidating close up. Must weigh a hundred-fifty pounds, easy. And they've got tusks the size of rhino horns sticking out from their bottom jaws. They're both staring at me with itty bitty black eyes sunk deep among the bristles. Sizing me up as a potential snack, no doubt. I hear pigs can eat every part of a human body.

"Except teeth."

Frankie has read my mind.

"They'll crunch up bones, no problem, but can't digest teeth."

"Good to know for when I next need to dispose of an enemy."

Frankie hands me a plastic bowl. In it are a stump of

lettuce, four wrinkled carrots and an indeterminate number of cabbage leaves.

"They'll take the food from your hand," she says. "Just don't let them eat the actual flesh."

She enjoyed my humiliation last night and she's enjoying this. But as I said, no Durant walks away from a challenge, even if we risk losing all our fingers. I pick out a carrot because it's the longest, lean over the pen railing and gingerly dangle it in front of—

"That's Ham Solo," Frankie informs me.

"How can you *tell*?"

"Ham's got the lighter skunk stripe above his snout."

She really digs these pigs. Ham takes the carrot, and demolishes it, grunting and crunching. My fingers remain intact. I offer a carrot to the other pig, who grunts and crunches with an enthusiasm that's actually kind of endearing.

"And who's this guy?" I ask. "Or gal?"

"Guy," says Frankie. "Luke Skyporker. My brothers named them."

I know just enough about farming to know that most animals are expected to earn their keep … and that most of them don't get named. These guys are definitely freeloaders.

"Why do you have pigs as pets?"

I can only see Frankie's profile, but her jaw muscle gives a telltale twitch. Interesting.

"One of Mom's rescue missions."

Her tone is casual, but I'm not fooled. Something more is going on here.

"Morons buy potbellied pigs when they're super cute

babies," she says. "But they don't bother to even google what they might look like when they're fully grown."

I find Ham and Luke more appealing now that they've shown a preference for food scraps over body parts. But it's true. They're about as soft and cuddly as a saguaro cactus.

"These two were found wandering on a hill trail by one of our vineyard workers. He managed to entice them up a ramp and onto his truck, and brought them here," Frankie continues. "Mom decided to keep them. Soon after, both my brothers left home, and Shelby was busy with Dad learning the wine trade. Fell to me to be mistress of the pigsty."

Again, the jaw twitch. And the words hanging in the air, unsaid. I know what it's like to have a complicated relationship with a parent. In my case, my dad. I've only met Frankie and Shelby's mom a couple of times, and we never got beyond small talk. Lee Armstrong's the same age as my mom, late fifties, and if it's not weird to say this, they're both very beautiful women. Lee's a willowy redhead, an artist, serene, and with a strong streak of woo-woo. Come to think of it, she couldn't be more different from Frankie…

… who says, "Okay, we're done here." Grabs the bowl out of my hand and tosses the rest of the scraps into the pen. Ham and Luke set upon the pile and start chowing down exuberantly. I admire them. They love their life. They have no inhibitions. We could all benefit from being more pig-like.

"Coffee?" Frankie's expression is neutral, her tone now coolly polite.

"Hell, yes." Be enthusiastic. Be more pig. "My emotional support beverage. Bring it on."

Chapter Seven

FRANKIE

Pretty sure Danny wouldn't be so gung-ho for coffee if he'd tried my sister's brew before. We sent a sample to the poisons control center for testing – purely out of scientific curiosity, you understand – and apparently, it *is* fit for human consumption. It just happens to look and smell like it crawled out of the La Brea tar pits after 50,000 years of being entombed in pitch. Those who know call it The Black Death. Those who don't better have a defibrillator handy.

Nate stands well back while he fills Danny's cup.

"Bro, don't be stingy," says Danny. "Fill it to the brim!"

"This is Shelby's coffee," says Nate. "Not Starbucks."

"Hey!" Shelby protests.

She's at the stove making pancakes, bless her. I offered to, but she refused, saying she had to do something productive, even if it was only whisking milk into original fluffy texture pancake and waffle mix.

Danny's puzzled. "What's wrong with Shelby's coffee?"

"Nothing!" Shelby brandishes the whisk, scattering milky drops.

"Technically nothing," agrees Nate. "And yet…"

Danny takes a sniff, and then a cautious sip. "Woah!" He takes another sip. "This is incredible!"

"Seriously?" Nate and I are a disbelieving chorus.

"It's like a coffee bean survived a nuclear explosion and mutated to have superpowers."

"*Thank* you!" Shelby calls from the stove.

"You know your pupils are soup-plate sized," Nate observes. "If I were you, I'd steer clear of operating heavy machinery."

"I could lift up heavy machinery!" says Danny.

"My point, exactly," says Nate. "No second cup for you."

Nate carries the ancient, possibly cursed, stovetop maker back to the safety of the kitchen counter. I glance at Danny – who winks at me over the top of his coffee mug. Normally, I'd be instantly ready to counterpunch unwanted gestures from men, but either I've been mildly sedated by the smell of pancakes cooking or the gesture isn't as unwanted as it might be.

As usual, when I'm caught on the hop, I suppress all reaction. Which, so I've been told, gives me resting bitch face.

"Let me guess," Danny says, with a sigh. "Winking is sexist."

"It's in the same ballpark as being told to smile," I say. "One of the gauntlet of microaggressions we women run on a daily basis."

Danny looks glum. "My sister, Izzy, talks about

microaggressions all the time. You get a lot of them when you're a woman in science, apparently. Macro ones, too."

"Law's the same," I confirm. "As is any field that used to be dominated by men. Which is pretty much every field."

"My sister, *Ava*, on the other hand," Danny goes on, "is a can of whoop-ass waiting to be opened. When she's pissed at you, she lies in wait, then leaps out and gives you a snake bite arm burn. Her technique is exquisitely painful."

I need to clarify. "You mean, she did this when you were kids?"

"Last Christmas!" Danny says. "I ate a piece of gingerbread that she'd earmarked for a midnight snack. I wasn't to know this, seeing there was no note, but I paid the price nonetheless."

He rubs his upper arm, like it still hurts. Shelby talks about Ava a lot, but I've only met her in passing. While I'm here, I must get to know her better.

"Pancakes are ready!" my sister calls. "Come and get 'em!"

Hot damn. I've been looking forward to these all morning. There's a huge stack, and I help myself to four, which I douse with maple syrup and top with a half-stick of butter. I see there's fresh fruit on offer as well. Someone will enjoy that.

When you grow up as the youngest of four, especially with two older brothers, you don't wait to be told to eat. Mom used to try to say grace, or some hippy words of gratitude that were her version, but it was hopeless. Soon as food was on the table, we'd grab it. I completely understand Ava wanting to hurt someone for stealing her gingerbread. Jackson snatched a chicken drumstick from my plate once and I would have stabbed him with the carving fork if Dad hadn't caught my hand.

So, I'm back at the table and happily munching away, licking the occasional trickle of buttery syrup off my fingers, when I notice Danny staring at me. He hasn't moved. Still sitting there with his coffee gently glooping away like a primordial mud pool. Of all the things that rile me – yes, obviously, there's a long list – being stared at while eating is near the top. Above it sits comments like, "Are you really going to finish all that?" and "No salad?" and the best one of all, "Good to see you enjoying your food", which translates as "Oink, oink".

"What?" I demand. "You've never seen a girl eat a pancake before? Have carbs and sugar finally been outlawed in L.A.?"

My god, he blushes. He actually goes bright red. And *springs* out of his chair to leave the table. Is he embarrassed because I called him out for being bad-mannered yet again? Or because he got caught staring? If the latter, why was he staring? Perhaps he never *has* seen a girl eat a pancake before? Rich people are weird about food, so it's possible.

Nate and Shelby are both at the table now, eating, though I do notice that Nate first checks his pancakes for any lumps of mix that haven't quite been incorporated. I know from experience that my sister's cooking, indeed her whole life, can be a mite haphazard. I also know that Nate cooks, and I assume he does it like he does everything else, with finicky perfectionism.

Danny slinks back into his chair, avoiding my eye. I get busy giving him a good hard payback stare. He senses it because he hunches lower over his plate, but he still won't look at me.

Nate, however, misses nothing.

"Frankie," he says, quietly, "you promised."

I did, didn't I? And I am a woman of my word. Damn it.

"After breakfast, I thought we could get our heads around the next couple of months," Nate says. "Agree roles and responsibilities, set goals, align our expectations, etc."

Unexpectedly, Danny flashes a glance my way. He's grinning again.

"Are we going to throw stuff against the wall and see if it sticks?" he asks his brother. "Or run it up the flagpole and see if it salutes?"

"I'll throw *you* against a wall," says Nate. "What's wrong with what I said?"

"Nothing," says Danny. "If you studied business at Harvard. The real world, however, is a little less … uptight."

"Are you going to be an asshole the whole time? Or just every second day?" Nate's getting hot under the collar.

"Please don't fight!" says Shelby. "I'm an invalid, remember!"

Danny looks sheepish. "Sorry, Shelby," he says. "It's an ingrained Durant habit to bust each other's balls. Apologies, bro. I'll do better."

"Apology accepted," says Nate, still tight-lipped.

"How about *I* run the discussion?" I suggest. "I've got a special pen, just for meetings."

"For taking notes?" says Shelby, my faithful stooge.

"For threatening to jab in people's eyeballs if they get off track. It's a fountain pen. Pointy nib."

"Sounds good to me," says Nate. "Give me twenty minutes to clear up, and we'll get started."

Chapter Eight

DANNY

It wasn't my fault, I swear. I just happened to look over while Frankie was licking syrup off her fingers and then I couldn't look away—

Shit. I need to get these thoughts under control. Before I start imagining a fully naked Frankie Armstrong covered in whipped cream and sweet, sticky syr—

Jesus, Danny! Go find a bucket of cold water and stick your head in it! And leave it under until the bubbles stop because you're making a huge *ass of yourself!*

I settle for heading outside into the fresh air and breathe deep to regain control. It's being back around family that's the problem. Every time I'm in the company of my siblings, I regress. Old habits; right from when I was little, I was always the prankster, the entertainer, the court jester. When you don't fit the Durant mold, you have to find some way to stand out. But it's not a talent that ages well. I need to step up and be better. In particular, I need to be better than Frankie Armstrong.

Now, that's a complicated thought. Do I want to be better than her, so she'll finally take me seriously? Or am I channeling the Durant competitive spirit into yet another challenge: which of us, Frankie, or me, gets to be the MVH, most valuable helper?

No point in unpicking it any further. Whatever my underlying motivation, the end game's the same: to win.

A rattling rumble down the driveway signals the approach of some aging vehicle. I'm always interested in vehicles, no matter how old and crappy, so I wait to see what it is. In doing so, I forget to wonder about *who* it is.

An ancient Dodge pick-up truck pulls up and stops with a judder of brakes and, I swear, a whistle of steam.

"Hey, Danny!" calls a voice from the open passenger window.

Crap. It's my sister, Ava. Haven't seen her since last Christmas. I resist the urge to rub my arm because it'll make her cackle with glee.

She hops out of the cab with her usual speed and agility. Ava is tiny, with short dark hair and Nate's gentian blue eyes. She lives in all-black activewear, and zips around like Tinkerbell's evil twin. She used to be an exercise rider for a top Kentucky racehorse stable but got burned out and quit. Before she was diagnosed, she was tested for all kinds of frightening conditions, so the burnout verdict was a big relief, especially for my mom. Secretly, none of us other siblings thought Ava would have the patience for the extensive rest that's needed if you don't want burnout to turn into chronic fatigue. But by that stage, she was in a committed relationship with Cam Hollander, Flora Valley Wines handyman and barrel maker, and the slowest moving human on the planet, so she was forced to chill. I can see Cam now, just starting to think about getting out of the truck. Meanwhile, Ava is already across the gravel and up in my face.

"What are *you* doing here?" I demand.

Attack is the best form of defense when you're a Durant.

"Same reason as you," she says. "Cam and I are part of Team 'Make Sure Nate Doesn't Have An Aneurysm'. Shelby will be fine, as we all know. It's Nate who's most likely to push himself to breaking point."

"Yes, but why *you*? Cam works here. He's already part of the team. You're still supposed to be taking it easy, aren't you?"

"Doesn't mean I won't have a useful role," she says. "For example, I could train *you*."

"To do what? Trot on command?"

Ava smiles and pats me on the arm. I try not to flinch.

"I already trained you to do that years ago," she says. And heads past me to the house.

Goddammit. I walked right into that one.

Cam's finally made it across the gravel. He was a soldier, served in Afghanistan, and he's a big unit, a head taller than me and Nate, and built like the kind of tree he makes barrels from. Despite it being high summer, he has on his usual plaid flannel shirt, sleeves rolled up, and old work-roughened jeans. I suddenly become a little self-conscious of my sage green polo shirt and chinos. Told you I should be wearing overalls.

"Hi, Cam. Good to see you again."

As well as being the slowest human in existence, Cam's also the least verbal. He lifts his chin in response. Could mean, "You, too." Could mean, "Still haven't forgiven you for teaming up with Jackson Armstrong last year and roasting me about my love life."

I give it a fifty/fifty shot. Nate was teasing him that night, too, and Cam and Nate are best buds now. Nate's probably closer to him than he is to me.

"Danny."

Speaking of. My beloved bro appears, to summon me curtly from the house. Ava's right: Nate's in stress mode, which makes him extra impatient and officious. I breathe in some more fresh air, so I can deal with Nate being overbearing, Ava looking for every opportunity to goad me, Cam possibly plotting retribution, and Frankie being ... distracting.

I could, you know, stop thinking about her in terms of competition. I could offer to collaborate, work with her. That way I could keep the promise of good behavior I made to Shelby and Nate. It would bring Frankie and me closer, and who knows where that might lead?

Or I could accept that I'm a Durant and we'd sacrifice vital body parts before conceding defeat.

I square my shoulders and walk back inside.

Chapter Nine

FRANKIE

So, this is Ava Durant, the sister in between Nate and Danny. As I said, she and I have had limited interaction thus far, but given what I've heard about her, I have a feeling we'll get on like a house on fire – or a nuclear power plant exploding. She's sitting opposite, giving me the kind of stare I could take offense at, except that there's no judgment in her expression, only curiosity and anticipation, like she can't wait to see what I'm made of, too.

Cam ambles into the kitchen at his usual leisurely pace and smiles at me. I've known Cam since I was fourteen and have watched him evolve from borderline-feral drifter to settled, skilled craftsman. Ava is the first serious relationship he's had in all that time. Well, apart from my mom. I don't believe that they did the actual wild thing, but they were very close. Dad never minded because, like I said, he had an iron-clad sense of self-worth, which allowed him to be generous and forgiving. I *did* mind, but by then, I was used to being overlooked. Although Cam has never done anything intentionally to hurt me, wouldn't be capable of it, I still have mixed feelings about him. He knows nothing of this and never will. So, I smile back.

"Hey, Cam," I say. "How's the new place?"

This is another story. Cam and Ava rent a cute bungalow on a decent-sized piece of land outside of Verity. The house used to be owned by my late aunt, Debra, my mom's half-sister. Debra was adopted out when my grandmother was very young, and she and Mom didn't know the other existed until last year. By the time the two reconnected, Debra was dying of cancer. I got to meet her only once, at the hospice, where she laid out her plans for her will. Having no immediate family of her own, she left us four Armstrong siblings fifty-thousand dollars each, and her house, for us to keep or sell as we wished. My brothers and I had no plans then to return home, so we agreed to rent it to Cam. The tiny house he built beside the workshop had room only for one, and he and Ava were an item by then, so it seemed a good solution: house got cared for and we got to share in a little rental income. I'm practical first, and emotional second, so I could put aside any ambivalence I have regarding Cam. I mean, he's not shacking up with my mom, is he? That would be a whole different basket of snakes.

"House is great," says Cam, in his usual fulsome manner.

"Come and visit," Ava says to me. It sounds more like an order than an invitation. "You too, Danny," she adds, as her brother finally joins us at the table. "Come and witness me being all cozy and domestic."

Danny gazes at her aghast. "Doesn't that breach some law of the universe? Like dividing by zero?"

"Ava's asked for Mom's jelly recipes," says Shelby. "Their garden has a lot of fruit."

"Jesus." Now Nate looks aghast. "Have you alerted emergency services?"

"I remember when Ava made a volcano for school science class," says Danny. "The kitchen counter had to be completely replaced."

Ava grins, happily. She's obviously impervious to insults. No doubt because she knows she can dish them out better than anyone. And if that doesn't work, she's always got snake bite arm burns to fall back on.

She smacks the tabletop.

"Let's get on with this meeting, people," she says. "I have things to do, surfaces to scorch."

Nate looks to me. I have a notebook and my trusty fountain pen. I'm ready.

"Right," I begin. "The purpose of this meeting is to figure out how we can all work together without killing each other, so that Shelby can have a restful last six weeks of pregnancy, and Nate can feel confident that the business won't implode the instant he takes his hands off the reins. Is that a fair summary?"

"Except that Nate's hands will be cold and dead before they loosen their grip," says Danny.

"Not helpful," I say, before Nate can retort. "But a good example of how we're *not* going to behave over the next two months."

Danny's mouth tightens in annoyance. Too bad. I've been handed control here and we'll run things my way.

"Shelby?" I ask. "Have you got a big jar?"

She hops up and fetches a preserving jar from a cupboard. Every year, at seasonal intervals, Mom made at least ten thousand pounds of preserves, and roped in us kids to peel, pit, de-seed, and chop. We were at it for days. I'm meanly satisfied to note that this empty jar is one of a whole empty-jar collection. My sister has clearly never made another preserve since, either.

"Perfect." I take the jar and set it in the middle of the table. "You know how some families have swear jars? This is our insult, barb, jibe, slur, backhanded compliment, aspersion, and put-down jar. Every time we commit an offense, we put our name on a piece of paper and drop it in. On the day of the crush, the person with the highest name count gets to take a punishment chosen by everyone else. Fair?"

"That's genius," says Ava. "I like the way you think."

"I'd take that as a compliment," Nate tells me. "Even if it sounds like a threat."

"Name in the jar!" Ava insists. "That was a slur!"

"It was a statement of fact," Nate protests. "And everyone here will back me up on that."

"People!" I raise my voice, and they quieten down. "Now we've established our code of conduct, let's talk about who's doing what. Let's start with Cam because he's easiest."

Cam looks alarmed, as he always does when he becomes the focus of attention.

"Cam keeps on doing what he's doing," I say. "Repairs, maintenance, barrels." I look up at him. "What else? Leafing? Crop-thinning?"

"Leafing's done," he says. "Crop-thinning soon."

"Okay, what are those?" Danny sounds reluctant to admit that he's the only one of us who hasn't a clue.

I'm about to answer him, but unusually, Cam speaks up. I

sense a small powerplay here. Cam isn't the macho type at all, but by claiming ownership of the knowledge, he's asserting dominance over Danny. Intriguing. I wonder what Danny did to get Cam's goat.

"Leafing's when we remove about a fifth of the grape leaves," say Cam. "Gives the grapes air and sunshine. Prevents disease. Crop-thinning happens if there's too much fruit on the vine for it all to ripen properly. It's been a heavy crop this year, so we'll thin pretty soon."

"You'll liaise with Javi and Doug to organize additional labor?" I ask.

Cam confirms with a nod.

"And then it's veraison!" says Shelby. "My favorite part of the year!"

"Verayzhun?" Danny's a little pink around the cheeks. I should feel sorry for him, but if the tables were turned, I know he'd be gloating.

"It's when the grapes change color," says Shelby. "So exciting! That's when we start doing a heap of lab testing, to check on acid and sugar levels, how the flavor's developing. You can pretty much tell then if it's going to be a good vintage."

"You have *some* idea," says pessimist Nate. "But until those grapes are safely harvested, you can't count your chickens. Anything could happen before then. Rain, hail, fire—"

"Plague of locusts," says Danny, attempting and failing to make a joke.

"There actually *was* a locust plague that ruined vines, in Jerusalem in 1915," says Nate. "Laid waste to every piece of vegetation. Broke into beehives, too, and ate the honey and the bees. Truly biblical."

"Well, there's an easy way to avoid that," says Ava. "Don't open the Ark of the Covenant."

"I think we can rule out locusts," I say. "Nate, you'll help Shelby with testing, right? I'll put my hand up for lab runs. I like the drive to Martinburg."

Danny's head shoots up like a dog spotting a rabbit. "Where's your car parked? I didn't see it."

"Far side of the Flora Valley Wines pick-up," I reply. "It's small. Easily hidden."

"What make is it?" he says eagerly.

"Car-talk later, Danny," warns Nate.

Danny slumps back in his chair. I almost feel sorry for him. I also observe that the petulant look does good things for his mouth, making it fuller, not tighter. He's mussed his hair in frustration, too. It's cute. Suits him.

Focus, Frankie!

"The instant the grapes are fully ripe, we push go on the harvest," I say. "Because we don't do anything the easy machine way at Flora Valley, it will be all hands on deck for the picking. Except Shelby, of course—"

"I'll be huge by then!" she says, cupping her bump. "Size of a planet!"

"Not Ava, either," Cam says, giving her a look. "It's hard, physical work. Too hard."

"I love it that you care," she replies, with a smile. Though it doesn't exactly sound like she's agreeing.

"It *is* hard," I confirm. "Plus, we work all night."

"All *night*?" Danny asks.

"Too hot during the day," says Cam. "Grapes stay fresher. So do we."

"I asked Danny to help only with admin," says Nate. "So, he can bow out of the labor if he wants."

Because Nate is earnest and sincere, he has no idea he's just confirmed his brother as a soft-palmed city-slicker who wouldn't know hard work if it bit him. Danny understands, though, and he's not happy.

"I'm in," he says, curtly.

"Then the famous Flora Valley Wines crush event," I say, "where the whole community comes out to watch the grapes getting stomped. We'll need all hands on deck again. Or all feet, whatever."

"Can I organize that?" says Ava. "I have terrific people skills."

There's a pause. Everyone looks at the insult jar. Everyone keeps quiet. Ava cackles, delighted.

"As it happens, I've already asked Jordan and Chiara if they'd help," says Shelby.

Jordan and Chiara are her two best friends.

"Great!" Ava resists all hints. "We'll be like Charlie's Angels! The Angels of the Crush!"

"And Danny and Nate will divvy up the admin." I might as well push on. "Don't need to hear the details. You'll work it out."

I set down my pen. "Consider me a floating helper," I say. "Though Shelby gets first dibs."

"So I don't go stir crazy," she says, "Frankie and I are going to binge watch ridiculous movies like *Ghostbusters*."

"Again?" Nate's expression is pained.

"And *Broadcast News* and *Gross Pointe Blank*," I add. "Joan Cusack is my idol."

"Ooh, good choices!" says Shelby. "And can we also re-watch *Gilmore Girls*?"

"If I can watch *The Princess Bride*," I bargain.

"Of course!" says Shelby. "No ridiculous binge-watch is complete without it!"

I close my notebook. "And on that note, I declare this meeting over. Everyone clear? Everyone pumped?"

Nodding of heads all round.

"Nice job, Frankie," says Nate.

Praise from my brother-in-law is high praise indeed. I'll take it.

"Danny, you can go look at Frankie's car now," he says to his brother.

"No, thanks." Danny gets up from the table. "I've got to make some calls. If that's alright with you?"

His tone is neutral, but the message is clear. Danny's pissed with us.

"It's fine," says Nate. "Meet me in the office in an hour?"

"Sure." And with barely a nod to anyone else, he stalks out.

"What's up with Danny?" says Ava. "Apart from his usual sore-loser attitude?"

"Ahem." I rip a strip from a page in my notebook, hand it across. "Name in the jar."

"I'm first!" says Ava, gleefully. "Yuss!!"

Nate rolls his eyes at me and shakes his head.

"Buckle up, Frankie," he says. "It's going to be a bumpy ride."

Chapter Ten

DANNY

I should be used to it by now – feeling like the odd one out, the dumb one, the laughingstock. No matter how well I do in life, what I achieve is never going to be respected by my family. I mean, I've just ended a call with a producer who's raving about me as a new TV talent. He says I've got real screen presence, like a preppy James Dean – which I'll take as a compliment. Most car shows are hosted by guys with fat mustaches and tattooed biceps, or Jay Leno. I'll be the first to appeal to a young female audience as well as the dudes. The producer's managed to get a pitch date with Netflix. He's talking big time worldwide syndication. I could be famous. A global celebrity. A "*Car*-dashian", lol.

But even if I was on the cover of every magazine and hordes of adoring fans followed my every move, my nearest and dearest would still find a way to put me down. My dad would call me out for my inflated ego – a Durant can win, but you've gotta stay humble. Nate would nag me about fame being fleeting, and when I'm no longer flavor of the month, he'd say he told me so. Ava would probably troll me on social media and undermine every compliment I receive. Izzy and Max wouldn't even notice because they're too busy with their own amazing achievements. Mom? She'd worry about me like she always has. Mom's a kind person but it's always been obvious that I was the one kid she lacked confidence in. The one with no discernible talent except making jokes. The one who could never keep up with his siblings. The one who left home with no qualifications or prospects, at least none that would sound good in the Durant family Christmas newsletter.

Fuck it. I have to shake myself out of this funk and focus on what's good for me. I have to be my own cheerleader, my own best friend. I have to keep trusting my instincts because they've served me well so far. I can't let myself be rattled by anyone, especially not Frankie Armstrong. She's spending too much rent-free time in my head at the moment, and I need to evict her. Best way to do that is to find another pretty girl to take my mind off things. Might spend this evening at Bartons Hotel. Even if there's no one to hook up with, I can guarantee I won't run into family there. Nate's too much of a homebody now; Ava, too. Frankie's a beer girl and the only beer they serve at Bartons is top drawer, such as a German fermenting lager for forty-five bucks or a vintage Danish brew that costs a hundred. I doubt even Frankie loves beer that much.

Now I have something to look forward to, I feel better about returning to the fray. I walk back from the workshop. Being among the trees and vines clears my head. Living in L.A. has all the advantages you'd expect from a big, vibrant city, but I make a point of getting into nature whenever I can. I have a place in Santa Monica, and from there I can get to Topanga

State Park, hike, or run the trails. Keeps me fit, blows away the cobwebs. Think I'll look up the best trails around here. It'll give me an excuse to get away on weekends. If Nate allows it. Or rather Frankie, seeing as she seems to have appointed herself boss.

She's in my head again.

Focus on the trees, Danny. Smell the summer air. Feel the sun on your skin. Look how the light bounces off that chrome bumper…

That's a 1967 VW Karmann Ghia convertible. On the far side of the winery pick-up. I jog over to take a closer look. It's in mint condition, not a speck of rust. Original pale blue paintwork. Dark blue soft top. Pristine white interior. Two doors, four-speed stick shift and a capable 1500cc motor. A perfect example of its kind, and still coveted by a certain type of buyer. Those who love that retro vibe.

Shit. This is Frankie's car. Hastily, I check to see if she's watching. Cars are my area of expertise. It's natural for me to show interest. But I don't want Frankie to think she has leverage over me because she owns a car that's desirably tradeable. Best thing to do is pretend I'm only mildly impressed, as if mint classic Karmann Ghia convertibles are a dime a dozen in L.A. Besides, even if Frankie was tempted by my offer, she'd refuse it on principle. Principle being that it will be a cold day in hell before she allows me anything I want. Including my dignity.

Time to meet Nate at the winery office. I have a lot of skills with admin, so I can be useful to him. Plus, the office fits two people maximum, and Nate, I hope, will be off most of the time doing wine-making stuff and caring for Shelby. With luck, I'll have the place all to myself.

Kiss My Glass

As I'd hoped, Nate shot the gap after a couple of hours and left me to it. It was fun getting under the hood of a different type of business. Pun intended, of course. Nate's got systems up the wazoo, so it was simple enough to get a picture of how Flora Valley Wines operates. Nate was right about the skinny profits. They rely on a solid, loyal base of customers, who in good years, take everything they've got and don't quibble too much about price. In bad years – well, it looks like there've been a few of those.

Nate and Shelby do have plans. Shelby's going to make a special higher-end wine for Bartons Hotel, but that will take another year to perfect. Nate and Shelby would love to build a wine tasting space, so they can be part of the whole Sonoma county experience. But construction costs money. The fifty grand Shelby inherited from her aunt would have helped, but now they've got a kid on the way, so my guess is they'll want to put that money into a college fund. No kid of Nate's will be deprived of a first-class college education.

But those are problems for the coming days. Right now, I'm back in my cramped quarters getting spruced up to go to Bartons. They have a strict dress code, but I'm in the mood for pushing it a little, so I ditch my usual preppy style and adopt a Euro-look, a light-wool double-breasted blazer and matching pleated pants, with a classic white T-shirt. The blazer and pants are light gray with a subtle crosshatch pattern and pale green buttons. White leather sneakers and a pair of vintage Armani sunglasses and the look is complete. No tie, but I think they'll let me in.

In case you've been wondering, I didn't drive up here in a classic car. They're fun but can be unreliable over long journeys, so I'm here with a 2009 BMW M3. Rear wheel drive with a 420-horsepower V8 engine. Goes like greased lightning. This evening, however, I will be leaving it at the workshop and going by Uber. As I said, the cops around here are pitiless, and as I'm currently dressed like the kind of guy they'd love to throw in jail and strip search, I don't intend to take the risk.

The doorman at Bartons lets me in without fuss. Nate says he finds the interior like being in a David Lynch movie, and it *is* pretty surreal. Blue and gold velvet, subtle concealed lighting, and artfully arranged twigs. Booths for privacy, tables for those who want to gawk. No seats up at the bar so everyone has a clear view of the bar staff at work. They have flawless good-looks, and their movements are weirdly precise. After a few drinks, you might start to believe they're androids.

One charming young android shows me to a table. Being a good salesman means you know how to size up a room quickly and unobtrusively. Mainly an older crowd tonight. A business vibe, and by business I mean the petrochemicals and diamond mining kind. Numbers with more zeros than seem possible. Who knows how these people get in and out of Bartons without being spotted anywhere else. Teleportation? Secret tunnel system built for international espionage?

"Danny Durant, as I live and breathe."

Speaking of espionage. At my elbow is Chiara, one of Shelby's two best friends. Chiara knows everything about everyone. According to Nate, that's why her name includes the letters C.I.A.

"I heard you were in town," she says. Of course. She probably knew I was coming to Flora Valley before I did.

"You're looking good," she adds. "Extra kudos for the green buttons."

Chiara works here at Bartons as a hotel receptionist, but she's obviously not on duty now. She's wearing a shimmery gray rib-knit dress. Because it's high-necked and maxi length it should look demure. Because it's skintight it does not.

Now, before there's any misunderstanding, I do not want to hook up with Chiara. She's as beautiful as a model, her looks a striking combination of her Italian father and Afro-Caribbean mother. She's also made it very clear that she has aspirations beyond Verity, and even beyond the rarefied atmosphere of Bartons and the obscenely wealthy connections she can make here. In a couple of years, when she's saved enough to give her parents a decent nest egg, she'll be jet-setting away. I admire her ambition, and I enjoy her company. But I also like to keep her at a safe distance. Who knows what dude with a private army might take exception to me horning in? Chiara knows martial arts, so she can protect herself. Me, not so much.

"You aren't waiting for anyone," she says. It's not a question.

"Nope," I reply. "You?"

"Probably," she replies, but slides into the chair next to me, anyway.

"Am I going to get a poison dart in the neck if you sit with me?"

She smiles, which isn't reassuring. The android waiter slides up beside us and dispenses two glasses of sparkling water.

"Good evening," they say. "Our feature cocktail tonight is an homage to Moorish Iberia, with vintage Armagnac, Dutch jenever, crème caramel tea, vermouth, an acorn infusion, and a cacao leaf tincture."

"Two, thank you, Aubrey," says Chiara.

"No octopus milk? I'm disappointed."

Chiara ignores me and my lack of class.

And says, instead, "So – you and Frankie. When will you accept that you have a thing for each other?"

PSA: never take a mouthful of sparkling water before Chiara plays her opening gambit. Some minutes later, after I've stopped coughing and the last bubbles have drained from my sinuses, I'm able to speak.

"What the actual?" I say. "Frankie Armstrong hates me!"

"Yes, I gather you've been bickering like cats," says Chiara. "It's always fun when a relationship starts off that way. Spices it up no end."

I'm goggling at her, mouth open like a fairground clown.

"You're insane," I manage. "Frankie and I will never have a relationship. For one, I'm not attracted to her."

"Is that the smell of pants on fire?" Chiara says, with a smile. "It could be woodsmoke birch spirit, but I think not."

I give up. I know when I'm beaten. Even Ava bows down to Chiara's skills.

"Okay, so she's gorgeous," I admit. "But come on, she'd rather see me tarred and feathered than naked in her bed."

Of course, that's exactly when the waiter appears with our cocktails. This being Bartons, not a flicker of surprise crosses their face. They've probably overheard plans for world domination, so rough justice with a hint of nudity is a mere trifle.

"You know that for certain, do you?" Chiara asks, after the waiter has glided away. "Without a shadow of a doubt?"

"I don't suppose I can ask *you* to confirm or deny, can I?" I say. "It would save me a lot of time, and potential humiliation."

"I've got you this far—" Chiara removes an entire ikebana arrangement from her glass. "You now accept the possibility of an alternative perspective. That a relationship with Frankie Armstrong is a viable goal. A point to which you were very easily led, might I add. I thought we would have needed at least two cocktails to get you to cave."

"Gee, thanks."

"But now the baton is in your hand, and you need to run with it."

She sips her cocktail. Seems to find it palatable. I suspect that even if it were pure cyanide, she'd have trained herself to overcome its effects.

"Why do you do this?" I ask. "Get involved in people's love lives?"

"Because they need me to." Chiara clinks her glass on mine. "Bottoms up."

Chapter Eleven

FRANKIE

You know when a fly's been buzzing around a room that you're in, and even after it's flown out, you can still seem to hear it? Well, all this afternoon, I've been bugged, so to speak, by the phantom buzz of Danny Durant. After he stormed off in a huff this morning, I didn't see him again. I know he was in the office because Nate came back to the house to nail Shelby down to a winemaking schedule. Shelby's more a seat-of-the-pants operator, which drives methodical Nate insane, but they worked it out together with minimum fuss, even though I did see Nate pause for a few deep breaths during the discussion. I'm not sure Shelby's blood pressure is the only one under strain here, but it's not my place to say.

Afterwards, Shelby and Nate went to meet Cam to talk winemaking and barrels and stuff, and I was left to my own devices. I decided to set up my home brewing kit in the shed space Shelby earmarked for me. I could have brought more gear, but my car is small, so I packed the basics: kettle, hydrometer, couple of carboys, testing jar, stirrer, sanitizer, and, of course, bottles and caps. I didn't bring all the ingredients I need with me because I want to check out what's available around here. Might visit the new local craft brewery Nate mentioned. It'll probably be run by a couple of blowhard bearded dudes sporting beanies and tattoo sleeves, but their beer was pretty good, so I'll chance it.

I sound super chill, don't I? But no matter what I did today, the whole time, my mind kept circling back to Danny. I'd expected to see him back at the house at the end of the day, and when he didn't appear, I confess I went to the office looking for him. I had no idea how I was going to explain myself, but as it turned out, I didn't have to. Office was empty. Pride meant I couldn't bring myself to ask Nate or Shelby where he'd gone, so I cooked dinner for us three, and ate it hoping that somebody would comment on his whereabouts. And then I had to excuse myself because when I'm frustrated, I am not my best self.

"You all right, Frankie?" Shelby asked me, as I headed upstairs early.

"Sure," I said. "I think the long drive has caught up with me."

"Okay," said Shelby. "Sleep well!"

Spoiler: I did not sleep well. I didn't even try to sleep. I heard Nate and Shelby head up to bed around ten, and I continued to lie awake for hours, wondering where Danny was, but most of all, wondering why the heck I cared.

End result: this morning, I'm a grouch. I have a cold shower to see if that helps. Now I'm shivering as well as grumpy. I dress and schlep downstairs to the kitchen, only to be greeted by my ever-cheerful sister.

"Hey!" she says. "Coffee?"

Why not? I can be cold, grumpy, and now wired.

"Granola or eggs?" Shelby asks.

"Eggs!"

Why did she even ask? She knows my views on the edibility of seeds and nuts.

Shelby's unfazed. "I'll make them scrambled, and not too sloppy, the way you like them."

"You're the best sister in the world," I say, and I mean it. I'm starting to feel better. No bad mood can withstand the combination of Shelby's sunny nature and her coffee.

"Nate out organizing?" I ask.

"He and Danny have actually gone to visit their parents," says Shelby. "Their dad, Mitch, kind of insisted they went. They'll take their mom out for lunch. Mitch will stay home because he's a little ... obsessive about what he eats. They'll be back for dinner."

So, that's another whole day I won't see him. Damnit, what's wrong with me? Why do I care?

Shelby places a plate of eggs in front of me. She's spooned the scrambled eggs into two piles to make eyes and curved bacon rashers underneath to make a smile.

"Cute," I say. "Sorry for being bad-tempered. More than usual, I mean."

"You're probably still tired," says Shelby, sitting down to her own eggs. "Unless it's something else?"

My sister doesn't have a sneaky bone in her body, but I still go on the defensive. "What kind of something?"

She frowns. "Well, I know it's hard for you to be back here. At first, I was sure I wouldn't ask you, because it didn't seem fair to put you in this position. But I really needed family, and—"

"Mom wasn't here," I say, bluntly. "So you were stuck with me."

"No! You were my first choice!"

"I was?" My sister is a horrible liar, so I know she means it. I'm just confused that she chose me over Mom. "Can I ask why?"

Shelby pinkens with embarrassment.

"Okay, here's the truth," she says, rapidly. "I'm glad Mom's overseas right now. She's great, don't get me wrong, but I always feel like she wishes we'd sold Flora Valley Wines. That it was gone and out of the family forever. I feel…" Shelby gets to grips with her thoughts. "I feel like Mom genuinely has to force herself to visit me here. Like being back here saps her soul or something. Does that sound crazy?"

No, it does not. A little woo, but fundamentally sane. I tend not to share personal stuff with anyone, especially family, but this revelation of Shelby's has sparked one in me.

"She was over the winery life years ago," I say. "All my childhood, I felt like she wasn't present. Like her body was here but her inner being was somewhere else."

"Oh, Frankie." Shelby looks stricken. "I always worried that you felt you were on your own."

She reaches out and squeezes my hand. "I'm so sorry. I should have been a better older sister."

"How?" I'm not saying it to be rude. "We were all in the same boat. Caught between parents who loved us, sure, but didn't value us, not really. Mom and Dad never saw us as us. As Jackson, Tyler, Shelby, and Frankie. We were cogs in the big

Armstrong family/Flora Valley Wines machine. We were Borg. No individual identity."

I've gone too far. Shelby's face is all pale and tight. Teach me to break my rule about sharing personal stuff.

"Ignore me," I say, brusquely. "I'm in a bad mood. Let's talk about something else."

Shelby is never upset for long. Sometimes, I marvel that we're related.

"How about you and I go somewhere for lunch?" she suggests. "Somewhere close, so I don't get overtired. Like Iris's café? Or The Silver Saddle? We could get a burger there."

I wonder where Danny, Nate and their mom are going to be. Probably that upmarket place in the center of Martinburg that sells chi-chi kitchen wares. It's well patronized by ladies who lunch.

Before I can respond, Shelby's phone beeps. Again, she frowns.

"It's Chiara," she says. "But I've no idea what she means. It says, '*One down. One to go.*'"

Chiara, Jordan, and Shelby have been a ride-or-die trio since elementary school. They were nice enough to me growing up, but I was never going to be invited into their group. I had my own friends at school, but we've all long since drifted apart. Chiara, Jordan, and Shelby will be tight forever. And, yep, I'm envious.

I'm also wary of Chiara. Jordan's like Shelby, outgoing, cheerful, and kind. Chiara likes knowing things you don't, and she uses her beauty as a weapon. As I said, both of Shelby's besties treated me well, but I've always had the sense that

Chiara views me like a cute, short, bad-tempered toy, an angry Furby. One she could play with, if she had the mind.

Shelby texts a reply. Another beep. "Oh, goody. Chiara can come to lunch, too! She gets off at twelve thirty, so we'll meet her at The Silver Saddle at one."

Oh. Goody.

Chapter Twelve

DANNY

I thought I'd have time to prepare for the first family visit, but no. Mitch rang Nate at the crack of dawn and insisted we both present ourselves mid-morning for parental inspection. As Nate said to me when he roused me out of sleep, might as well get it over and done with.

I'm not hung-over, but I'd like to be. Having dropped her bombshell, Chiara set a limit on cocktail consumption because I need to be on my best form to impress Frankie. A wasted effort, because now I might not see Frankie at all today. I'll be interrogated and disparaged by my father instead. If I were hungover, I'd have an excuse to imbibe hair of the dog. Being slightly drunk would at least cushion me against the worst of it.

"You were at Bartons last night," says Nate.

Luckily, he's driving, otherwise I might have veered into the other lane in surprise.

"Does everyone know my business?" I'm pissed, and I think I have a right to be.

"It was a guess!" protests Nate. "Bartons has this unique aroma, and I thought I could smell it on you."

"Aroma?" I sniff my shirt, even though it's clean on today. "Of what? Money?"

"I think it's more likely to be the bouquet of a thousand and one bonkers cocktail ingredients quietly mutating in the Bartons cellar."

"My drink had acorns in it," I say. "And some kind of tincture. I'm not even sure what a tincture is."

"Meet anyone?" Nate asks, all casual-like.

"No," I reply, curtly. "Had two cocktails. Avoided the gaze of the international arms dealers. Went home."

"Good call," says Mister Play-By-The-Rules Nate. "Three cocktails and I might be bailing you out of a Turkish jail."

"Turkish jail could be more fun than what we're about to do," I point out.

"Well, there's one bright side." Nate turns off the road and starts up our long driveway.

"What's that?"

"They're short-staffed at the riding center," says Nate, as he parks outside the house. "Ava was too busy to come."

Our mom, Ginny, is outside on the front steps, waiting for us. Dad Mitch will be inside because God forbid that he should show enthusiasm about meeting his two oldest sons. To be fair, he has mellowed a lot since his heart scare. But that's like saying there's been a little erosion on Mount Rushmore. He's fundamentally the same rigid disciplinarian.

As I get out of the pick-up, I wonder what Frankie is up to today. Admitting to Chiara that I find Frankie attractive was strangely liberating. Like it removed a blockage and now I can access a bunch of other feelings I didn't know I had. How much I admire Frankie's strength, for example. Her determination. The way she takes no shit at all. I wish she was here now because I could use a dose of that myself. With Frankie as my wingman (though no doubt she'd correct it to wingperson), I feel like I'd have the confidence to meet Dad head on. Say what I really mean, instead of biting my tongue, so as not to upset Mom.

Ava was never afraid to go toe-to-toe with Dad, and he respected her for it. Even gave her a nickname, Little Missy, which wasn't exactly complimentary, but it was more than he gave any of us other kids. Again, I wish Frankie was here. I get the feeling she had to battle to be recognized by her parents, too. It'd be good to have someone to be honest with about this stuff. Despite our competitiveness, Ava and Nate would both stand up for me if I asked them to. But they've got their own issues with Dad. I don't need to burden them with mine.

"Nate! Danny!"

Mom kisses and hugs us both. She and I are the most alike in the family, with our fair hair and eyes the same shade of blue. Nate and Ava are Dad clones, but if it weren't for the fact they both have the Durant cheekbones, Izzy and Max might be changelings. The twins have dark red curly hair like Irish Setters, and a far more secure sense of self than their older siblings. I guess there's a certain safety in numbers being a twin, and maybe also in being the youngest. By that time, there are fewer parental faults to inherit.

"Come inside." Mom hooks her arms in ours. "I've made cookies."

Other people meditate or take St John's wort. Mom bakes cookies.

"Mitchell!" she calls upstairs, soon as we're in the house. "The boys are here!"

She ushers us into the kitchen because Dad will take his sweet time to come down. Mom sits us at the kitchen table and doles out the cookies (and side plates and folded cloth napkins, because we're that kind of family).

"Coffee?" she offers.

"Yes, please," we chorus.

Not that long ago it would have been glasses of milk. Okay, no, that was a long time ago. It's just that whenever I'm back here, I feel like a little kid again.

"My cookie has more chocolate chips than yours," says Nate, quietly.

"Yeah, but I'll get to take the leftovers home because I'm Mom's favorite."

"Great to be home, isn't it?" Nate says.

"It's where the heart is," I agree. "I can hear it beating behind the walls."

"Nate. Danny."

Dad has entered the kitchen. And though the words of his greeting are identical to Mom's, he sounds more like he's about to disclose that he's cutting us out of his will.

"Hey, Dad," I say. "How are you keeping?"

"Very well," he replies. "I take no sugar, alcohol, wheat, dairy, or caffeine. If we all avoided those, most debilitating health conditions would be permanently eradicated."

The cookies on our plates emit a radioactive glow, and the

steam from our coffee turns toxic green. But it will take more than Dad's lectures to stop Mom baking.

"Tea, Mitchell?" she offers him. "It's organic and herbal, with filtered water."

"Thank you, Ginny."

Dad sits down at the table. Fixes his gaze on me.

"Nate tells us you're helping him at the winery, Danny. Is your business in trouble?"

Straight into it. Cool, cool, cool.

"No, Dad. My business is growing. I can run it from wherever I am, and I'm quite capable of multi-tasking."

"But you're still a one-man band?"

"It's how I like it. I don't want to be weighed down by overheads. I want to be nimble and agile."

"That means you have no exit plan," says Dad. "No one will buy a sole trader business."

"I can sell cars until I die, Dad." My voice sounds even but I might be crushing a cookie between my fingers. "I don't need an exit plan."

Nate steps in. "Dad, you don't give me a hard time and the winery is barely solvent."

"It won't be for long," says Dad. "*You* have the skills to significantly grow that business."

For fuck's sake.

"Mitchell." Oh great, now Mom has to defend me. "Danny loves his work, and he's very busy with it. He's doing Nate and Shelby a big favor by coming all this way to help out."

"But don't let that throw you off, Dad," I say. "I'm sure you haven't finished pointing out my shortcomings."

On Dad the Durant cheekbones are like flint arrowheads. It

seems impossible for his lean face to tighten any further, but it does.

"It's important for you all to think about your future," he says. "I know you're young and retirement seems a long way off, but the years will pass in a blink, and if you're not well set up, your golden years will be a struggle."

Is that supposed to mean he's fault-finding because he cares about me? Sure. Yeah. I'll buy that.

"Noted, Dad," says Nate, with a warning glance at me. End of discussion. For now.

"Nate, dear, how is Shelby?" says Mom, relieved to be able to change the subject.

"She's doing fine," says Nate. "Having regular check-ups and taking it very easy. And now we have Danny and Frankie here to help, she won't have to do anything but look after herself. And the baby."

He says "baby" like an afterthought, as if he can't quite believe it's real. It does seem weird to think of Nate as a father. He's not even thirty yet.

Holy shit. And Dad and Mom will be grandparents.

"Mom, what do you want your grandma name to be?" I ask, with a grin. "Grammy? Meemaw? G-Madre?"

Mom is taken aback. "Oh! I haven't thought—"

"We will be Nana and Grandad," Dad announces. "That's what I called *my* grandparents."

"Both sets?" Nate frowns. "How did they know which of them you were talking to?"

Dad briefly, and incredibly, blushes. "I called my father's parents Sir and Ma'am," he says. "But I feel that could be a little too formal."

Nate catches my eye, and we nearly burst a blood vessel trying not to laugh. I really wish Frankie was here. She needs to witness this shit first-hand, because it will sound too unbelievable if she hears it from me.

Maybe I'll tell her tonight. Maybe I'll ask her out for a drink. To anywhere other than Bartons.

"Dad, you're welcome to join us for lunch," says Nate.

He's being polite because he knows Dad will refuse. Least, he'd better refuse. I'd walk back to Flora Valley before I'd spend another couple of hours with the old grouch.

"No, thank you," says Dad. "I'm not entirely convinced by the provenance they claim for some of their produce."

"Okay, Mom, it's you and us boys," I say. As a parting shot, I add, "And lunch is on me."

It won't change Dad's opinion one iota, but it feels like a small victory, nonetheless.

Chapter Thirteen

FRANKIE

Part of me hopes that Danny is having a worse time than I am. Part of me hopes he isn't, because not even Danny deserves that. Another small but insistent part wishes he was here. I could do with some back up. And a witness, because I'm pretty sure this violates some international human rights treaty.

I'm at The Silver Saddle with Shelby and Chiara. Brendan, who owns the place, gave up long-haul trucking to buy the bar, but he still looks like an extra from *Sons of Anarchy*, blond and beefy with a bunch of dubious tattoos. He also holds the title of all-time most ornery in a proud tradition of ornery barkeepers. Luckily, he adores Shelby, so I'm acceptable by association. Although Brendan's default expression is "bite me", I detected a flicker of mistrust when Chiara approached. A hundred percent warranted, as I'm now finding out.

At first, I think I'm safe; Shelby and Chiara catch up about Shelby's health, and then feel obliged to discuss their other bestie Jordan's renewed crush on Brendan, despite him being ten years older and showing no interest in her whatsoever. I say "renewed" because apparently Jordan was miffed to discover (from Chiara, of course) that Brendan had a secret girlfriend, an actress, who lived in L.A. and sneaked up here undercover for their trysts. When Chiara subsequently informed her that the actress and Brendan had broken up, Jordan was even more miffed because he'd failed to tell her himself, and so she didn't speak to Brendan for a couple of months. But now – and I promise this story will be over soon – Jordan's back on her Brendan-crush bullshit. When I ask the obvious question, has Jordan told Brendan how she feels, both Shelby and Chiara stare at me like I've grown two heads.

"Of course not," says Shelby. "That would kill the crush buzz."

"You mean, Jordan wouldn't be able to gaze longingly from a distance when she's here?" I clarify. "Or continue to wallow in completely pointless emotions instead of channeling them productively into a real relationship?"

"Precisely," says Chiara. "And speaking of relationships…"

At this moment, I sense the conversation is about to slide rapidly downhill.

I am correct. Because Chiara follows up that opening with, "When will you and Danny Durant admit you have feelings for each other?"

"Frankie!!" Shelby's wide-eyed and grinning like a loon. "You and Danny! That's adorable! You're such a cute couple!"

I'm not normally at a loss for words, but then I'm not normally surrounded by people who've gone collectively insane.

"Back the truck up!" I insist. "Danny and I are not a couple!

We will never be a couple because my only feelings for him are—"

"Complicated?" says Chiara. "Conflicted?"

She's playing with me. Winding me up like those clockwork teeth on legs, so she can watch me dash madly in all directions, gnashing away.

I engage lawyer voice mode. "I am not having this discussion. Not now, not ever. Got it?"

"You two have more in common than you think." Chiara has failed to get it. "You should set aside your grudges and take time to get to know him."

"Grudges?" She's chosen that word on purpose, to wind me up further. "You mean, perfectly reasonable objections to toxic male behavior?"

Chiara smiles. She's enjoying this, damn her. Most people probably cave in to her immediately, so a bit of cut and thrust with me is an entertaining novelty.

"I admire that you're not afraid to call out poor form in others," she says. "I also think you look for any excuse to keep your distance. How many long-term boyfriends have you had, Frankie?"

Shelby's shifting in her seat, discomforted by Chiara's full-frontal attack. Me, I want to smash a beer bottle and threaten Chiara with it. But I'll settle for taking her down verbally.

"My personal life is none of your business," I say. "And you have no idea which way I lean. Could be gay or bi, could be asexual. Don't impose your cis-het norms on me."

Chiara sits back in her seat. Taps her immaculately manicured and nonsensically long nails on the table.

"Hmm," she says, apparently to herself.

Before she can regroup for a second charge, Brendan appears with food. Cheeseburgers and curly fries all round. Hot damn.

"Jordan not joining you?" he says.

His tone suggests he couldn't care less either way. The fact he uttered words when his usual demeanor is a surly silence says otherwise.

"It's summer camp season," says Shelby. "She's taking a whole group of teenagers rock-climbing and abseiling. I don't know how she does it. I'd be terrified!"

"Of heights?" I ask.

"Teenagers!!" Shelby replies.

"Oh, come on, Shel," says Chiara. "We weren't exactly saints ourselves."

"That's what I mean!" Shelby pats her bump. "When this one is born, I'm locking them away until they're thirty-five."

Brendan is still hovering.

"Can't imagine you and Jordan misbehaving," he says to Shelby. "*You*, however"—he nods at Chiara—"were born trouble."

"That's the nicest thing you've ever said to me," says Chiara. "Now, go away. Frankie and I are sparring."

"Wrong. I'm eating." I pick up my cheeseburger and say to Brendan, "And I'd love another beer."

He shrugs, which means, "Sure thing, coming right up," and walks off back to the bar without a second glance at his now nemesis, Chiara.

"You know, Jordan's right," says Chiara, who ignores everything that doesn't suit her, "he does have a fine rear end."

"I suppose," says Shelby, reluctantly. "Nate's is cuter."

"You think Nate's *nasal* hair is precious," says Chiara. "You are not an objective observer."

"Poor Nate," says Shelby, with a sigh. "He really didn't want to visit his parents today. Hope his dad hasn't been too difficult."

"What's Danny's relationship with his father like?"

I have to admire Chiara's ability to pivot. Getting nowhere with me directly, she's now trying the oblique route.

Shelby, of course, is oblivious to devious tactics. "Nate says his dad gives Danny a hard time because he didn't go to college. Says his dad doesn't mean to be harsh, but he has very firm ideas about the correct pathways to success, and he's worried that Danny's strayed off them."

"But Danny's business is doing very well, isn't it?" Chiara appears to be looking directly at Shelby, but I know she has a corner of her eye on me.

"Yes!" says Shelby. "And Nate says he's been asked to be on TV! To present some car program!"

Okay, now I'm listening, but I refuse to give Chiara the satisfaction. I focus intently on eating my curly fries.

"Tough business, television," says Chiara. "I wonder if he has an agent, or someone with legal experience. He'll need help fighting his corner when it comes to rights and remuneration."

She may as well be spelling my name out in neon. Subtle.

"Danny's super savvy," Shelby says. "Nate's always said he admires his instincts, and his tolerance for risk."

"Typical outgoing, adventurous middle child." Chiara casts yet another fishing lure my way. "Although the youngest is often the most rebellious."

"What about only children like you?" Shelby asks.

"Oh, we're a perfect combination of every birth order trait," says Chiara, smugly.

Brendan sets my beer down with a pointed lack of care. "Last orders," he announces. "I'm closing up in fifteen minutes."

"According to the sign on the door, you're shut between three and four-thirty," Chiara says. "It's only one forty-five."

"My joint, my rules," says Brendan, and walks off again.

"Wow,' says Shelby. "He's really mad at you."

Chiara sighs. "I'll make it up to him."

What about *me*? I want to ask. Any chance of an apology for the torture session I just endured?

I drink my beer, instead. And by one fifty-nine, we're standing outside on the pavement, The Silver Saddle's door shut firmly behind us.

"Bye, sweets." Shelby kissed Chiara on the cheek. "Thanks for lunch."

Chiara paid, which seemed the least she could do. Brendan managed to avoid looking at her for the whole transaction.

"Goodbye, Frankie," Chiara says. "And remember, you and Danny do have more in common than you think."

She walks off in the direction of Bartons, where she may as well live. Did Danny get tortured by Chiara, too? Maybe I'll ask him; maybe I won't.

We took my car because Nate has the pick-up. I'm just pulling the keys out of my bag, when said pick-up pulls in behind us, and the driver hops out.

"*Nate!*"

In this respect, Shelby's a lot like a dog. Even if Nate's only been gone five minutes, she acts like he's been away for years.

"How was lunch?" he says, after they've kissed hello.

"Weird," says Shelby. "How was yours?"

Nate pulls a face. "On brand."

He looks at me. "Don't suppose we can swap?"

"What? Cars?" I ask.

"Passengers. So, I can drive home with my beautiful wife."

Danny's leaning on the pick-up. He lifts his hands to make it clear this is not his idea.

My thoughts are – yes, damn you, Chiara – complicated and conflicted. I want to show my car off to Danny. I want to ask him quite a few questions. I would also sooner eat leafy greens than give Chiara an inch. What will it be, Frankie?

"Sure," I say. "Danny. Hop in."

Chapter Fourteen

DANNY

This is ... unexpected. I'd expected a flat out "No" to Nate's request, but now it looks like I'm riding shotgun in Frankie's Karmann Ghia convertible. Top down. Wind in our hair and all that jazz.

"Do you think I can door-hop in here like they used to do in those 70s TV shows?" I ask, assessing the distance from pavement to passenger seat.

"You mean *The Dukes of Hazzard*?" says Frankie.

"They went in through the windows," I reply. "And only because The General Lee's door handle got broken in an early chase scene."

Only a true vehicle nerd would know that. Frankie remains unimpressed.

"Try it if you want," she says, with a shrug. "But if you land ass-first on the gearshift, don't come crying to me."

Fair point. I'll use the door. I get in and have to push the seat back a mile because Shelby was in here last and my knees are up round my ears. Frankie's still on the pavement, but whatever second thoughts she's having about agreeing to this, she sets them aside and gets in.

I'm used to classic cars being on the compact side. I'm not prepared for how it feels being so close to Frankie that I can feel the warmth from her bare arms. She's wearing another retro sundress, this one in tangy orange. She looks sweet, juicy and edible, and she smells amazing, an almost masculine musky scent that, if I didn't know better, I would swear was Old Spice, and I need to stop thinking those thoughts right now or the second she glances my way, she'll know. I could lift her tote bag off the floor and onto my lap, but that would be more obvious. I think about Dad, instead. Works instantly, like a swift tap with a cold metal spoon.

Fully present and re-focused, I note that Frankie is an excellent driver. Confident and alert. Changes the gears smoothly, which isn't always easy in these old cars. I watch her hand manipulate the gearshift and hastily picture Dad again. And start looking at the passing scenery because I obviously can't be trusted to keep my thoughts above my waist.

It's not a long drive from Verity to Flora Valley Wines, but it's a pretty one. My family tends to think of me as a city boy now, but I love being out in nature. Often when I run or hike the Topanga trails, I take a moment to stop and sit and take in what's around me, the colors and textures, scents, and sounds. I've become adept at identifying different bird calls. It's amazing what you can observe when you slow down and look outside of yourself.

"Do you miss living around here?" Frankie's first words to me in two miles.

"Truthfully? No," I reply. "Every time I come back, I feel

like I'm being crushed by the pressure of my family. I know that's a me-problem, but I haven't been able to rise above it so far. It's only when I get away that I can breathe free again."

Don't know why I said all that. Frankie doesn't strike me as someone who welcomes oversharing.

Sure enough, she goes quiet again. I look out at the passing fields, irrigated and green or crispy summer brown, other vineyards, the distant hills. Frankie deftly and courteously overtakes a bunch of cyclists. They look like serious riders, not wine tourists. The lead cyclist waves in appreciation of us not forcing them into the ditch.

"I think you broke a country code, there," I joke. "Most of the pick-ups round here have stencils of bicycles on the door, like the bombs on the old World War II planes."

"I'll lose my job if I get a conviction," she says. "Plus, I'm not an asshole."

Another Danny joke crashes and burns. I prepare to sit out the rest of the drive in silence.

Two minutes later, she says, "Shelby says your father's hard on you. On all of you Durant kids, I mean."

Okay, so she's not giving me the silent treatment. Surprising. Also confusing. I feel like I'm trying to retrace my steps back through a minefield using pure guesswork, where even a toenail in the wrong place spells instant death.

"It's possible he means well," I say. "The jury's still out on that. For me, at least."

"I've always thought it's one of life's great rip-offs that we can't choose our family," says Frankie. "Think of all the drama and therapy bills we'd save if we could."

Because Frankie's keeping her eyes diligently on the road, I can't tell if she's lightening the mood or deadly serious.

"Uh, yeah," is my lame response. Do better, Danny. "Would you choose any of your family?"

"Tricky," she replies. "Sometimes I'm convinced I'd have been better off as a turtle. Hatching out of an egg buried in sand, then running like hell to the ocean before the birds catch me. No need to worry about family then, only survival."

"That's an interesting take," I say. "But it didn't answer my question."

"I know." I finally see her smile. "I'm a lawyer. We never give a straight answer."

"I'd pick Mom and Nate," I tell her. "Izzy and Max are great but they're too much of a tight unit to be close to me. Dad's, well … you've got the idea. If I was in a real bind, Ava would support me, no hesitation. But until such time, she'll continue to torment me because she can."

"Like Chiara," says Frankie. "She enjoys being a puppet master way too much."

Does this mean what I think it means? Did Frankie get the Chiara interrogation treatment, too?

"Chiara claims she does it for people's own good," I venture. "But then, wheat grass is supposedly good for us and it tastes like garbage."

I can see a muscle working in Frankie's jaw.

"Chiara has a theory…"

She's being cautious, and I think I know why. But I'll be cautious too, because if I'm wrong, I'll be hitchhiking home.

"Chiara's theory," Frankie continues, "is that you and I have more in common than we think."

"Yeah. She mentioned."

Not cautious enough. Frankie flicks me a fierce glance, her eyebrows slanting down in a way that makes her look exactly like an Angry Bird. It's cute. And I will never tell her because I value my body parts.

"Chiara said the same thing to *you*?" she demands.

"Yup. Last night. Ambushed me at Bartons."

"Bartons? Why were you at Bartons?"

Her tone's starting to irk me, but I don't want to start a fight.

"Because I needed a break," I say. "And apparently a drink with acorns in it."

"Acorns, huh."

Good call, Danny. She's calmed down.

"Chiara ambushed me at The Silver Saddle," Frankie says. "Managed to enrage both me and Brendan."

"Brendan's in a permanent state of enragement, isn't he? I thought he hated everyone?"

"True, but he achieved an extra level of animosity towards Chiara today."

Frankie sounds gratified. Me, I've experienced enough of Brendan's customary attitude to not want to imagine him when he's really provoked.

We're coming up to the winery turn-off, and suddenly, I don't want this drive to end. Up until now this day has been a write-off. Lunch with Mom should have been nice except that I couldn't shake my resentment towards Dad. It sat like a vulture on my shoulder the whole time, digging its sharp, mean claws into my flesh. Nate tried to cheer me up on the way back, but it wasn't until we spotted Frankie and Shelby in

Verity that I felt my mood lift. This drive with Frankie has been surprising, but in a good way. A very good way. I wish I could magically lengthen it by twenty more miles.

I'm not prepared for when Frankie swerves onto the grassy verge and hits the brakes.

"Oof." I catch my breath and gaze at her, wildly. "What was that about? Skunk on the road?"

The engine is idling. Frankie swivels in her seat to face me. She leans forward, and for a micro-second, I think she intends to kiss me. But seems it was a figment of my imagination. Her back is upright now against the driver's seat and she's glaring at me. Not with the full Angry Bird eyebrows, but I brace myself anyway.

"Chiara's also of the opinion that you and I are attracted to each other," she says.

"Uh—" This conversation is going places I never anticipated in a million years.

"Well? Are you?"

Jesus, what's the right answer here? I suppose I'd better opt for the truth.

"Yes," I say. "I am extremely attracted to you. Even though you seem to hate my guts."

Her big blue eyes search my face, scanning for clues to my sincerity. It was the truth, but I bet I still look shifty as hell. Being scared for one's extremities will do that to you.

"I'm not sure I hate your guts as much as I thought I did," she says, and winces as if immediately regretting it.

"That's good to hear." I smile to try to lighten the moment. "I swear I'm not that bad once you get to know me."

Of course, that comes out sounding shallow and

unconvincing. Frankie's eyes narrow a little, and I'm sure I've blown it.

"All right, then," she says. "Let's get to know each other."

Again, not what I expected. "Uh, get to know each other as in…?"

"I want to stress-test Chiara's theory," she says. "I want us to find out what we do have in common. And whether that's enough to base anything more serious on."

"Okay." Seems a sound idea, though currently lacking in executional detail. Which is why I say, "Thoughts on the best way to do that?"

She chews on her full, luscious pink bottom lip. I might have imagined her wanting to kiss me, but I sure as hell want to kiss her. On that lip, and the one above it, and then—

Focus, Danny!

"How about we take turns introducing each other to stuff we care about?" Frankie is saying. "Things we love to do, hobbies, sports, special interests, etc.?"

"Like your beer brewing?"

"Just like that," she confirms. "I've got a few other niche pastimes, too."

She makes that sound slightly ominous, and my apprehension must show in my face because Frankie grins.

"Backing out already?"

"Hell, no," I say. "I'm in, boots and all!"

My enthusiasm lands badly. Frankie's face closes up like a clam.

"I won't rush this," she says. "I won't be pressured. Understood?"

"It'll take the time it takes." I nod my assent. "I'm good with that."

She eyes me, warily. "Why are you good with it? You have a choice, you know."

"I do," I agree. "And I choose to do this at your speed."

Frankie still doesn't seem convinced, so I add, "Just because I live in L.A. and like cars, doesn't mean I'm addicted to the fast lane. Sure, my work keeps me busy – at times I'm hustling like a crazy man – but I always carve out time for stillness and peace. Sometimes I like nothing better than to sit on a tree stump and listen to the birds. Call me Opie or Abner, I don't mind."

To my amazement, Frankie gives me a smile, a dazzlingly gorgeous one. It takes all my effort not to pull her into my arms and kiss her for a really long time.

I settle for asking, "So what now?"

"Now," she says, "we head back home and go our separate ways. Tomorrow morning, we can share our top four … activities with each other."

She puts the car in gear and pulls back out onto the road. This day has improved immensely, and I'm looking forward to tomorrow.

At least, I think I am.

Chapter Fifteen

FRANKIE

"What. The hell. Is pickleball?"

Danny and I have swapped lists. We're at the kitchen table. He's already drunk two mugs of Shelby's coffee but looks like he could do with a third.

Mind you—

"Does this say 'running'?"

"Or hiking," Danny replies, with a grin. "Great hill trails around here."

Beyond the kitchen door, I hear urgent whispers. Nate and Shelby left the room after breakfast but now they're back.

"*You* ask," Nate mutters to Shelby.

"No, *you*," insists Shelby. "Invalid, remember?"

"You can both do it," I call out. "Danny and I have nothing to hide."

"We don't?" Danny gazes at me, alarmed. "Do we really want this to be broadcast across the entire Flora Valley community?"

"It will be anyway," I shrug. "Chiara's got spies everywhere."

"Probably bugged this whole house," agrees Danny, glumly.

His mouth does that cute pout thing. He will never know how close I came yesterday to launching myself at him and kissing him passionately. I hung on to enough self-control to avoid making a fool of myself that way, but not enough to avoid coming out with the crazy "getting to know you" plan.

I blame Chiara. It's totally her fault that I did the most irrational thing in my life since buying my Karmann Ghia. Okay, so I do love that car. But I refuse to think too far ahead about what might happen with Danny. I don't trust easily enough to take more than cautious baby steps. Baby hiking steps by the look of it. Because running is absolutely out of the question.

Nate and Shelby sidle into the room and take a seat each at the table. Nate stares at Danny and Shelby stares at me. Danny catches my eye, and we share a smile.

"I hate you two already," says Nate. "Tell us what's going on or I'll withhold privileges."

"Such as?" Danny inquires.

"No idea," says Nate. "It was the only threat I could think of."

"You'll make a great dad," says Danny.

"Shut up and spill the beans," Nate insists.

Danny looks at me. "Want to do the honors?"

"Sure." I address Nate and Shelby. "Yesterday, Danny and I concluded that there are grounds for progressing our incipient friendship to an advanced level of affiliation, and we intend to compare our compatibilities in order to affirm whether forward movement in that domain is appropriate and/or mutually beneficial."

Nate gives me an even stare. "You're getting to know each other better before you decide whether or not to leap into the sack."

"Gold star for you," I say.

"Wait— Chiara was right? You two do have feelings for each other?" asks Shelby.

Danny and I exchange another glance. Neither of us wants to credit Chiara with anything after the way she treated us, but the alternative is answering this question with a lie.

"We're exploring the possibility," I say, but I can feel my face grow pink. A dead giveaway.

Nate spots my blush and grins, but fortunately – for him – doesn't push it.

"So, how are you going to get to know each other?" Shelby asks, excitedly. My sister is a sucker for romance.

This time, Danny does the honors. "Frankie had this idea that we should participate in each other's hobbies and interests. If we don't want to kill each other by the end, we've likely got a decent basis for a relationship." He waves the piece of paper I gave him. "We listed our top four, which we're now reviewing."

"That's ... sensible, I guess?" says Nate. "Though I have to admit, I'm getting an *Annie Get Your Gun* vibe."

"Are you implying that this will turn into a competition?" I enquire. "As in 'anything you can do, I can do better'?"

"Well, does the word 'competitive' seem apt when applied to you two?" is Nate's rejoinder.

I'm not going to look at Danny. I'm not going to look at Danny.

I look at Danny. He's got his poker face on, which means he's ready and waiting for the starter's gun. Competitive it is.

"Can you bake a pie?" I ask him.

He shakes his head. "Never tried."

"Neither have I," I say. "Happy to eat one, though. Any kind except pecan. I have strong opinions about nuts."

"Oh, she does," Shelby confirms. "Some kids have nut allergies. Frankie has nut hostility. You can imagine how our hippy mom felt about that!"

"No home-made granola?" Danny suggests.

"No walnut cake." Shelby counts off on her fingers. "No chestnut stuffing, no crushed peanuts on banana splits, no peanut *butter*, not even extra smooth—"

"No Smuckers at all?" Danny's grinning at me. "Not even Goober Grape?"

"Disgusting," is my final word.

"What's on your lists?" Nate forces us back on track. "Unless it's private. Or kinky."

"No kinky stuff so far." Danny scans my list. "Though I have my doubts about pickleball."

"Fastest growing sport in America," I say. "Anyone can play. All you need is a wiffle ball and a paddle."

"Happy to say I have neither," says Danny.

"New sports store in Verity," says Nate. "Called Ball's. With an apostrophe."

"Because it's owned by a Mr or Mrs Ball?" Danny asks.

"If only," says Nate. "Anyway, what else?"

"Uh—" Danny scans the list. "Beer tasting! Now you're

talking. Shopping for vintage clothing, okay… Lindy Hop. What is *that*?"

"A dance!" says Shelby. "Like swing and jive. Super fun."

Danny narrows his eyes at me. "Seriously?"

"Are you suggesting I don't look like a dancer?"

"No-o," says Danny, evenly. "But that definitely sounds like you need prior training."

"You'll catch on." My smile is only slightly evil.

"What's Danny making you do, Frankie?" Nate asks.

"Hiking." I'm not smiling now. "On the trails."

"We'll skip the scroggin." Danny is grinning from ear to ear. "Given your nut aversion."

"Go karting," I continue. "Could be fun. What's next? Karaoke!!"

I look up and glare. "Who does karaoke these days?"

"You used to *love* SingStar when Chiara brought round her PlayStation," says Shelby. "You shrieked if we tried to take the microphone off you."

"I was eight years old!"

"Karaoke?" Nate's giving Danny the side eye. "Since when?"

"Since I ended up drunk in a bar a couple of years back. Seems I can sing."

"Drunk singing isn't singing."

Danny smiles tightly. "Think you can do better?"

"And lastly—" I interrupt before this escalates. If Danny's going to compete to the death with anyone around here, it'll be me. "The final item on the list is … twitching…"

I squint just in case I've read it wrong. I have not. "Twitching?"

"Bird watching," says Danny. "Particularly rare ones. It's the British term but I prefer it."

"Uh huh." I'm not convinced he's for real. "What kind of rare birds are around here?"

"Western tanager," he says. "Yellow billed loon, sage thrasher—"

"You are making this up!"

"Google it," he says. "I started noticing birds when I was out hiking. Became a little bit obsessed."

"This is the Durant way," says Nate. The two of them fist bump.

"We can't come and watch any of this, can we?" Shelby sounds disappointed.

"No!" Danny and I chorus.

"I don't want to be a buzzkill," says Nate. "But will you two actually have any time to help as promised?"

"Of course," I say. "All of this will happen in our downtime."

"Don't worry, bro," says Danny. "Unless we get eaten by bears while out hiking, you can rest assured that everything will be taken care of."

Chapter Sixteen

DANNY

"So? You and Frankie?"

I'm impressed. Nate made it through a whole hour of work before cracking.

"It's not me and her yet," I reply. "I've got to dance, shop, and brewsky-taste my way into her good books first."

"Not to mention the ol' pickleball," Nate reminds me.

"Can't be harder than tennis, can it?" I say. "I've had plenty of experience being run all over the court by Izzy and Max. Should have built up *some* skills. Aside from losing, that is."

This morning, Nate asked me to help him set up an online sales system. Before he took over, Flora Valley Wines' sales were made entirely via personal phone calls, last year by Shelby, and in all the years before that by her dad. Orders were written down in a notebook that was stored alongside the family photo albums. Because their customers are like family, according to Shelby. This year, Nate also wants to run sales through their new website, but tech isn't his forte, and he wants my advice on the system that will work best. I'm not super tech-savvy myself, but I do know what customer information is most useful to collect. It's not what you might expect, either. All the usual data online forms insist on gathering, such as age, gender, address, purchase history, etc., doesn't get to the heart of *why* people buy. Crack that code with a few pertinent questions, and you'll be streets ahead of any competitor.

I'm aware of the irony. I still have no idea why Frankie suddenly came up with this plan. Until then, I'd been under the impression she still considered me on a level below a parasitic flatworm. And the more I replay that conversation in the car, I more I realize how much she didn't say. My guess is that Frankie keeps her emotions on a tight leash, and on the rare occasions they slip their collars, she has a hard time pulling them back in line. I think it's possible that she did try to kiss me, and that I didn't imagine it. Then again, I'm often guilty of wishful thinking.

As if he's read my mind, which I sincerely hope he has not, Nate says, "So you two *are* telling the truth that you haven't yet—?"

"Schtupped? Done the nasty? Spelunked the Bat Cave?"

Nate winces. "I'm regretting the question, but yeah."

"Nope," I say. "Not even a little kiss."

"Really?"

Reasonable of Nate to be surprised, I guess, but I can't prevent a flash of resentment.

"You assumed I would have made a move on her already, because I have no self-control." I try not to sound huffy. "Frankie's a cautious person. And I'm happy to go at her speed."

"I admire your newly found restraint," says Nate.

He just had to get that dig in, didn't he? Time for the boot to go on the other foot.

"And how long after you met did you and Shelby get jiggy with it?" I ask.

Us Durant siblings do have masterful poker faces. But as Ava's long pointed out – and he's long denied – Nate has a tell. A tiny twitch of his left eyebrow. I spot it now, and smile on the inside.

"Few weeks," he says.

"Four? Six? Eighty-five?"

"Maybe three."

There's no "maybe" about it. Nate is fanatically precise. He'll remember to the *minute* when he and Shelby first knocked boots.

But I won't push him. Mainly because, though I'll never admit it to him, Nate does have a point. I've never needed to wait for sex before. I've also never wanted anything more than a fun time, so I've never minded if it didn't last. I'm twenty-six and not a complete schlub, so why would I?

But it feels different with Frankie, and I'm not totally sure why. Yes, she's gorgeous. Yes, I'm attracted to her. Yes, I like a challenge. There's something more going on, though, which I can't put my finger on. Chiara claimed we have a lot in common, and I'm *starting* to see that. Maybe all will be revealed when we start uncovering deeper layers of connection.

Shit. And what if we start peeling back the onion and Frankie finds I've got nothing below the surface? Dad's always implied that I'm not a serious person, and what if this proves it? Proves I lack substance, grit, and forethought? I'll have no chance with Frankie at all.

When I told Dad I refused to go to college, he naturally asked me why. I replied that I didn't need a degree to be successful in business. Dad dismissed this as eighteen-year-old arrogance, and he was partly right. But I was making six figures by the time I was twenty, so it wasn't all bravado. It also wasn't the whole truth. I didn't want to go to college because I knew I didn't have what it took to match Nate and Ava. I never could in high school, either, but I was way more popular and that made up for it. But in college, being the guy that everyone wanted to be friends with would count for nothing. I couldn't face four, maybe five years of underachieving by Dad's standards. So, I lit out for L.A. And, luckily, didn't have to crawl home in disgrace.

I'm good at what I do, but it's the *only* thing I do. I'm a one-trick pony, and when it comes to Frankie, I'm not sure one is the magic number.

"Danny?"

Nate has something else on his mind.

"What?"

"Don't take this the wrong way, but Frankie isn't an ordinary girl. She's family."

I get it. There's a lot more riding on this than hurt feelings. A lot more riding on me. Don't fuck it up, is what Nate's saying. More than that – he's saying don't place him in a spot where he's forced to choose between his brother and his wife.

I could plead my case, promise I'd never do anything to hurt Frankie, but I won't because there's only one way I can take that comment. If Nate trusted me, he would never have said it.

Thanks for the vote of confidence, bro. You and Dad have a lot in common.

"I've got some ideas about your data capture," I say. "Want to hear them?"

Nate searches my face but I'm pokered to the max.

"Sure," he says. "Fire away."

Chapter Seventeen

FRANKIE

About me and Danny, Shelby only says, "I'm so happy for you!"

Hearing her gives me mixed feelings. I've been coming up with so many objections – to this bananas plan I seem to have concocted and to the possibility of it succeeding. Even if Danny and I sail through every challenge and find we're the most compatible two people on earth, is a relationship the right thing? I'm twenty-six and I do well on my own. Statistics show that single women live longer than their committed counterparts. And where would we live? No way will I move to L.A., but I can't see Danny trading down to San Diego. And what if my law firm asks me to relocate to another office again? Somewhere even colder than Minnesota, like Alaska? I'm pretty sure there isn't a flourishing classic car trade in the frozen north. And what about the future: does Danny want children? Kids have hardly been top of mind for me, and I'd prefer it to stay that way for a while. It'll be me whose career is most interrupted, and that feels unfair. And considering I didn't much enjoy my own childhood, I'm not sure that I want to risk my own kid feeling the same.

And-and-and ad infinitum… I can come up with a million reasons not to do this, but deep down, I know they all have the same root cause. Fear. Of being vulnerable. Of being rejected. Of being forced to be someone other than my true self. I know all this because I'm the kind of person who likes to solve problems. Even the weird, knotty tangles of my own psyche.

But just because I know all this doesn't mean I want to open myself up. Not yet anyway. That's the advantage of this plan: it buys me time.

Besides, Shelby can find reasons to be happy about pretty much anything. If an asteroid turned the world to dust tomorrow, she'd get one of those tiny rakes and make Zen gardens.

It's mid-afternoon and she and I are headed to the main shed to hang with Cam, Doug, and Javi, who are meeting to discuss the vineyard work schedule. Shelby didn't tell Nate she planned to crash the meeting, and perhaps I shouldn't have agreed, but I know it's important to her to feel part of things. I suspect it's a distraction, too. I'm not the only one with underlying fears, and if Shelby sits around the house too long, she starts to focus on them. Plus, it's a beautiful day and a short, easy walk to the main shed. Shelby can sit and rest while the guys sort out who's doing what when.

Cam, Doug, and Javi are already there, seated on empty barrels arranged around an old trestle table. The Flora Valley Wines actual office only fits two people at most and thus is currently fully occupied by Nate and Danny. A part of me wishes they were here, too. Just because I'm being cautious doesn't mean I want to avoid Danny altogether. It's weird – ever since Chiara informed me that I had feelings for him, I've been able to let go of my grudge and appreciate his good points. It's like Chiara acted like human Drano and cleared a bunch of blockages. Now I can admit to myself that I like Danny's ready smile, and the way he always looks to catch my eye first when someone's said something funny. I like his dress sense, the way he's not afraid to wear color. I like his energy and how his body moves with an easy athleticism. I like to imagine how his mouth would feel against mine and—

Focus, Frankie. You need to keep an eye on Shelby. One minute, you're lost in a sexy fantasy, and the next, your frail pregnant sister is trying to build a wine tasting room with her own bare hands.

"*Muy buenas*, Frankie!"

Javi, short for Javier, has only been part of the Flora Valley Wines team for six or so years, so I don't know him that well at all. But I think I must remind him of Dad, whom he loved, because he's always super glad to see me.

Javi kisses me on both cheeks. He's short and slender but has a serious presence – you wouldn't want to mess with Javi. His main place of employment is actually Bartons Hotel, where he's the concierge. His boss, Ted, gives him time off to work for the winery. Ted says it's because he wants to support the wider community, but it's more probably because Javi can source anything from anywhere and Ted would hate to lose him. If you want a bejeweled elephant for your private birthday party on the Bartons lawn, just slip Javi the word and a suitable amount of currency, and voila, Bulgari-encrusted Jumbo.

"Hey there."

This is Doug's standard greeting. He's in charge of mowing

but gets roped in to most other outdoor tasks. Doug's of indeterminate age and looks like he's made out of knotted rope and cowhide. His full gray mustache makes him look like a cross between Sam Elliott and Mark Twain. He's also known as Toothless Doug, even though he has a full set of teeth. Don't ask.

I don't expect anything more than a nod from Cam, but to my surprise, I get, "Good to see you, Frankie." And to Shelby, he says, "You doing okay?"

"Ye-es," she replies, heavily. "Bored. Trying not to freak out. Did I mention bored?"

Corner of Cam's mouth lifts. "Not sure a work scheduling meeting is going to help with that."

"Oh, it will," insists Shelby. "It'll be like listening to a meditation guide, only without the weird 'om' sounds."

Turns out she's not wrong. There's something immensely soothing about listening to three people who know exactly what they're doing, and who get on and do it without fuss. Cam and Doug have slow bass voices, while Javi has a sharp, quick tenor. It's like lying on your back in a grassy field, staring at the sky, while two bulls and a goat have a friendly conversation over the nearby fence.

Every so often, kindly, and unnecessarily, one of them will turn to me and Shelby to get our opinion. The meeting takes around forty minutes, then Doug and Javi say their goodbyes and leave us. Javi probably has to source a bottle of 1945 Romanée-Conti, or a new identity for an international art thief. Doug will have something to mow.

Shelby and I are left with Cam. Who obviously has

something on his mind. I suspect I know what, and really wish I wasn't around to hear it.

Sure enough…

"Have you heard from your mom yet?"

As I said, I'm pretty convinced Cam and Mom never got it on, but he was like her faithful dog for years and that's a hard habit to break. I wonder how Ava deals with Mom being a third wheel in their relationship. Probably ignores it. Good approach. I should try it some time.

Shelby glances at me before answering. I make sure my face doesn't give anything away.

"Nope," Shelby replies. "And I don't expect to. She's doing that big spiritual pilgrimage walk, the one that's, like, three hundred miles across France and Spain. She even refused to take her phone. Said she'll call from a hotel if there's an emergency."

"Debra's death really hit her hard, didn't it?" says Cam.

"I think it wasn't so much her death as the fact Mom never knew she had a half-sister," says Shelby. "Mom always prides herself on being kind of intuitively connected, and my guess is she feels like she'd failed Debra."

"By not sensing her presence somewhere in the universe?" I have to comment, because … come on!

Shelby scrunches up her face in embarrassment. "I know! It sounds crazy! But … well, you know Mom."

"Do I?"

It's out before I can stop it. Cam's attention turns my way. He has big brown eyes and most of the time, they're calm and gentle. Now, I catch a flash of emotion. I look away before I can identify it. To be honest, I don't want to know what he's feeling because I don't care.

But it's Shelby who responds first, of course. "Oh, Frankie. You and Mom are just so different. You were always destined to butt heads."

Cam's still staring at me. Is this news to him? If he'd had eyes for anyone but Mom, he might have noticed what was going on. But then again, if he had, he would have sided with Mom because he worshiped her. So perhaps it was for the best that Cam stayed oblivious? Means I only resent him a little instead of hating his guts.

I've got to get out of here before I say something I regret. Shelby and Cam can talk about Mom all they like, but not with me around.

"Shel, are you okay if I take a walk?"

"Sure!" she says, slightly startled. "Meet you back at the house for dinner? I thought we might start rewatching *Gilmore Girls* after?"

I manage a smile. For her. Cam, I ignore.

Outside the shed, I gulp down air. And berate myself for getting over-emotional. It's ridiculous that my mother has this effect on me all these years later. I'm a grown-ass woman and my childish grievances should all be behind me.

I'm walking but have no idea where. Maybe out of the winery and down the road a while. It's quiet and rural and I'll be all alone.

As I round the corner that will take me past the house, I spot Danny coming out of the office and hang back to spy on him. He crosses the gravel where the cars are and starts up the path through the trees that leads to the workshop. He's walking jauntily, with a swing in his step, and I think I can hear him singing.

I blame a recent excess of emotion for what I do next. If I were in total control, I'd keep on going down the driveway and out onto the road. What I do is follow Danny. With not a clue how I'll explain my presence when I end up at his front door.

Chapter Eighteen

DANNY

All up, it's been a pretty good day. Nate was genuinely impressed with my suggestions for improving his customer data, and I felt like he saw me with new respect. That's the thing with my family – the Durant career path as laid down by Dad is traditional and well-worn. No surprises, and not a lot of new thinking. My own career path has been forged through trial and error, but on the whole, my instincts have served me well. I focus on what really matters to people, not what they *think* matters. Or what family or society has always told them matters. Today, Nate suddenly understood that distinction and saw how it could help Flora Valley Wines forge stronger bonds with the customers they have and connect with new customers who share the same values.

Of course, his response was the usual low-key Durant one of, "Good job." Like I'm a little kid who's managed to tie his shoelaces. But Nate's never been one to gush, so I'll take it.

I have more ideas about how the winery can communicate better with its customers, and even how it could promote via social media without spending a fortune. Those will keep for another day. Right now, I'm going to head back through the woods to Grandma's house and google how to Lindy Hop. Forewarned is forearmed and all that.

On the way, I'll also practice my stand-out karaoke number, "Sweet Child O' Mine" by Guns 'N' Roses. The falsetto at the end is pretty challenging, but I've nailed it before so I should be able to nail it again.

Nobody's around, so I give the ending a shot in the glade just outside the workshop. There's a raucous squawking and a gang of Steller's jays flap off out of the trees. Philistines. Bet they would have hung around if I'd been singing boring old "My Way". Probably would have joined in. Steller's jays are talented mimics – can imitate cats, squirrels, chickens, and even machinery. Old Blue Eyes should be a cinch.

I open the front door and am once again struck by how ridiculously compact this place is, and yet how well every part of it's been thought out. Cam built it with his own two hands, because of course he did. The last thing I built was a Porsche 911 RSR out of Legos. The age minimum was 10+, so it wasn't all *that* simple.

But despite my resentment of Cam's manly skills, I have to appreciate his handiwork. At the risk of sounding like an estate agent, the storage solutions are both creative and functional. The whole space under the stairs is filled with drawers and shelves. I snooped in every single one, and most are empty, but I did unearth a first aid kit, and next to it, a half-filled bottle of bourbon. The compact fridge has a tiny compartment for ice, and so I'm all set. I'll check my emails, google dance moves, and chill out for an hour before dinner. Nate's cooking for us all tonight.

I've left the front door open because while this place is built perfectly for winter, it's a little close in summer. The hot air rises and if I forget to leave the window open, the bedroom's a sauna. I should have bought an electric fan in Martinburg after lunch with Mom, but Nate and I were in too much of a hurry to get away. There's a hardware store in Verity called Screw It. Next time I'm in, I'll check out their range of small appliances. Maybe I can ask Frankie to come with me, and we could go for a drink at The Silver Saddle? As long as Brendan hasn't banned everyone who's even remotely connected to Chiara.

Cam's table folds down from the wall and fits my laptop and not much else. I'm checking my in-box, when through the open front door, I hear more squawking. Some people use geese as guards, but frankly, any loud bird will do. Someone, or something, is in the woods, and the jays are shouting a warning. I was joking with Nate about bears, but maybe I should err on the side of caution and close the door?

"Shit!"

I appear in the doorway at exactly the same time as Frankie arrives outside it. We both take a startled step backwards.

"Hey," I say. "I … er, wasn't expecting you…"

Frankie gives me a "No shit, Sherlock" look. "That's because I didn't let you know I was coming."

I notice a tightness about her mouth, like she's fighting whatever impulse brought her here. Of course, my first hope is that she's changed her mind about the no hanky-panky rule. But if it's important enough for her to come all this way to see me, it's much more likely to be something else, so I'll put my libido to one side and be a courteous host.

"I've just poured myself a bourbon on ice," I say. "Want one?"

"Yes," she says. "Thank you."

I open the door wide for her, and she enters a little hesitantly, stops and looks around.

"I've never actually been in here before," she says. "This was Cam's private space."

"It's barely big enough for me," I say, fetching a second glass. "Cam could probably stretch out and touch all four walls at once."

"Mm," is Frankie's response. I'm guessing she's not here to talk about Cam.

She peers up the stairs. I'm a tidy guy so I've nothing to hide.

"Take a look if you want," I say.

"I'm good," she says.

"Bourbon time it is, then." I make another and hand it to her. "Do you want to sit outside? I'll bring the second chair."

"Sure." She seems to realize that her answers have been a mite abrupt and makes an effort to smile. "Should be rocking chairs, don't you think?"

"So we can sit there and whittle? Maybe play a tune on the old harmonica?"

"And shoot a few varmints while we're at it?"

She's smiling properly now, with that full gorgeous mouth, and my libido pops up again to say hello. *Down*, I tell it. Frankie has initiated a rare and unexpected opportunity to connect, and I will not fuck it up.

For a while, we do nothing but sit and sip. It won't be dark for a few hours, so the birds are still noisy in the trees.

"What're those birds?" Frankie suddenly asks. "The ones that sound like squeaky toys?"

I listen. "Chickadees. Mostly juvenile. This is the time of year where a lot of young ones are figuring out how to bird."

"You mean, learning to fly?"

"And what's food and what's not."

"Seems a little haphazard," says Frankie. "What if they eat something bad?"

"More likely to get eaten themselves," I say. "Nature is pretty brutal."

Frankie nods, and we sit and sip some more. I'm dying to ask her why she's here but I know that'll spoil whatever this is. I sense a vulnerability in her, but that's for her to share when she's ready.

Apart from a half-melted ice cube, my glass is empty. So is Frankie's.

"Another?" I ask.

She makes a face. "Better not. I'm not used to spirits."

"Cam and Ava took the beer cooler with them," I tell her. "Even though Ava's not supposed to be drinking, and Cam's given up in support, Ava said it had 'sentimental value'."

"A *beer* cooler?"

"Apparently yet one more remarkable thing that Cam made by hand."

I wince at how petty that sounds. The bourbon has loosened my tongue, and my insecurities are taking advantage.

Frankie's laugh has a slight mocking tone. Fair, I guess.

But then she says, "Do you think Cam and your sister are happy together?"

"Uh … I assume so," is my best answer. "Ava doesn't exactly have a high tolerance level, so if she was *un*happy, I'm pretty sure she'd have left by now."

Frankie nods again. I sense she's working up to something, and a good salesperson knows how to stay quiet and not be tempted to fill the space. The more you yap, the less trustworthy you seem, and the more likely you'll end up with a shitty deal.

Finally, she says, "I'm not sure why I came here."

She doesn't look at me, stays staring out into the woods. I wait.

"I pride myself on being able to keep my emotions in check," she goes on, "because that's what my job demands. But the instant I'm here at Flora Valley, it's like I become an emotional blender, with every conceivable feeling churning around inside me. I hate it, and what I hate even more is that I've no idea what to do about it."

"Oh, man," I say. "I know how that feels. Away from home, you can kid yourself that you're a grown-up who's got it all under control. Soon as you're back, you're ten years old again, wondering what it will take to get your father to show you some love."

Shit. I didn't mean to say all of that out loud. Thanks, bourbon.

To cover my embarrassment, I change the subject. "We'd better get going. Nate and Shelby are expecting us for dinner."

Frankie turns and looks me squarely in the eye.

"Or how about we make our excuses," she says. "And go upstairs to your room?"

Chapter Nineteen
FRANKIE

It's like I've smacked Danny across the face. His mouth is moving but no sound's coming out. Luckily, that gives me an opportunity to backtrack, or better still, act like it never happened.

"Come on." I get to my feet. "Dinner time."

"Frankie!" Danny leaps up so fast, he kicks his chair into the glade. "Shit!"

In the time it takes him to fetch and right it, I've placed my empty glass in the sink and am back out on the porch ready to go.

"Frankie." His hair has fallen over his forehead, but he doesn't seem to notice. "Sorry for the possum in headlights act back there. You just ... took me by surprise."

Guess pretending it didn't happen is now out of the question.

"I know," I admit. "I took myself by surprise, too. Sorry. I was ... feeling weird."

"Okay, so..." Danny's still a little breathless. "Uh, is your offer still open? Or do you want me to forget this ever happened?"

His goddamn hair is curling over his forehead and my fingers are twitching, desperate to gently coax it back in place. I've had an emotional afternoon and one fairly strong bourbon, and I should trust my ever-cautious instincts and back away. I *should* but I don't.

"I can't tell," I say, honestly. "Like I said, I have all these stupid emotions churning around in me, and sometimes I don't know what the hell I feel!"

Damn it. Danny's calm enough now to realize his hair's messy and he pushes the curls off his forehead. I feel like an idiot dork but his smile is kind. I'm not the super huggy type but I'm about a second away from throwing myself into Danny's arms. So maybe there's my answer?

"Okay," I say. "I do want to … you know … but I also want to stick to the plan and get to know each other properly. And I don't know how to reconcile the two."

"Can I make a suggestion?" Danny says. "Feel free to ignore it if it's dumb."

"Well, I have nothing," I tell him. "So even the dumbest suggestion's better than that."

"How about we tell everyone that I've asked you to give me dance lessons?" says Danny. "In private, so no one can laugh at me. Nate will buy that. Then we can come back here, dance a little in case anyone snoops, and see how we feel after that. No pressure, I promise."

"Shelby wants to watch *Gilmore Girls*," I say.

"You're not leaving for a while," Danny says. "Might not be

time for all seven seasons of *Gilmore Girls* but you can certainly fit in the four-hour 2016 special."

"How do you know so much about *Gilmore Girls*?" I demand.

"I'm also very well informed about *Dawson's Creek* and *Felicity*," he replies. "There was a distinct viewing divide in the Durant family, and on the whole, I preferred hanging out with Izzy and Mom."

Then he adds, "Anyway. Dumb suggestion?"

He sounds hesitant, unsure, and I think that's what tips the balance.

"Not dumb," I say. "But I can't promise anything."

"I won't expect you to," he says. "Truly. Whatever you want to do is good with me."

We both stand there, not quite knowing whether to smile or not. I decide to take charge.

"We'd better go, or we'll be late for dinner," I say. "Despite Shelby doing her best to drive it out of him like a demon, Nate still insists on punctuality."

"That he does," Danny agrees. "Give me a minute to lock up, pardner, and we'll skedaddle."

Dinner is fine. Just fine. Danny spins the line about dance lessons, and Shelby buys it without question. Though she's disappointed.

"I was really looking forward to watching TV with you," she says.

"Let's do a binge-watch tomorrow night," I offer. "The whole *Year in the Life* special in one go."

"Okay!" My sister is easily pleased.

Nate, however, is more naturally suspicious. "How will you do dance lessons in that tiny house?"

Luckily, Danny is prepared. "We'll use the workshop. There's enough clear area in there."

"There's also a lot of sharp tools," Nate points out.

"We'll be careful," says Danny. "Given I don't even know the basic steps yet, I doubt we'll be getting too physical."

A piece of food goes down the wrong way, and I have a short coughing fit.

Nate stares at me and then at Danny, who meets his brother's stern eye with a face-full of innocence.

"Don't break anything," are Nate's final, and somewhat ambiguous, words.

When we reach the path through the trees, Danny stops and says, "It's not too late to change your mind. About everything, including the dance lessons. Because I googled the Lindy Hop, and I don't mind admitting that it intimidated the shit out of me."

"I don't want to change my mind." I sound *way* more confident than I feel.

"Okay," says Danny. "But be gentle with me."

Suddenly, I'm torn. I want to walk on and I want to pull back. I want to laugh and get close to Danny as he learns to dance. I want to run away and never see him again. I want to kiss him, and maybe go further than that. I want to wait, possibly forever, so I'll never make any mistake that might cause myself a power of hurt.

"Hey…"

Danny's quiet voice breaks through my thoughts.

"Say the word and I'll walk you back," he says.

Say the word...

"I hate that I'm nervous about this," I tell him. "I hate feeling less than in full control."

"Nerves aren't always the enemy," says Danny. "Sometimes you should trust them."

"Do you *want* me to back out?" When in doubt, make it the other person's problem.

Danny grins. "You forget, I'm a Durant. Powerplay tactics like that will never work on me. This is your choice. And whatever you choose, I'll respect it."

Damn it. Okay, breathe, Frankie. You only need to take one step at a time. Focus on the first one and go from there.

I grab Danny's arm. "Let's go dancing."

The workshop is where Cam makes barrels but I do my best not to think about that. There's an area in the far corner that's room enough for some simple first moves. Danny sets up his Bluetooth speaker, and I play the old standard *In The Mood*, just to, you know, set the mood.

"That's a heck of a pace," he says, looking wary.

"Don't panic," I say. "We won't try to dance to it yet. I'll teach you a basic rock step, and then we can try a side pass and tuck turn. I'll keep count. Slowly."

Lindy Hop is an African American jazz dance related to swing and jive, and it's fast and athletic. When I first started learning it four years ago, I thought I'd never master it. But my dance group was super supportive, often literally, catching me as I tripped, so I kept it up. It helped that they're also a bunch of eccentric weirdos, and of all ages and stages of life. All sizes and shapes, too, so I never felt out of place like I might have done if I'd taken up tango or ballroom. Sure, not every partner is strong enough to hoist me into the air but there are so many moves to choose from that no one cares. It's fun. It keeps me fit. It suits my style.

I tell Danny all the above in between keeping time and teaching him moves. He's only partly listening. The competitive Durant spirit has been awakened and is determined to conquer. His focus is intense and his coordination excellent. He has a natural dancer's ability to move the top and lower halves of his body independently. Might surprise people, but I have it too. By the end of the hour, we're dancing a pretty capable six-count circle. Still a little stiff, sure, but not bad. Not bad at all.

And I was concentrating so hard, I barely noticed the physical connection with Danny. It was pretty tame, mainly holding hands, occasionally in each other's arms as we practiced the turns. Now, we're both sitting shoulder-to-shoulder on the workshop floor, resting our backs against the wooden wall, out of breath and laughing.

"You know what?" says Danny. "We could tick this off as task complete. Unless you have some *Dirty Dancing* type contest in mind for us to enter?"

"No way I'm getting in a lake with you," I say. "I like activities that keep me warm."

The silence where we both realize what I've said is long and highly charged. I guess, given all the opportunities to back out that Danny's offered me, I'd better be the one who breaks it. I took the first step, and now it's time to decide whether or not to go to step two.

"I've been having fun," I say to him. "And you know what? I'm not ready to stop."

Chapter Twenty

DANNY

I'm trying to decide exactly what Frankie means, when she clarifies by straddling my lap and kissing me. We've both worked up a sweat and her musky Old Spicy-style scent is strong. I'm tempted to grab her hips and pull her hard against me, but I resist. She's kissing me with some urgency but I think it's best I take it slow. So, all I do is gently twine my fingers in her hair and kiss her back, our mouths opening, our tongues touching and teasing. I can feel her body soften with desire, while mine actively does the opposite. But I won't rush. I'll let Frankie set the pace.

She lays her hand on my erection. I guess that's a sign we're moving things along. But this floor is as hard as I am, and I've already got enough bruises from bumping myself on wooden objects. Time to suggest we vacate the workshop.

"Bedroom?" I murmur.

"No," she breathes. "I want you to take me on the bench."

The bench. The hard, unforgiving wooden bench. With the

vises and other metal implements attached. And the possibility of splinters in places where no splinters should be.

Frankie's unfastened my pants and now her hand is inside my Calvins and reaching for my fully primed cock. Bench it is.

Except—

"Condoms are upstairs," I say.

Frankie halts. She slides her hand out of my pants, which is good because if she'd got a firm hold on my guy, I suspect there might have been an embarrassing incident.

"You could go get them," she says.

"I could," I agree. "But upstairs there's also a big soft, comfortable bed that isn't covered with dangerous metal things and would allow for unrestrained freedom of movement."

Frankie smiles. "City-boy wimp."

"Guilty and unrepentant."

"Oh, all right…"

With the athleticism she demonstrated at our dance lesson, she hops off me and holds out a hand to pull me up. As my pants are falling half off, I have no dignity to preserve so I take it. She hauls me to my feet like it's no effort at all.

"You have some serious strength there," I remark. "I'm impressed."

I take a step and my knee twinges. Not used to those quick swivel turns.

Frankie catches my wince, and grins. "Want me to fireman's lift you up the stairs?"

Okay, I have a shred of dignity left. "I'll manage."

"Huh," says Frankie when she sees the bedroom. "There's a bed, and—nope, that's it. Spartan."

"I half expected the sheets to be plaid flannel," I say. "But they're white cotton. Good thread count, too."

"City boy."

Frankie says it half-heartedly, like her mind is on something else. I wonder if it's the history of this particular bedroom. I suppose it is a bit weird to think the last people who had sex here were Cam and my sister, though Shelby assured me they'd taken the old mattress with them.

The bedroom only has one window, which given the steep pitch of the roof is more of a skylight. It's just after sunset and the glimpse of sky through the trees is an intense indigo blue, pin-pricked by the first stars. I've switched on the bedside light, but it's still dim in here. So dim, I can't fully make out the expression on Frankie's face.

I move towards her, slowly, and just stand there, with my arms by my side. She looks up at me, her eyebrows at half-Angry Bird. I worry that she's judging me and I'm falling short. I really hope that's not the case.

Then she says, "I've worked hard to love my body. But I'm still self-conscious about getting naked for the first time."

Relief. It's not about me.

"Especially with someone like you," she continues.

Okay, so it's a little about me.

"You're in the perfect body category," Frankie says. "Like all your family, and most of mine. Shelby and Tyler have always been slim, like Mom. Even though Jackson and Dad were bigger, people referred to them as 'burly' or 'solid'. I'm the only one who ever got called 'fat' at school."

"Kids are assholes," I say. "And if it helps, I had a late growth spurt. For all of elementary and most of middle school,

I was really small. Even my kid brother Max was taller than me at one point. So, until I finally did a heap of growing between fifteen and sixteen, even my friends called me Danny Du-Runt. Fun times."

I've made her smile. It's reluctant but it's a smile.

"No lingering insecurities?" she says.

"Hell, no," I reply. "Self-esteem solid as a rock."

Frankie lifts her eyes to the ceiling. "I'm going to ask this once, and then we will never mention it again. Do you think Chiara is a witch?"

"I think she makes it her business to notice things about other people," I say. "But I'd love to know how hard she looks at herself. Not that I'll ever have the courage to ask her that, of course."

Frankie moves a fraction closer, and my breath catches. I want her so badly, but I have to be patient. I want to tell her how gorgeous she is, how I love her curves, but I know that could have the opposite effect. When I was short, people used to think they were doing me a favor by citing all the famous people who were height-challenged. All it did was highlight that being short was seen as a social disadvantage and I'd need other attributes to compensate. Frankie's body isn't something I need to comment on. How it feels to touch her, be close to her, that's what matters.

"It's possible I'll freak out part way through," she says. "Just so you know."

"All good," I say. "We've got time. Maybe not for all 157 episodes of *Gilmore Girls*—"

"Danny," says Frankie. "Shut up and kiss me."

I shut up and kiss her. Slowly and then not slowly at all. We do the clothing fumble, trying to take off each other's before giving in to practicality and removing our own. Then we're on the bed, limbs entangled, hands and mouths everywhere, following our mutual lustful instinct. The only part of me I steer her hand away from is my erection. I want this first encounter to be about her pleasure. Mine can wait. Well, it can if she doesn't get a hold. If she starts giving me a hand-job I will not be answerable for the consequences.

"Will you *stop* that?" Frankie protests, after I've yet again forestalled her hand. "I want to touch you."

"And I very much approve of you touching me," I say. "But Lil Danny is on a hair trigger right now and I'd like this to last."

Frankie raises one eyebrow. "*Lil Danny?*"

"Could be worse. Could call it my joystick. Or my lightsaber. Or—"

"Stop right now or I'll do Big Danny an injury."

"Seriously," I say. "I promise to give you access at the earliest opportunity, but right now, I think you should relax and let me do this…"

"Ohh…"

Frankie arches her hips as I put my fingers and thumb to good use. She is slick and tight and hot, and the hair on Lil Danny's trigger is now one of those nanowires measured in atoms. I take her nipple in my mouth and tease it gently, which doesn't help me one bit, but does send Frankie right to the edge. I know this partly because I can read the physical signs, but mostly because she's swearing at me, ordering me to get inside her right now.

The condom is within reach, and I have honed my ability to

remove it from the packet and roll it on with one hand (and some careful tooth-tearing action on the foil). Frankie's breathing is shallow and rapid, and her whole body has tensed up. I stroke my thumb over her sweet spot one last time and, ignoring her furious demands to hurry up, enter her slowly and steadily. I maintain control until I'm right up to the hilt and then it's all on. Frankie shudders and grabs onto my arms as her orgasm rushes through her, and I drive myself into her hard and fast and shout out loud as I come in perfect gratifying sync.

Now's my favorite part, the come down, if you'll pardon the pun. The gradual slowing of heart rates and breath, the tingle of the aftershocks through our nervous systems, the melting of tension as we lie together in a sweaty, mellow tangle. The pleasure of satisfaction achieved. And a tiny hint of smugness on my part.

"You're smirking," says Frankie.

"It's how I smile!" I protest.

"You ignored my requests," she adds.

Sounds like I'm being cross-examined, which I react badly to.

"I figured you'd want more than a two-minute bang."

"*Bang!* Did you seriously just use the word 'bang'?"

This seems to be going downhill fast. Time to put on the emergency brakes.

I roll over on my side, prop myself up on my elbow. "Frankie. Did you enjoy it? Because I certainly did, and I would like to do it again. Many times."

Her expression is more amused than annoyed, I'm relieved to see.

"Yes, Danny, I did enjoy it," she says. "But let's take turns calling the shots, okay?"

My mind fills with a raft of possible ways that could play out, and it's enough to stir Lil Danny from his post-sex coma.

"Okay, but no whips and chains," I say. "City-boy wimp, remember?"

Frankie reaches up and pushes a wayward curl off my brow.

"No whips and chains," she promises. "But I've still got my eye on that workshop bench."

Chapter Twenty-One

FRANKIE

Just because I have some self-consciousness doesn't mean I avoid sex. Nor am I short of opportunities to have it. In the immortal words of Amy Schumer, I can catch dick whenever I want. And yes, there are a lot of jackasses online, but if you're willing to sift, you'll find decent guys. Most of the men I've hooked up with, though, I've met by chance, at community events, through pickleball and dancing, even once at the dog park when I was minding my neighbor's dog, Murray.

What I have avoided up till now is a relationship. I've invited men into my bed and then I've politely (mostly) shown them the door and declined any future requests to meet. This can get a little tricky if you know you'll see them again, for example, when you're paired up on the dance floor, but I'm a skilled communicator. I make my position crystal clear, leaving no room for the slightest misinterpretation. And I never change my mind.

That's why this whole thing with Danny has got me so

flustered. Despite my considerable initial misgivings, I've found myself falling for him. Only not falling as in a pleasant floating sensation, but more like that sudden anxious jolt when you misstep. Or those hypnic jerks you have when you're drifting off to sleep, that cause your eyes to fly open and your brain to go, *What the fuck?*

I thought I'd been smart and in control when I came up with my get-to-know-each-other plan. But we've barely ticked off one item and here I am naked in his bed. Or to be accurate, Cam's old bed, but let's not go there.

And it was good. Ridiculously good, even though it wasn't my style at all. Normally, no surprises here, I like to take charge. I don't mean to make it sound like I treat the guy like a programmable sex robot; I'm as fond of being carried away by passion as the next person. But I like to set an expectation of "my bed, my rules". And most guys have no problem with that. In fact, I think they find it kind of a relief.

I don't know why I expected it to be the same with Danny. Nothing else with him has gone as it should. It's like Flora Valley is Wonderland and I'm Alice, and I'm now trying to work out a whole new set of rules in a place where everything is topsy-turvy.

Thing is, I don't hate it. It's new and confusing and part of me still wants to run away screaming, but overall, I'm willing to see where this leads. I'm willing to see if this could turn into my first real relationship.

However, I'm also going to ensure we stick to the get-to-know-each-other plan. This means ignoring the fact that we jumped the gun by having sex. Because now that line has been crossed, I am not going back, so we'll have to run the plan in parallel. I guess it'll be like straddling two trains, one foot on each roof as they rattle along, and hoping like hell that the tracks don't suddenly diverge.

From downstairs, I hear a muted, "Ow, fuck!"

I'm lying here in bed trying to get my thoughts in order (spoiler: I haven't) while Danny's on a mission to dispose of the condom and fetch us water. Important to stay hydrated.

His footfall sounds on the stairs and then he appears, a glass of water in each hand, scowling.

"How the fuck did Cam the Giant survive in this place?" He hands me a water glass and slides back into bed. "Every time I turn around, I smack some part of me on a hard wooden edge."

"Evolution moves faster than Cam," I say. "That probably helps."

"And who doesn't build some kind of closet?"

"A man who doesn't have clothes that need hanging," I point out.

"I guess I can be thankful that the bathroom isn't a long drop," Danny mutters.

He senses my side-eye and screws up his mouth.

"I know, I know – city-boy," he says. "Though technically, I grew up in a semi-rural area. But in a ten-bedroom house. With a tennis court. And a mile-long tree-lined driveway. So … yeah."

Right. Sometimes I forget that the Durants have money. Well, Nate doesn't right now; he and Shelby are teetering on broke. But unlike us Armstrongs, he did grow up with money. And so did Danny. It grates a little, but I have to admit, I'm curious about how the other half lives.

"What was it like, being a rich kid?" I ask.

"We hung out mainly with other rich kids," he says with a shrug. "We went to private schools, and Mom and Dad's friends all have money, too. So, I guess I'm saying that while I knew we were wealthy, it seemed normal." He frowns at me. "Does that sound super arrogant?"

The fact that he's worried about that makes me consider my answer with more care.

"Not arrogant exactly," is my reply. "But a little narrow and entitled."

"I guess that's true," says Danny, with a grimace. "Though unlike most of our friends' parents, Dad made it clear that he and Mom would never bail us out. We'd have to build our lives and careers ourselves. And if we failed, too bad. We'd have to suck it up and deal."

"You haven't failed, though, have you," I say.

He smiles. "Nope, not yet."

I smile back. "There you go."

"Though it's possibly because I refuse to look down at what's circling in the waters below me," he says. "And I'm not too sure Dad approves of that as an approach."

"*My* Dad would have," I tell him. "He lived his whole life pretending financial crisis wasn't sawing a hole under his feet."

I drink some water. It's cold and refreshing. "Then again, that kind of confidence is catching. Flora Valley Wines wouldn't be here today if Dad hadn't been so relentlessly optimistic."

"You must miss him a lot," Danny says gently. "He died pretty young."

My first instinct is to say I don't think about it anymore. That I did my grieving for Dad on my own, and in my own way, and then I put that grief aside and got on with my life. But that's my defense response, my armor, and a big, fat lie. Plus, I'd be a hypocrite to ask Danny personal questions without being willing to answer his questions of me.

"I miss him every day," I say. "And it's bullshit what they say about grief. It doesn't happen in stages. It happens randomly, unexpectedly, like you're strolling along and someone lobs a grenade in your path. And I have not got to the acceptance stage, either. I'm stuck on sadness and anger—"

I stop because I'm about to cry. I hate crying. I hate leaking stupid, weak tears.

Danny sets his water glass on the floor and shuffles closer but doesn't reach out to hug me. He's being cautious and fair enough; my whole body is rigid and I'm clutching my own glass in both hands, like it's a weapon.

"Sorry, Frankie," he says. "It was thoughtless of me to bring it up. Are you okay?"

"No," I reply. "But that's not your fault."

"Do you want a hug?"

His earnestness makes me burst out laughing. Danny looks as if he doesn't know whether to be offended or join me.

"We just intimately connected a whole bunch of body parts," I explain. "It's adorable that you're asking permission to put your arms around me."

Danny turns on the full-wattage smile. Pretty sure I can guess what's coming. And who.

I was right. Relentless positivity *is* catching. I'm suddenly once again in a good mood.

"Want to give the body parts another workout?" he asks. "You can call all the shots this time."

I turn on my best single eyebrow arch. "Sure you're ready for that?"

He lifts the sheets and shows me Lil Danny. *He's* ready, but Big Danny, I feel, is overly – no other word for it – cocky.

"All right then, let's get this show on the road." I set my water glass down and rub my hands together to warm them and give the impression I'm scheming. Which I am.

"First, you'll need to be condomed-up."

"Really?" Danny frowns. "No foreplay?"

"Not for you," I reply. "You're on the sidelines until I summon you."

Danny eyes me warily. "Summon?"

My smile is my answer. Slowly, teasingly, I lower the covers until every inch of my bare skin is exposed. Danny's got the condom packet in hand but freezes as I begin, gently and leisurely, to pleasure myself.

"Shit," he mutters. "Could you wait a second until I get this on?"

"Don't look?" I suggest, with a lazy smile.

"Impossible," he says, and hastily rolls on the condom. "Made it. Just."

There's lube by the bed but I don't need it. I close my eyes, and revel in the sensation, the delicious tension that's building in my whole body.

"Shit," I hear Danny mutter again. It's time.

I open my eyes and smile up at him. Honestly, his jaw is so tight, he looks like he's undergoing surgery without anesthetic. Pity it's not going to get any easier.

"Sit up and stretch your legs out," I tell him. "You'll need to lean backwards and prop yourself up on your arms."

"Okay." He's fully focused. No wasting energy on excess words.

"Right, I'm going to lower myself onto you," I say. "But you're not to move. I'll do everything for us."

Facing him, I lower myself onto his erection and hook my legs over his thighs. Then I lean back, too. His eyes are dark with lust and his breathing is rapid and shallow. But I now control the speed and depth of the thrusts and unless he does an Incredible Hulk and flips me over, there's nothing he can do about it. So, naturally, I take it slow. And because I can, I continue to pleasure myself.

Poor Danny. His arms are trembling and he's trying to lift his hips up to get more traction but he's effectively trapped. I lean back a little further and the electric sensation of the new angle makes me gasp, and I quicken the pace of my fingers. That takes me right to the cliff-edge of orgasm, but the slowness of the thrusts means I hang there, teetering, unable to go over. It's torture and it's exquisite and I become a lot more vocal.

My partner is also becoming louder, though less appreciative, judging by the fact he's just yelled "*FUCK!*" But the sex gods are merciful because at that instant, my orgasm breaks, and now both of us are shouting. Any night birds outside will be wondering what the hell is going on. Danny's arms give out and he collapses backwards, and I'm left straddling him, limp and wrung out and laughing with the joy of it all.

Danny's eyes are closed, his arms splayed out sideways like

a scarecrow's, and his chest is heaving. He's also muttering a stream of what sounds like curse words.

"I did warn you," I say.

He squints at me. "That was the kind of warning like 'Parental Advisory', which is basically an encouragement. You did *not* say I'd be taken to the brink of insanity."

Lil Danny is still inside me, and the condom will soon be a hazard, so I gently lift myself off. And lie down beside Big Danny and nuzzle his neck.

"You did well, young apprentice," I say. "Now, we should sleep."

"Nate and Shelby will know you didn't come home," he points out. "They also know there's only one bed here."

"Sleep," I insist. "And we'll deal with our beloved families in the morning."

Chapter Twenty-Two

DANNY

Of course, we both have to get up in the night to pee, but only I almost fall down the stairs. I blame Frankie for the fact that all my muscles have turned to cheesecake. I had an easier physical workout competing in a Tough Mudder race a couple of years back, where crawling along under barbed wire and scaling a mile of ten-foot mud mountains were only two of eighteen demanding dirt-themed obstacles. I was sore and crusty after that, but at least I could still navigate a set of stairs.

I rummage in Cam's first aid kit for some pain killers but there's only an herbal balm with a strong odor of Pine-Sol. I don't want to go back to bed smelling like disinfectant, so I pass. It occurs to me that Frankie's mom, Lee, might have given the balm to Cam, and I wonder if anything went on between them back in the day? Might explain why Frankie is so down on her mom, though she's been civil enough with big man Cam so far. Ava would never tolerate anything but single-minded devotion in her relationship, so I'm certain that if there was ever anything between Lee and Cam, it's long over.

Rough for Frankie to lose her dad so young, when she obviously got on better with him than her mother. I'd be bereft if Mom died and, yes, if Dad died, too. I know this because he almost did die last year, and I realized that despite our constant clashes, he's my dad and I love him. Just wish he'd accept me for who I am instead of trying to make me fit some perfect Durant mold.

Going back up, I take the stairs carefully. My knees are still twinging and my quads and glutes are on *fire*. Forget beer, Frankie should start a fitness regime – Lindy Hop lessons and torture sex. A little niche, but I think it has potential.

Frankie's fast asleep. Gingerly, I get back into bed, and check my phone, out of habit. Nothing urgent. Haven't heard back from the producer guy yet. Despite his enthusiasm, I know it's a long shot, but there's part of me that really does want it to happen. I told Frankie I hadn't failed yet, but that doesn't mean I'm a success. No matter how good I am at it, being a car salesman isn't like being a scientist or a Harvard MBA graduate. But if I have my own TV show, and it becomes popular … that's something people might respect.

I fall asleep while rehearsing my speech for the Emmy's…

…and wake to find all the covers have been stolen in the night. Okay, now I'm more alert, I can see that the covers are still here but are tucked around Frankie. She's rolled herself up in them like a burrito. Hasn't left me even a corner of the sheet.

I nudge her shoulder and hear a snarl. Lil Danny might be raring to go again, but Big Danny has survival instincts, and they're telling me to put on some pants and go make coffee.

The smell of fresh brew precedes me through the bedroom door and it's enough to rouse Frankie from slumber. She fights off the covers like it's their fault she's trapped, and blinks at me, disheveled and cross. Wild guess? Frankie is not a morning person.

She is, however, naked, and her luscious breasts are on full display. I can't help it; my eyes have a mind of their own.

"Are you ogling me?" she demands.

"Yup," I admit. "I also come bearing hot liquid. Want a shirt?"

She sees the coffee mugs in my hand, and realizes it'd be smart to cover up. Scalded bare flesh isn't a fun way to start the day. I set the mugs down carefully on the floor because there is no side table as well as no closet in this room and fetch a shirt out of the drawer in the bed base. First one I lay my hand on happens to be a pink polo.

"This all right?"

"Give," she says, and pulls it on.

Oh my. My shirt has never looked so sexy, and I say that as a person of not insignificant vanity. Lil Danny stirs in my Calvins but the need for coffee overrides everything. I hand Frankie her mug and carefully slide in beside her holding mine.

"Don't speak," she says.

No problem. Morning coffee is a sacred ritual and woe betide anyone who interrupts before the requisite level of caffeine is ingested.

We sip in worshipful silence until Frankie says, "Is it early or late?"

"It's ten past seven," I reply. "So … neither?"

"Shelby and Nate usually have breakfast at eight," she says, without enthusiasm. "I guess I'd better be there."

"I have granola and fruit downstairs," I suggest.

"Ugh." Frankie shudders. "Breakfast can only be eggs, toast, hash browns, waffles, or pancakes. The only acceptable side is bacon. No tomatoes or mushrooms ever."

"Any style of egg?"

"Well-cooked scrambled," says Frankie firmly. "Or an omelet if it's not gooey inside. Plain only. None of those spinach and feta abominations."

"We should *both* go to breakfast," I say. "Not fair on you to take all the heat."

Frankie sighs. "Why does life have to involve other people? It'd be way less complicated if we were all in our separate bubbles."

"No dancing in separate bubbles," I say. "No torture sex, either."

"I warned you," says Frankie, laughing. "And I also said we could take turns."

"True…" I give her a hopeful look. "I don't suppose—"

"Nope," she says, pushing away the covers that she stole. "If I'm going to face the court of Nate and Shelby, I need to look my best. First dibs on the shower, and if it doesn't have a decent-sized water tank, then tough luck."

Chapter Twenty-Three

FRANKIE

Oh boy, good times. Danny and I walk into the kitchen to find not only Nate and Shelby, but also Cam and Ava. And not one of them, not even Cam, is pretending they don't know exactly what went on last night.

"I'll make double the amount of eggs," says Shelby, beaming from ear to ear. "Figure you'll be extra hungry after all that *'dancing'*."

She makes air quotes with her fingers because of course she does. It's a wonder she doesn't also jiggle her eyebrows like Groucho Marx.

Even Nate is grinning. I realize I'd expected him to disapprove of our – *my* – flakiness, but I suspect the Durant siblings relish any opportunity to get one over each other. I'm trying not to look at Danny but I can't help one glance to see how he's taking all this. He's got his poker face on, which means he's doing better than I am, but I'm not sure he'll be able to keep it intact. I can see Ava's itching to pile on in.

"It's that house," she says. "It's so small, you can't help

getting horny for each other. I mean, Cam and I were at it within minutes," Ava persists. "Maybe it's the way the wood smells. It's like a timber aphrodisiac."

Cam leans back and raises his eyes to the ceiling, like he's praying for some kind of natural disaster, a meteor strike perhaps, to intervene and make it stop.

Nate's not happy, either. "Must you?" he protests. "This is only one step away from talking about our parents having sex."

"Well, I hate to break it to you," says Ava, "but that's how they came to have five children."

"Doesn't mean I have to think about it," says Nate. "Change of subject."

And he turns to me, damn him. "How did Danny acquit himself with the Lindy Hop moves?"

I tell the truth. "Danny's a natural."

"Oh, you'll have to show us!" says Shelby, eagerly, from by the bench where she's cracking eggs into a bowl.

"That will not happen in our lifetime," I tell her.

I'm thinking the subject is closed, but it seems Nate's not done with me. "So, I assume the plan's now void?"

"What plan?" says Ava.

Do she and Cam have to be here?

"Frankie concocted a plan for her and Danny to share in each other's top four hobbies." Nate is showing no mercy and I will not forget it. "So, they could get to know each other better before becoming ... more intimate."

"I like that plan," says Ava to me. "It failed its Beta testing but it was still a sound idea. You need more than scorching sexual compatibility for a great relationship. Isn't that right?"

She pats Cam on the shoulder.

"No comment," says Cam. "Nate invited us here to talk about the crush, and call me crazy, but I was kind of hoping that would be the main subject. Seeing as I have to get to work soon."

That's a big sentence for Cam and an unusually assertive one. I guess, being with Ava, he's been forced to come out of his shell. Not that I've thought about this much, but if Cam was going to end up with any woman, I'd always assumed she'd be like him, a quiet working-class girl who grew up scratching a living on a farm. Rich, mouthy Ava Durant could not be more opposite to that.

But despite Cam's small display of tetchiness, he's smiling lovingly at Ava. I suddenly realize that he's happy with her and feel a weird twinge in my gut that I can't easily identify. Part of me is glad that he finally found the right person, and part of me is still resentful that he took Mom's attention away for so long. Part of me really wants what he and Ava have: an equal, loving, well-grounded relationship. Although I had an amazing time with Danny last night, it's not been enough time for me to feel like I properly trust him yet. Damn it. I should have stuck to the plan. Emotional turbulence has a lot to answer for.

Shelby calls from the kitchen. "Eggs are ready! Come and get 'em!"

We form an orderly queue for toast and eggs. Shelby has made a batch just for me because not everyone likes their scrambled eggs without a single hint of moisture.

"And there's coffee on the stove," Shelby adds. "Help yourselves."

Danny is the only one who takes up the offer. He selects the largest mug and fills it to the brim. The steam from it coils like cartoon vapor emanating from a lethal potion.

"Mm-mm," he says, taking a sip. "That's a cure for male pattern baldness right there."

When Danny and I came in, we went straight to opposite ends of the table, before realizing that it was pointless to pretend that we hadn't been together all night. Now, Danny pulls out the chair right next to me.

"I'm happy to keep the plan going, by the way," he murmurs so only I can hear. "If you are?"

Am I happy to keep going? Or do I want to use this "failure" as an excuse to back away and stay safe? That's what tends to happen when I feel vulnerable, and there's nothing like a whole bunch of people judging you over breakfast to make you feel exposed.

But if I give up, then what do I lose? Even if Danny and I don't have a future together, we have this month. And if I say "yes" to pushing on with the plan, then I have a bunch of things to look forward to. Okay, not hiking, but I could make sure it's a short hike.

"It's your turn to pick an activity," I say.

Danny gives me a wide smile that's got more than a hint of surprise in it. Guess he expected that I would back out. Is that down to me and my commitment issues, or is he a little less self-confident than he appears?

"Go karting," Danny says. "Indoors. How about I book us a slot for an upcoming weekend?"

"You're going go karting?" Ava has the ears of a lynx. "Be

careful. Danny gets so competitive he's been known to shunt even his own family off the track."

"The only family member I shunted was you," says Danny. "And that's because you were weaving in front of me, refusing to let me pass."

"It's supposed to be a fun, friendly activity, not NASCAR," says Ava. "Another example of poor sportsmanship on your part."

Danny's holding his fork in a dangerous manner. "On my part?"

"Ahem," I say. "Remember the jar. No insults allowed."

"And maybe now we could discuss what we came here for," says Cam. "Nate? The crush?"

"Right, yeah, the crush," says Nate, slowly. Whatever's on his mind is weighing heavily.

"What I wanted to run by you all," he says, "is whether we should have the big party this year or hold off because Shelby might be giving birth in the middle of it. Well, she'll be in hospital, but you know what I mean."

"You can't hold off," says Shelby, immediately. "It's been a community event for ever. Everybody loves it, and everybody comes."

I get the feeling they've already talked about this and not come to any agreement, hence Nate bringing in the rest of us.

"They come because of you," says Nate. "The way they came because of your dad. And if you're having a baby, I'll be with you, and so will your mom and"—he glances at me—"whoever else in your family can be there. There'll be no Armstrongs at the crush at all."

"But everyone will still want to help out." Shelby's not giving in easily. "Jordan, Chiara, and Ava have already started making plans for it. They'll be *so* disappointed. Won't you, Ava?"

"A little," says Ava. "But I'm family, too, and Jordan and Chiara are your two best friends. We'll all want to be there for the birth, so I'm not sure who'd be running the event."

"I'm not sure that many people can fit in a birthing suite," says Nate. "Or in the hospital waiting room. You might have to set up a marquee in the parking lot."

"Argh." Shelby claps her hands over her face, then peers at us over the tips of her fingers. "Okay! But can we please keep planning until we absolutely have to pull the plug. I don't think I could bear it if we could have had a party but didn't just because of me."

Nate looks around the table. We all either shrug or nod.

"All right," he says. "Crush is on until we make the call. But we'll have to warn everyone that it might not happen, otherwise there'll be a community uprising."

"We'll handle that," says Ava. "Jordan, Chiara, and me. We'll spread the word and calm any ruffled feathers."

"You've never calmed a ruffled feather in your life!" protests Danny. "You're the one who causes the ruffling!"

"Name in the jar, Danny," I say.

"It's the truth!" Danny objects.

"Also an unprovoked personal attack," I say, firmly. "Name in the jar."

Danny gives me a look like I should be on his side. But I'm standing firm. About this, at least. He writes his name on a slip of paper with bad grace and shoves it in the jar.

"One each for you and me," says Ava, delighted. "Game on!"

"Okay – time to go to work." Cam stands up and starts collecting plates. "Thanks for breakfast, Shelby."

"Thank you, Shelby," we chorus.

Danny's pulled out his phone, probably so he doesn't have to look up and say goodbye to his sister, who's being hustled out the door by Cam. I sympathize, but he's got to stop letting Ava rile him up.

Like I have to stop letting Mom rile me up, which she does even when she's hundreds of miles away. Can't be a hypocrite now, can I? Although, as we all know, advice is a lot easier to give than to receive.

Nate's asking Shelby to go and sit down, saying he'll deal with the dishes. She wraps her arms around him and hugs him tight, or as tight as her baby bump will allow. He kisses her tenderly and then tells her to scoot and take a load off. She heads towards us, her whole face aglow with love. I feel that weird twinge in my gut again. My sister's so happy, and she's about to become a mother. I can only begin to imagine what that must feel like. Exhilarating and terrifying, peaceful and chaotic, overwhelming and purposeful – all the contradictory emotions all at once.

I glance at Danny to see that he's also watching Nate and Shelby. Maybe thinking the same thoughts as I am? Or maybe I'm the only person who struggles this much trying to work out what I want from life?

"So, what are you two planning for today?" says Shelby, as she joins us again at the table. "Nate and I have to go into Martinburg for my check-up, so that's our fun time sorted."

Danny says, "As it happens, I've just got a message from a guy outside of Verity who's got a car I might want to buy. Thought I might head out there mid-afternoon, maybe stop off for a quick drink at The Silver Saddle on my way back."

He looks my way. "Want to come with me?"

His mouth's curved in a small hesitant smile, and I sense an olive branch being offered. Unlike me, Danny doesn't stay mad for long. Suddenly, I realize why. Danny's instinct is always to connect, whereas mine is always to separate and create distance. Emotional and physical.

Weirdly, knowing this makes me want to say "yes" all the more. In fact, I'm alarmed by how much I want to go with him.

I check with Shelby. "Is that alright with you? I'll be back for our *Gilmore Girls* binge-watch. And how about I bring burgers home, seeing it's my turn to cook?"

"Promise?" she says. "It'll be the only thing I have to look forward to all day."

My sister is another one whose instinct is to connect. That's why she never hides her emotions. And it must be because mine are churning around in my internal blender that I have a rush of love for her. I'm so lucky to have Shelby as my sister and so grateful that she asked me to be here with her. If she hadn't, I'd never have had this opportunity with Danny. Shelby's always claimed our mom is a little witchy, but I suspect *she's* the one with special powers.

"Cross my heart," I say. "And I'll make sure Brendan makes your burger with your favorite spicy pickle."

Chapter Twenty-Four

DANNY

Man, I have to stop letting Ava rile me up. Every time I do, I lose, and then I look – and feel – like an idiot. It's my own fault, I know, but old emotional triggers are strong, and it doesn't take much to set them off. For me, anyway. No doubt other people have more self-control.

On the plus side, I bounce back quickly. Especially when I have the prospect of a perfect day ahead of me. A classic car treasure hunt with Frankie by my side. The only thing that will make it better is if the car turns out to be a rare beauty – like finding a first edition holographic Charizard Pokémon card in a junk store. The guy who messaged me didn't give details, so he's probably some crusty old farmer, a man of few words. Not even sure how he got my number – probably through the Flora Valley grapevine, pardon the pun.

And I was pretty sure Frankie wouldn't want to come with me, but to my surprise, she didn't hesitate. Given my previous advice to myself about self-control, I shouldn't get too excited about what this might mean. But then, advice is always easier when you're giving it to someone else.

Nate's dutifully rinsing off all the plates before loading them in the dishwasher. The hardest substance in existence isn't diamonds but cooked egg that's been left on a plate and put through a hot wash. Mom taught all us kids how to be useful in the kitchen. We may have been rich enough to have cleaners and gardeners, but the kitchen was solely Mom's domain and we learned to respect it from a very early age. I can make cutlery and glassware sparkle and was always the best at ironing and folding the cloth napkins. In the rare instance that I might be called on to polish forks and press table linen, I'm ready.

I watch Nate wipe up the bench. Pretty soon, he'll be changing diapers and whatever else parents need to do with babies. I'd better bone up quickly if I'm going to be any great shakes as an uncle.

"Hey, Nate," I say. "Got a burger preference?"

"Anything as long as it has no spicy pickle," he says. "I'd rather have a patty made out of roadkill than eat that stuff."

"If Brendan's still mad at Shelby and Frankie, a roadkill burger might be what you get," I say.

"He was only mad at Chiara," says Shelby. "And she will have made it up to him by now."

"I want to know how. And yet I really *don't* want to know." Frankie echoes my thoughts exactly.

"What will you do this morning?" Shelby asks her.

"Research," says Frankie. "Brewing supplies, vintage shops, craft beer tasting, pickleball courts, rare birds of Sonoma county." She pauses. "Where to buy hiking boots."

"Ball's," says Nate. "The sports shop in Verity also has outdoor gear."

"We can stop off there this afternoon," I say. "Get you kitted out." Now it's me who pauses. "And I guess I can buy a pickleball paddle."

"You should sell this idea to your TV producer guy," says Nate, with a grin. "Dating show meets *WWE Smackdown*."

"It's so cute that you're pushing on with your plan," says Shelby. "Even though you've already boinked."

"Boinked isn't even a real word," says Frankie. "Let alone a euphemism!"

"And on that note, it's definitely time to go," says Nate. "You ready, Shel?"

"I suppose," says Shelby, heavily. "Hospitals are not my favorite place."

"Mine either." Nate kisses the top of her head. "Now go pee because we don't want a repeat of the roadside incident from last time. I swear at least five thousand cars went past while you had your pants down."

Frankie catches my eye, and her expression clearly says, *Can we get out of this madhouse as soon as possible?*

"I'll be working in the office until after lunch," I tell her. "Then I'll go get my car and pick you up back here at two thirty?"

"Two thirty it is," she says, and her smile makes my heart beat faster. I'm going to work like a dog to make sure the morning flies by. Because I cannot wait for this afternoon.

Two thirty on the dot I pull the BMW M3 into the spot beside Frankie's Karmann Ghia. She's ready and waiting, and in the cutest outfit yet, yellow capri pants and a blue-and-white striped top, a yellow scarf holding her hair back and white espadrilles on her feet. Cute and hilarious because I've changed into a fresh set of clothes and happen now to be wearing a yellow polo shirt and a pair of seersucker pants in a pale blue and white stripe.

"Awkward," says Frankie when she joins me in the car. "Shall I put on a different shirt?"

"No time," I say. "We're due at our mystery man's house at two forty-five. We can always tell him we're twins who never got over being dressed in matching clothes."

Frankie buckles up. "Nice car," she says.

"It's not something I'd usually own," I reply, as I put it in gear and move off. "Nothing ever goes wrong with these, so there's not much opportunity to add value. That's why I'm excited to see what our mystery man has to offer. I'm expecting it to be a piece of junk, but there's always the possibility of a real find."

"And what's your professional opinion of my car?" Frankie asks.

I know a test when I hear one. Fortunately, with this subject, I'm on solid ground.

"I could sell it today if you wanted. Convertible in mint condition, could reach forty grand, maybe more if we got a couple of strong bidders."

"I bought it for twenty-five," says Frankie, thoughtfully.

I flash her my best salesman's smile. "Just say the word and I'm on it."

The navigation on my phone tells me the destination is coming up on our left so I slow down. The road is rural and quiet, and it doesn't look like there are many dwellings around here at all.

"Mystery man said watch out for an iron gate," I tell Frankie. "I'm guessing the farm kind."

"There's a gate." She points it out. "But it does not look like it belongs to Old Macdonald."

I stop the car outside what is most certainly not a typical farm gate. It's wrought iron and flanked by stone pillars. On one pillar there's a video-com unit. As I edge the car up to the gate, it starts to swing open. We've been spotted.

"Do you think we're being lured into the lair of a serial killer?" I say, only half joking.

"Should have bought your pickleball paddle before we came," says Frankie. "So we could use it as a weapon."

We motor slowly up a carefully swept gravel driveway formally lined with cypress trees and set among what can only be described as parkland, with mature oaks and chestnuts, and shrubs that have been trimmed into neat, curved shapes.

"They might be a serial killer," I say. "But they have excellent taste. And a load of moolah."

"Oh my," says Frankie, and I let out a whistle.

Holy shit. That's a palace. It makes my family home look like a dog kennel.

I pull up at the side of the big circular gravel area in front and cut the engine.

"Did you know this place existed?" I ask Frankie. "I've never even heard a whisper, and my mom and dad know everyone."

Frankie's smile borders on sly. "Bet you I know whose place this is," she says.

"What?" I'm taken aback. "Who?"

A series of wide stone steps leads up to the double front door that is right now being pulled open. Out steps an elegantly dressed blond man in his thirties, who smiles in our direction.

"Who else but the ultimate mystery man of Flora Valley?" says Frankie. "Known to us mere mortals as Ted."

Chapter Twenty-Five

FRANKIE

Ted seems like a decent human being but it's hard to tell through the layers of well-bred British courtesy. There are all sorts of rumors about him that not even Chiara has been able to confirm or deny. Given Chiara's powers, it seems impossible that she doesn't know, but Ted is her boss, and through her job at Bartons Hotel, she has access to the kind of connections she'd never make working at even the flashiest hotel in Martinburg. Chiara knows on which side her bread is buttered, as they say in Ted's home country.

Danny asks the most frequent of the Ted FAQs. "Does Ted have a last name?"

"Why don't you ask him?" I reply, as we shut the car doors and start to walk up.

"Because no one has before?" mutters Danny. "Or no one has lived to tell?"

"Frankie, my dear, what a lovely surprise." Ted kisses me on both cheeks, British style. He smells incredible, and not unlike a typical Bartons cocktail, with notes of warm spice, vanilla, and citrus zest.

He holds out his hand to shake Danny's. I watch for signs of macho grip-strength competitiveness but Danny's being sensible. One of the Ted rumors is that he was in the British SAS, their special forces whose missions are highly classified. If that's true, Ted may have killed people with the bare hand he's now politely offering in greeting.

"Thank you for coming on such short notice, Danny," says Ted. "I'm acting on behalf of an acquaintance who's been plunged into straitened circumstances and is hoping for an expedited sale of all their major assets, including this vehicle."

Being a lawyer, I'm used to unpicking sentences that on the surface sound clear and factual but in fact omit great chunks of vital information. In my mind, a James Bond scenario plays out, in which Ted's "acquaintance" is a rebel Russian oligarch with a price on his head, who needs to raise money quickly to employ his own private army.

"Happy to help," says Danny.

His face is alight with curiosity and eagerness to see said vehicle. He really does love his work. I hope he's rewarded with something special. My best ever vintage clothing find was a red silk Christian Dior gown in my size! I still have it and wear it when I want to make my best Jessica Rabbit impression.

"Nice place," I say to Ted.

"Yes," he says, vaguely, as if he's barely noticed that he's standing in front of a house to rival a Vanderbilt mansion. "Quite an interesting history to it."

Then he's all business again. "Let me show you to the garages."

The garages – plural – are way down behind the house, I suppose in order not to clutter up the entranceway. There are six, all with wooden doors that would not survive a ram raid, though security here, I imagine, is up to rebel Russian oligarch standards.

Ted lifts a remote from the pocket of his beautifully tailored linen trousers and opens the first garage. I can tell that Danny is holding his breath. He lets it out in a low whistle when the car is revealed. I recognize the hood ornament – it's a Rolls Royce. An older model, a two-door, goldish colored convertible with its top folded down, and that's where my knowledge ends.

"I realize it's not out of the absolute top drawer for this marque," says Ted. "And my acquaintance's expectations for sale value are reasonable."

Danny has snapped into professional mode and is walking around the car, peering at everything. He folds open the hood and scrutinizes the engine. Lastly, he runs his hand over the tan-colored leather seats, almost as if he's caressing them, and looks at Ted with a huge smile on his face.

"I'll have to sense-check my assessment," he says. "But my strong feeling is that this could fetch close to four hundred grand."

I practically choke. "Excuse me?"

Ted is unmoved by such numbers. "And how quickly do you think you could complete the sale?"

Danny pulls out his phone. "Let me make a few calls and I'll let you know."

"Splendid." Ted turns to me. "Frankie, may I offer you some refreshment while Danny conducts business?

"Yes, please." If it means I get to see inside the house, then I'll agree to eat anything, even sandwiches with cucumber in them.

Alas, Ted leads me around into a delightful garden area, with low formal hedges holding back an overflowing abundance of roses and other flowers I have no hope of identifying. A path made of golden gravel takes us to a paved circle in the center, where sits a French style café table and chairs painted a pale mint green and shaded by a modern cantilevered umbrella standing nearby. Whatever is on the table is covered by a white cloth.

Being a gentleman – he literally is a British aristocrat, but no one knows what kind – Ted pulls out a chair for me, and then removes the cloth to reveal a glass jug filled with a reddish liquid and topped with fruit, and a three-tiered stand holding miniature cakes, sandwiches and scones with jam and cream. It's so perfectly, ridiculously British that I can't help but laugh.

Ted, being perfectly British himself, ignores my rudeness, and pours me a glass of the red stuff. Fortunately, or perhaps intentionally having been forewarned of my tastes, he uses a strainer so the fruit stays in the jug.

"Pimm's," he says. "I can offer you tea if you'd prefer?"

I take a cautious sip. "Thank you, no," I reply. "This is weirdly delicious."

"A statement that applies to most traditional British fare," says Ted, with a smile. "Although often the word 'weird' alone suffices."

Set on the table before me is a white china plate with a gold rim, a crisp white damask napkin, and a pair of tiny silver tongs. Real silver: I spot a hallmark.

"Please."

Ted gestures for me to help myself, and I do. There's probably a correct order to eat these dainty morsels in, but I start with the scone. Jam is one of the few acceptable uses of fruit, so I'm not forced to surreptitiously scrape it off.

After the scone, I decide it would be polite to make conversation. Difficult to know where to start when I have so many pressing questions.

I settle for, "Have you lived here long?"

Ted smiles. He has hazel eyes with more green in them than brown, unusual for someone with such white blond hair. His skin is perfect, as are his teeth. He's either struck it lucky in the genetic lottery or he has a sizable personal grooming budget. As with everything about Ted, you'll never find out. Even if you ask him directly.

"Not long, no," he says.

See what I mean? That kind of evasion is … what's that British phrase? It's not cricket!

He must have spotted the determined glint in my eye because he swiftly changes tack. It helps that my mouth is now occupied with a miniature butterfly cake.

"How are things at the winery?" he says. "Do Nate and Shelby need any further help?"

"I'm not sure," I reply, truthfully. "It was pretty huge for them to ask Danny and me to come and stay, but that doesn't mean they'll confide in us completely. Shelby's always been an incurable optimist and Nate takes too much responsibility on his shoulders. So…"

I shrug my shoulders and take a tiny sandwich. It's smoked salmon, which is borderline but acceptable.

"I hear they may not hold the crush celebrations this year," Ted says. "It's a sensible precaution, given the timing coincides so closely with Shelby's due date. But I wonder—"

"Whether we *should* hold it?" I say. "We've talked about it, and the major issue is that all of the Armstrong-Durant friends and family will be supporting the birth if it does coincide, and it would be strange not to have them there."

"Sometimes community events become bigger than their founders," he responds. "And though the presence of the Flora Valley Wines families would be missed, I wonder if the event itself would be missed more."

I could interrogate him about why he cares so much about our little community when it seems like he'd be more at home jetting between international tax havens, but that feels churlish.

"Ava, Chiara and Jordan are the official organizing committee," I say. "Perhaps you should talk to them."

"Sound advice," says Ted. "Thank you."

There isn't a hint of disappointment in his tone but I still feel like I've failed some kind of test. Maybe I should take over organizing the crush celebrations? Maybe Danny and I should do it? Even if Nate and Shelby's baby decides to make its entrance on the day, it's not like that'll be our only opportunity to see our niece-slash-nephew. Maybe Danny and I should take one for the Armstrong-Durant family team and make sure our community doesn't miss out on the highlight of their year? I have no idea how we'd break it to Ava, Chiara, and Jordan, but it's possible they'll be relieved. Shelby will be overjoyed. She's determined that the crush will go ahead because it was always Dad's big day, and she wants to be loyal to his memory. Which I fully understand; Dad was larger than life and it's impossible to imagine a Flora Valley Wines event without sensing his presence.

While I've been thinking and, to be fair, eating another tiny cake, Ted has stepped away from the table to answer a call. It must be Danny because Ted's giving instructions on how to find us. Two minutes' later, Danny appears, a little flushed and breathless, which makes him look super cute and about fifteen years old.

"Three-ninety less ten percent sales commission, cash payment overnight and pickup within the week," he says to Ted. "Might get more at auction, but—"

"Excellent." Ted shakes Danny's hand again. "My acquaintance will be very relieved. Send me the details and consider it done."

He gestures for Danny to take a seat. "I think a glass of champagne to celebrate, don't you?"

"Not for me, thanks," Danny says. "I'm driving." He flashes me a grin. "And I haven't found out yet whether Frankie's a champagne drinker or not."

I am not. I know it's an elegant, sophisticated tipple, but to me, champagne always tastes like almond pastry. I like pastry but not when it's tainted by almonds.

Time to take our leave. I get up and stand next to Danny.

"Thank you, Ted," I say to him. "And I will think about what you said."

"Will you?" Ted arches one perfect blond eyebrow. "That's very good to hear, Frankie."

I offer him my hand, too. A tiny part of me would like him to bend and kiss it, but sadly, he gives it a firm single shake.

"I'll show you out," he says. "And thank you again for agreeing to come on such short notice."

"Our pleasure!"

I can see Danny fighting an urge to skip with joy. It's frankly adorable.

Back in the car, Ted having waved farewell and retreated into the mansion, Danny finally gives in and lets out a whoop.

"Holy shit!" He lifts his hands off the wheel. "Look! I'm shaking!"

"Let me guess?" I say, with a smile. "Biggest sale you've ever made?"

"Second biggest," he says. "I sold a Ferrari 550 for half a million a year back, but that was for an old friend of Dad's. I never thought I'd get a chance like that again. My sweet spot has always been classics between fifty and a hundred grand. Easy to find, easy to add value, easy to sell."

"So, who bought the Rolls? Another old friend of your dad's?"

"Friend of a friend of a friend." Danny's grin is slightly sheepish but mostly gleeful. "Never made so many rapid-fire phone calls in my life."

"And they had nearly four hundred grand in cash just lying around?"

"Well, yeah," says Danny, like it's not an insane amount of money to part with in one go.

"Wow," he adds. "My commission is ten percent…"

He gazes at me, eyes wide, as the reality of that sinks in. "Frankie! I made thirty-nine-grand in one afternoon!"

Wow, indeed. My *yearly* salary is eighty. I'm happy for Danny, but this is a world so far removed from mine it might as well be on an alien planet.

But now's not the time to kill Danny's buzz. That would be churlish.

"Drinks on you at The Silver Saddle?" I smile.

"Drinks for everyone," he says, firing up the BMW. "And curly fries all round."

Chapter Twenty-Six

DANNY

My mind's buzzing so hard trying to process what the heck just happened that I'm unusually quiet on the drive to Verity. It's only when we pull up outside the sports store that I realize Frankie's been quiet the whole way, too.

"You okay?" I ask her.

"Sure." She gives me a quick smile. "It's just been a weird afternoon."

"Surreal," I agree. "Do you think it was a dream? Am I actually asleep?"

She pinches me.

"Ow! Okay, not a dream." I rub my arm. "Good to have that cleared up."

The sports store, Ball's, has taken the place of a men's outfitter that I remember from my childhood. There are still old-fashioned mannequins in the windows, now wearing an array of sports attire, from fishing waders to tennis whites.

"Do you need special clothing for pickleball?" I ask Frankie.

"If you want to waste money," she replies. "Shorts and a T-shirt are fine as long as you can move freely in them."

"My old friend, nylon sports shorts," I say. "We meet again."

Frankie side-eyes me, amused. "Store closes in twenty. Let's go shopping."

I come out as the new owner of a pickleball paddle and a set of four yellow plastic balls with holes in them like spherical Swiss cheeses. I also got persuaded by Hank, the owner of Ball's (whose last name is Peterson), to buy a T-shirt that says, "Big Dink Energy". I have no idea what that means and am afraid to find out. I decided to stick with my running shorts, which are a merino-lyocell blend. Hank was dubious about their sweat-wicking capability, but I held fast to my no-nylon principle. Hank also complimented us on our coordinated outfits, which made Frankie immediately buy a pink-and-white argyle patterned golf shirt. It clashes with her yellow pants but looks amazing in all other respects. I had to fight down the urge to kiss her passionately right there in front of Hank. Much more reluctantly, Frankie also bought a pair of sturdy walking shoes. Hank urged her to break them in before attempting a hike.

We stow the goods in the BMW and walk down to The Silver Saddle. Frankie's still kind of quiet and I am most certainly still over-stimulated. For half a second, I consider slapping the bar in front of Brendan and declaring, "Bartender! The drinks are on me!" But one look from him re-activates my common sense, and I let Frankie do the ordering. A beer each and curly fries for now, and four burgers and more curly fries to go. Extra spicy pickle for Shelby.

Brendan's wearing his usual black T-shirt and jeans. The T-shirt is tight and emphasizes the bulge of his biceps and his pecs. He has multiple tattoos, including one down the inside of his right forearm of a skull with a sword through its mouth. When he hands me my beer, the skull judges me for wearing city-boy clothes. I'm tempted to say, "This city boy just scooped a cool forty-grand. How's your afternoon been?" What I say is, "Thanks" and pass over enough cash to cover everything plus a hefty tip.

"Frankie! Danny!" A cheery voice hails us as we're looking round for somewhere to sit.

"Okay," murmurs Frankie. "Now I know how Chiara got back in Brendan's good books."

Shelby's best friend, Jordan, is waving at us from a booth. Next to her is Chiara.

"Do you think we can run away?" I murmur to Frankie and am gratified to hear her laugh.

"They'd hunt us down," she says, and starts walking their way.

"Oh my god, you guys look so *cute*!" says Jordan as we join them in the booth. "All retro preppy like a 1950s beach movie!"

Jordan herself is wearing a blue athletic tank top and a pair of very short shorts. Her curly blonde hair is tied up in a ponytail and she has no makeup on whatsoever. Her fresh outdoorsy look and sunny open personality couldn't contrast more with Shelby's other best friend, Chiara, who is polished to the max and about as sunny and open as a nuclear bunker. But who am I to judge what attracts people to each other? I thought Frankie hated me and now we're a thing. Okay, not quite a thing. I might be feeling on top of the world right now, but I shouldn't leap too eagerly ahead. That way danger lies.

"How was Ted?" says Chiara, because of course she knows exactly where we've been.

"Ted-like." Frankie plays Chiara at her own game, and I am pettily delighted to see a hint of irritation in Chiara's face.

"Ted is the best," says Jordan. "You know, he donates money every year so we can run a summer camp for disadvantaged children?"

Her enthusiastic tribute coincides with Brendan's arrival with curly fries.

"Least he can do," says Brendan, dumping the plastic baskets on the table. "Got more money than God."

"But he doesn't have to spend it on us," Jordan points out. "He could spend it on … on…"

"Luxury yachts? Private islands? Graff diamond watches?" suggests Chiara, thus revealing three of her personal life goals.

"Exactly!" says Jordan. "Ted really cares about our community. We're so lucky to have him here."

I'm pettily delighted a second time to see the conflict in Brendan's face. It's clear he disagrees with every fiber of his being but does not want to upset Jordan. Last time he did that, Shelby told us, she shunned him for weeks.

"Another beer?" he says. Playing it safe.

"No, thanks," says Jordan, cheerfully. "Next kids' camp starts tomorrow and I've got to get up early and drive. But I'm glad Chiara made me come back here in between. It's been so nice to see you all!"

She says, "all" but she's smiling only at Brendan, who freezes for a moment like a deer in headlights before muttering, "Yup" and walking back to the bar at a pace a petty person might describe as hurried.

"God, his rear is delicious," says Jordan. "I can't wait for winter, when I can come here and ogle it all the time."

"Call me crazy," says Frankie. "But wouldn't it move things along faster if you told Brendan how you feel?

Chiara emits a disapproving tut-tut sound. Jordan gazes at Frankie as if she *is* crazy. I have no idea what's going on here.

"I don't want a relationship," says Jordan. "Not yet. I'm too busy. I'm happy to leave things as they are."

Frankie nods, apparently accepting that as an answer. I'm none the wiser but it seems the subject is now closed.

"What's next with you two?" says Chiara. "I hear the dancing was a success."

Yes, she does put subtle air quotes around "dancing". Shelby has spilled the tea.

"Oh, cute," says Jordan. "I can just imagine you two on the dance floor."

Okay, so Shelby hasn't spilled to everyone. Yet.

"Go karting," I say, and with a glance at Frankie, add, "Maybe a game of pickleball?"

"Fun!" says Jordan, who no doubt thinks every sport in the world is fun, including that old English one where they put ferrets down their trousers.

Frankie doesn't appear to be listening. Her perfect forehead is creased in a frown. Chiara says what I'm thinking. "Something on your mind, Frankie?"

"Um – yeah…"

Because it's so unusual for Frankie to be hesitant, we all

stare at her. She quickly gathers herself and addresses Chiara and Jordan.

"How would you two feel if I took over the organization of the crush party?"

Hello? News to me. Was this what was preoccupying Frankie on the drive from Ted's?

Jordan gives Chiara a worried look. "Babe, when Ava said she'd help, I was going to ask you whether I could bow out. I just have no *time*."

Chiara taps her fingernails on the tabletop. "It is a big commitment," she says. "And a potential conflict of interest. If Shelby goes into labor that day, I won't be leaving the hospital until we break out the cigars."

"How about you and Ava organize it, Frankie?" says Jordan. "Although isn't she supposed to still be taking it easy?"

Frankie's attention's now on me, and suddenly, I think I get it.

"How about us two do it?" I suggest. "It'll take the heat off everyone else. And it's not like the baby's going to turn into a pumpkin at midnight if it does come the same day. It'll still be a tiny red wrinkled thing the next morning."

"Sounds good," says Frankie, with a quick smile.

"So, who's going to break it to Ava?" Chiara's smile lasts longer and is ten times more evil.

I'm still pumped full of deal-fueled confidence, so of course I say, "I'll do it."

"Burgers up," Brendan calls from the bar. His tone implies that you better grab them right now or you'll never get takeout in this joint again. I swig the last of my beer and slide out of the booth. Frankie follows suit.

"Nice to see you, Jordan," I say, with a smile. Chiara gets a nod because I'm not a big fat liar.

"Nice to see *you*," says Jordan. "Shelby's so happy you two are here, and she's thrilled that you're together. Such a cute couple!"

I glance at Frankie but she's walking towards the bar. Probably checking Brendan hasn't rescinded our order.

When I catch up to her, I touch her elbow and she jumps a little, but then smiles at me.

"Care to join us in a *Gilmore Girls* binge?" she says.

"Tempting," I reply. "But I've got sales admin to complete. My accountant gets shitty if I don't keep my records up to date."

"Your accountant, huh," says Frankie.

I can't quite read her tone, but Brendan's holding out the takeout bags, so I'd better not keep him waiting.

"Thanks," I say, after taking the bags. He nods, which I suppose is a step up from overt hostility. Maybe Jordan's presence has mellowed him. Chiara certainly knows how to win friends and influence people, though "manipulation" might be a more accurate choice of words.

Frankie's already out the door, so I follow. There's still something on her mind, I can tell. My worry is that she's re-thinking how she feels about being with me. I liked the thought of us as a cute couple, "together", but though I had some luck today, I don't want to push it by asking her outright. Better to go with the flow and hope it doesn't carry me over a waterfall.

Chapter Twenty-Seven

FRANKIE

There's nothing I hate more than feeling like I've been played. I've got no evidence, only vibes, but my instincts have been sharpened by my time in court and I'd swear that Ted just manipulated me into agreeing to organize the crush. My guess is that he's convinced it's vital to the community that an Armstrong family member runs the event, and the only Armstrong family member who's present and not pregnant is me.

Chiara may also have hinted to him that I would prefer to see the baby once it had been cleaned of birth goo and swaddled in a fresh cotton wrap. That isn't entirely untrue. Mostly, I'd prefer to avoid listening to my sister in pain and worrying whether everything is going to be okay with her and the baby. If I'm running the crush celebrations, I'll be too busy to settle into full worry mode. I'll be able to reduce it to a mild background anxiety. As I said, I don't really know Ted but I do know he reads people well. And with Chiara feeding him intel behind the scenes, he'd be perfectly placed to play me like a Hammond organ.

Okay, so Ted couldn't have known for sure that I'd accompany Danny, but maybe he had enough Chiara-intel to assume it was likely that I would. Maybe he even contrived the sale of that Rolls Royce to lure Danny into coming, so that I'd come with him? Now, that's clutching at straws but it's not entirely impossible. Ted might not even have an "acquaintance". It might be his car and he might have five others, one in each of the other garages, so he could happily part with one. He distracted Danny and charmed me with tiny cakes, and I fell right into his genteel trap, curse him.

Ugh. No point in keeping up this line of thought because it's done now. Ted got his wish – I've taken on the organization of the crush. I've roped Danny in, too, and now we're both committed. No doubt Chiara will have texted Ted the instant Danny and I left the bar, so we can't back out. Curse them both.

But to be honest, my irritation at being used isn't my biggest concern. This afternoon, I got a proper glimpse into Danny's world, where money is plentiful and huge numbers change hands with barely a blink. All right, Danny was astounded by what happened, but it wasn't completely foreign to him, was it? When I inherited fifty grand from my late aunt, I thought it was a fortune. It allowed me to put a deposit on a house, which I didn't think I'd be able to do for at least another decade. Yet Danny made close to that amount in a single afternoon, and given what he told me about his business, a quick calculation tells me he could earn well over five times my annual salary. And who knows what kind of trust-fund income might be coming his way?

It's hard to tell how much money the Durants have, because having got to know the family a little better, my conclusion is they're what I call conservative rich. They think expensive cars and designer-label clothes are vulgar. They'd never own yachts or helicopters, and they certainly would not have gold taps in the bathrooms. They ensure any philanthropic work they do flies under the radar, no names on buildings or charitable foundations. God forbid that their photographs ever appear in the society pages.

But even if they're not the kind to flash the cash around, my guess is they still have, in Danny's words, a load of moolah. And today, I got to see how people like that operate, which is a stratosphere above anything I've experienced. I can guess why it shook me up so much. Danny and I might find we're perfectly compatible in every way, but I'm not sure I could ever feel comfortable in his world.

I've talked about my fears before, of being vulnerable, of being rejected. But my greatest fear is being forced to be someone other than my true self. And I would have to make so many compromises to fit in Danny's life. His family might have accepted Shelby but I am a whole different ball game. Shelby wins even the most curmudgeonly people over because she's relentlessly positive like Dad, whereas I tend to be cautious and suspicious and keep my distance.

And despite the fact she makes no effort at all, Shelby fits society's conventions about attractiveness. She and Nate were the picture-perfect couple on their wedding day, like they might as well have been standing on the cake. Danny likes to look good, and he cares what people think of him. It's possible that how I look and who I am might not measure up. And I refuse to be with someone whose life pressures mean they can't accept everything about me. That they can't recognize and honor my whole true self.

Danny noticed I was quiet on the drive back, but I told him I was thinking about what was involved with the crush. We sat with Nate and Shelby, ate our burgers, made jokes about the effects of spicy pickle. Danny was surprisingly low key about the sale of the Rolls, and now he's off completing paperwork and I'm trying to focus on Lorelai and Rory.

"We should watch *The Lost Boys* movie," I say. "Lorelai's dad is the head vampire in it."

"Ew no!" Shelby protests. "I can barely cope with the scary bits in *Ghostbusters*!"

I laugh. "There are no scary bits in *Ghostbusters*."

"My point exactly!" says Shelby.

"Weirdo."

"*You're* a weirdo."

Nate's in the kitchen doing ... something.

"Settle down, you two!" he calls out.

"Weirdo," whispers Shelby. "And you can't hit me! I'm an invalid!"

I might have lifted up a cushion.

"Don't make me come in there!" calls Nate.

Shelby and I exchange a grin and settle down to watch *Gilmore Girls*. Rory's in a bad mood. Luke's offering her pie.

"Does Luke remind you of Cam?" Shelby says.

"Apart from the flannel shirts, absolutely not," I reply.

"Cam would never run a diner, for one. He'd have to talk to more than one person a month."

Shelby goes quiet. Too quiet. Something's bothering her.

"What's up?" I demand. "Spit it out."

My sister screws up her face apologetically. "Cam thinks I should tell Mom right now about the pre-eclampsia. He says the baby's birth will be more important to her than any pilgrimage, and because there's a strong chance the baby will come early, I shouldn't risk leaving it too late to tell her in case she can't organize her travel back home in time."

I don't know why, but I'm suddenly furious. That's not Shelby's fault, so I take a deep breath before answering.

"Cam's an expert on Mom now, is he?"

Not deep enough. I sound very snippy. "Sorry," I mutter, ungraciously.

"It's okay," says Shelby. "I was cross at him, too."

"You were?" Shelby being cross comes round about as frequently as Halley's comet.

"Because I felt bad because he's right. I've been super selfish," says Shelby. "I've been using the importance of Mom's trip as an excuse to put off telling her because I hate feeling bad about her feeling bad whenever she's at the winery. But that's my issue to deal with and I shouldn't make it Mom's problem, too. She deserves better."

Unraveled, it's a fair point. "So, you'll tell her?"

On the TV, Lorelai and her mother are having a to-and-fro. Our mom is not the kind of person you to-and-fro with. She's the kind who makes you herbal tea and threatens to read your aura.

"That's what I'm worried about: I'm not sure how to tell

her!" says Shelby. "She hasn't got her phone with her, and she didn't leave me a copy of her itinerary. This was meant to be a proper pilgrimage, with no outside distractions."

"Did she leave an itinerary with Cam?" I'm back to being snippy.

"He'd give it to me if she had."

Shelby rests both hands lightly on her baby bump, caressing it. As I watch, I see the bump shift, as if a tiny internal earthquake has caused the surface to ripple like a wave. It shouldn't be a surprise, but it is. There's a real, live baby in there! My niece-slash-nephew! The first Armstrong-Durant grandchild!

Mom's first grandchild…

Damn it.

"You know which route she's taking, though, don't you?" I ask.

"I think so. She said she was starting in France, and that the whole walk is about three hundred miles. She's spreading it out over two months, so she can get to know the towns along the way. There are set places people stop at, apparently, and she wants to spend a few days in each one."

"There you go," I say. "If we look online, we can figure out how far she might have come, and where the next stop is. We might even be able to find out where people doing the walk usually stay. If not, we'll just call every hotel. We'll track her down."

Shelby's smiling and frowning at me. "Are you okay with this?"

"Doesn't matter," I say. "It's the right thing to do."

"I'm glad you're here," says my sister. "I couldn't have managed all this without you."

That's definitely not true, but I appreciate the vote of confidence. I want to tell her about taking on the crush, but Danny and I agreed that he should tell Ava first. He said he'd call her this evening, and that he hoped Chiara hadn't beaten him to it, otherwise he'd be getting a snake bite burn first opportunity. I said I thought Chiara knew the score on that front, but he shouldn't wait too long.

I check my phone but there's no text from Danny yet, and I'm not sure if I want to text him first. It's ironic. I can come up with a plan to track down my mother like I'm Carmen Sandiego, but I still can't figure out how to navigate my own feelings.

Shelby's cueing up episode five. I usually love *Gilmore Girls*, but tonight, it makes me feel like I'm gently drowning in a giant tub of molasses. Could be worse, I guess. Could be in a tub of lima bean puree.

My phone buzzes. Text from Danny.

Told Ava. She seems OK. Going 2 watch my back tho.

I text back.

Sleep with 1 eye open. C u tmrow. If u survive the night.

He texts back the scream-face emoji and two love hearts. Funny guy.

"Ready?" Shelby's poised to hit play on the remote.

Good question. Not sure what my answer would be if she was asking me about my life. But seeing it's about the goings on in Stars Hollow, I feel reasonably safe making a commitment.

"Sure," I say. "Let's do it."

Chapter Twenty-Eight

DANNY

Ava took the news better than expected. I suspect Cam has been quietly but firmly advising her against taking on too much. And from what Nate's told me, organizing the crush party is a lot of work. I've never been to it but it sounds like it's going to be huge. Up to three hundred locals of all ages setting up picnic blankets in and around the vines, the grapes having been harvested a couple of weeks before. People can bring their own food or buy what's on offer. Iris from the Cracker Café grills Cuban sandwiches on site. Chiara's dad owns a business that supplies Italian pastries to restaurants, and he brings along enough cannoli to feed the entire population of Sicily. Local growers bring baskets of watermelons and peaches, cherry tomatoes, and sugar snap peas. Ted's team at Bartons serve up non-alcoholic drinks because this is a family-friendly event. The actual crush itself is done in a line of big plastic bins, set up so everyone can watch, and anyone who's brave enough can leap in bare-foot and help the main Flora Valley Wines crew stomp the grapes.

Nate told me that for ages, the crush party was super small, just winery workers and their families, and it was Shelby's mom who did all the catering. Gradually, it got bigger and bigger, but it's only possible because the community makes it so. The local businesses that provide food and drink either do it for free (Ted) or only charge enough to cover their costs. There've also been the odd donations from anonymous benefactors. Likely suspects are Ted (again) and more recently J. P. McRae, majority Flora Valley investor. It's also possible that our dad's now a donor as well. He and J. P. are old friends and therefore intensely competitive. Dad wouldn't consider for a second investing in anything as flaky as a family winery, even one run by his own son, but he'll match every cent J. P. donates to charity. And let's face it, Flora Valley Wines is as close to a charity as you can get without actually standing on the street corner rattling a donation box.

All the more reason for the crush party to be a success. Having strong connections to its community is how most small businesses survive. Because that's how they become the businesses locals recommend to visitors. This might sound strange coming from a car salesman, but my business depends on a community, too, of car enthusiasts and mechanics and parts suppliers and restorers. I'm a competent mechanic myself but I'm always coming up against stuff I don't know or can't figure out. For every favor I ask, I make a point to give back whenever I can. And I don't expect every favor I do to be returned. Generosity isn't weakness. It's the oil that keeps relationships running sweetly.

And generosity doesn't have to be a big sweeping gesture,

either. Sometimes it's as simple as bringing a super stressed person coffee. Especially when that person is me.

I've run out of ground coffee for the machine. Should have picked some up in Verity yesterday but I did not. I got a pickleball paddle and four yellow plastic balls, and they are caffeine-free. It's only six in the morning, too early to walk to Nate and Shelby's.

Okay, so I'm pacing up and down. Is there a word like hangry for being coffee deprived? Stresspresso? Ragey-au-lait?

That's it. I'm walking to Nate and Shelby's. Coffee brewing is quiet. I won't wake anyone. Unless Shelby's ancient coffee pot finally explodes.

Sun's coming up, and it's another day in paradise. As I walk, I start thinking about yesterday, and how I couldn't wait to tell Nate about the deal with Ted, right up until we were all together eating burgers. I looked across at Nate and saw our dad, and in my mind, I heard him say that money wasn't a subject for polite conversation. Unless you're nagging your children about planning for their futures, of course. Also, Nate and Shelby aren't starving, but they're hardly well off. I'm happy to compete with Nate when we're on an equal footing, but it feels wrong to brag when we're not. I'd come across like Scrooge McDuck diving into his cellar full of gold coins.

Mom and Dad gave us Durant kids every advantage, it's true. But we all know how privileged we are and we also know that Mom and Dad expect us to make our own way now, without their help. Dad in particular was always super clear about that. It's why he gets so down on me – because my way's not the way he'd have chosen. I could call him up now and tell him about the success I had yesterday, but deep down, I know it wouldn't make any difference. He'll point out that it was a flash in the pan, a one-off favor from Ted, like the one-off favor his friend with the Ferrari did me. He'll ask me when the next big sale is coming and all I'll be able to say is, "maybe next week, maybe never". He'll point out how flaky and risky that sounds, and I'll end the call before I say something I regret and spend the rest of the day feeling like a shitty loser. I love my dad, but sometimes he makes it hard for me to like him.

Huh. There's a light on in the kitchen. With luck, it's Shelby, and she's already got the coffee brewing on the stove.

It's Frankie. Sitting at the kitchen table, scowling at her laptop. She's concentrating hard and hasn't noticed me. It's one of those moments where you don't want to startle someone but you know you're going to.

I settle for a cough as the least disturbing announcement of my presence. Fail. Frankie leaps like I've stuck her with a pin.

"What are you doing here?" she demands in a stage whisper. "It's the crack of dawn!"

"Ran out of coffee," I say.

She rolls her eyes. "If Shelby's coffee maker bites your hand off, don't come crying to me."

Frankie's cute when she's annoyed, and I will never, ever say that out loud. I do stand behind her and plant a quick kiss on the nape of her neck. I half expect her to swat me away like a fly, but she thumps back in her chair and lets out a frustrated, "Gah!"

"What's up?" I ask. "Anything I can help with? After I've had coffee, I mean?"

She exhales a long breath. On her laptop screen I can see a route map, of...

"The Camino de Santiago? Isn't that the trek your mom's doing?"

"Yup. My guess is she's somewhere between here"—Frankie points her finger at a spot marked PAMPLONA, in Spain—"And here." Her finger moves to a spot further west marked BURGOS.

"And this is important why?"

"Because Mom decided to go all authentic medieval and not take her phone," says Frankie. "So, I need to track her down so I can leave her an important message."

Lack of caffeine makes me a little slow. "How will you do that?"

"I'm going to contact every possible place of accommodation along the route. I can eliminate any big chain hotels – Mom would sooner sleep in a bus shelter – but it's still a loooong list. And I could be completely wrong about where she is, which is fun."

"Will coffee help?" I admit it, I'm on a single track here.

"No, Danny," she replies, turning around so she can give me an even stare. "I am dialed up to eleven right now. I am at Defcon one and my hand is on the big red button. If I get any more wired, I will launch into hyperspace."

I wait a beat. "So, I guess a quickie is also out of the question?"

She's got a good aim. Her pen almost clips me on the ear as I make a run for it.

"I'll fix you breakfast!" It's my plea for mercy. "Whatever you want!"

I'm safe. Frankie is smiling. A little wryly, but still.

"What I want," she says, "is to not have so many issues with my goddamn mother. I'm too old for this shit."

"I hear you." I really do. "Let me get some nuclear-powered liquid in me and I'll sit down and help you out."

Chapter Twenty-Nine

FRANKIE

I threw my pen at Danny but what I really wanted to do was say, "Yes, please, fuck me now, as hard and fast as you can, so I don't have to think about my mother and her five hundred possible locations."

But that would wake up Nate and Shelby. If we did it right.

I missed being in Danny's bed last night. But I also enjoyed hanging with my sister. I realize we haven't seen that much of each other in the six years since I left home. Ironic that we were watching *Gilmore Girls*, where Lorelai is forced to reconnect with parents she's been estranged from for years. And although it's a feel-good show, it doesn't make the family reunion look like sweetness and light. Maybe this is a message for me? A higher being is teaching me life lessons via the medium of a critically acclaimed comedy-drama? Maybe I do have my mother's woo-woo powers? Or possibly I just need a break. And food.

Shelby comes downstairs and into the kitchen just as Danny's dishing me up eggs. He's been paying attention and they are scrambled and well-cooked. The toast is buttered but not too heavily. He's made coffee, too, but does not offer it to me again because he knows that if he does, I really will injure him.

"Danny!" Shelby's hair is all mussed, like she had a rough night's sleep. "You figured out the coffee maker!"

"Yes, he uttered the correct incantation to unlock its arcane secrets," I say.

Danny grins at me. "The demon inside it escaped," he adds, "but that was a price I was willing to pay."

"Don't tease, I'm exhausted." Shelby lowers herself carefully into a chair, holding her bump. "The baby was thrashing about for hours last night. It was like I'd swallowed a disco ball and the soundtrack to *Saturday Night Fever*."

Danny, who's had at least three cups of coffee, suddenly launches into the falsetto chorus from "Staying Alive".

"Jesus." Nate's here, and not looking any more well rested than Shelby. "We could sell you to the army as a sonic weapon. The dogs are howling outside the back door and I don't think it's because they're hungry."

"Can you feed them, sweetie? I can't move," Shelby says. "Well, I can but I don't want to."

"I'll do it," says Danny.

The dogs used to sleep inside at night but Nate put his foot down when he moved in, saying that sharing a bedroom with four cats was enough. To appease Shelby, he paid Cam to make a luxury kennel for them, so now they have the most comfortable sleeping quarters in the whole vineyard. And having been rigorously trained by Cam and Doug, they're well behaved enough to be allowed to roam around the property at will. These three are the latest in a succession of rescue mutts that have ended up here. I like dogs well enough but never bonded with any of them the way I did with Ham and Luke. Those guys and I have a real understanding. If my neighbors wouldn't complain and it didn't breach a bunch of bylaws, I'd have them in my own back yard in a shot.

Danny, however, obviously thinks the dogs are great. He's left the back door open, and I can hear him chatting away to them as he dumps kibble in their bowls and freshens their water. The conversation's pretty one-sided and limited to variations on the theme of "who's a good boy, yes, *you're* a good boy", but it's sweet. Dogs know who's kind and who's not. They're smart like that.

I wasn't aware of having a fond, gooey smile on my face, until Shelby says, softly, "You really like him, don't you?"

Nate's rattling around fixing breakfast, so only I hear her.

"I do." My reply is short and businesslike because I hate being caught out. "But it's still very early days."

Shelby smiles but she knows better than to push. Danny comes inside and shuts the back door.

"I should get a dog," he says. "They're awesome."

"Take one of those," says Nate. "Take all of them."

"Ignore him," says Shelby. "He's sleep-deprived."

"Well, that's not going to get any better once baby's in the world, is it?" says Danny, cheerfully.

"Don't you have somewhere to be? Such as anywhere else but here?" Nate's clutching his coffee mug with both hands like it's a life preserver.

"Nope!" Danny pulls up a chair next to me. "I'm gonna help Frankie track down her mom."

Shelby looks guilty. "I'd help, too, but I'm not sure it'll be good for my blood pressure."

"Won't be good for mine, either," I say. "But sooner we get onto it, sooner it's done."

"How's your Spanish?" Danny asks me. "Mine's got better living in L.A. but I'm definitely not fluent."

"Won't be reading *Don Quixote* in the original any time soon," I reply. "But I've googled 'Do you have Mrs. Lee Armstrong as a guest?', 'Thank you', and 'Goodbye', and with luck, that'll be all I need."

"How many places do you have to contact?" says Nate.

"*Muchos*," says Danny. "That's Spanish for—"

"Yeah, I got it."

"Spain is nine hours ahead, so we'd better get started," I say. "How about I do Pamplona and you take Burgos? I'll send you the list."

"*Bueno*." Danny scans his email. "Okay, then." He starts pressing numbers on his phone. "*¡En sus marcas, listos, fuera!* Or as you monoglots know it: on your marks, get set, go!"

"It's not a race," I protest, but Danny holds up his finger for quiet. "*Buenas tardes*," he begins.

Okay, so it's a race.

Shelby and Nate retreat and leave us to it.

Two hours later, I'm about to run outside and yeet my phone into the vines, when I hear Danny say, "*Si, si. Señora* Armstrong! A message for her, *si*—"

He covers his phone, and hisses, "What *is* the message?"

"Call Shelby ASAP," I say.

"Er, *teléfono* Shelby, *su hija*, her daughter, *por favor*," says

Danny. "And ... er, *los antes posible*? As soon as she can? *Si. Muchas gracias. Adiós.*"

"You did it!" I say once he's hung up. "You actually did it!"

Danny stands up and takes a bow. Then he flops back down into the chair. "Oof," he says. "And I'm used to making a shitload of calls."

I resist an urge to lay my head on the table and close my eyes.

"It's only mid-morning," I say. "Feels like it should be beer o'clock."

He grins at me. "How about we take the day off? Do something on your list? Like vintage clothes shopping."

I perk right up. "I've earned it, haven't I?"

"Or…" Danny's grin is now accompanied by an eyebrow raise. "We could go back to my bijou accommodation for some more 'dance lessons'."

We could. I did miss being with him last night. I'm also cautious about things moving too fast. Then again, I'm tired of constantly overthinking things. Sex with Danny is fun and it doesn't mean we're committed to each other. Why don't you pick what you *want* to do, Frankie, not what you think you ought to, otherwise known as the safest options.

Thing is, though, Danny's already uttered the magic words that trump all others.

"We're going vintage clothes shopping," I say.

"That's your choice?" Danny sounds more amused than put out.

"I don't see this as an 'either/or' situation," I elaborate. "More 'now this and later that'."

"How much later?"

"Depends," I say, truthfully if annoyingly. "On what the shops have in stock."

Danny makes a rueful face. "I'm going to spend a lot of time sitting outside changing rooms, aren't I?"

"And in them," I reply, with a grin and an eyebrow raise of my own. "I'll be choosing some outfits for you, too, don't you worry."

"Not matching?" says Danny, dubiously.

"Hell, no," I assure him. "That was humiliating. We looked like novelty salt and pepper shakers."

"My car or yours?" he asks.

"Mine, of course," I say. "If we're going retro for the day, may as well go the whole hog."

"Can I drive?"

"Absolutely not." I get up and wince. Chair's hard and my butt is soft, which is why it's aching. "I'm going to freshen up. See you back here in ten. Don't forget your wallet."

"Wait—?" Danny calls after me. "Am I paying?"

Of course he isn't, I'm a modern woman. But it's fun to wind him up.

That said, the guy did make thirty-nine grand yesterday afternoon. I think I can be old-fashioned enough to let him buy me lunch, at least.

Chapter Thirty

DANNY

Frankie plans her shopping like she's in charge of D-Day. She's plotted out a route map that takes us around her strategic choice of locations in the shortest amount of time, no dilly-dallying. She's also picked a spot for lunch. It happens to be a place us Durant kids took Mom last year. It's kind of kitschy, which doesn't seem like Frankie's style, so I suspect she's only chosen it because it's en route. Hope she likes floral-patterned teapots and being surrounded by small porcelain animals dressed in British Edwardian clothing.

Me, I'm happy to be pulled along in Frankie's slipstream. It gives me time to fantasize about what I'd like us to get up to when we're back at my place. I feel a need to pay her back for the torture-sex session. Immature, I know, but fun to imagine. Though I'd better stop imagining now as we're entering our first vintage store. A bad look to enter boner-first.

Needn't have worried. Frankie races in before me like a whirlwind and starts flicking through the racks with the speed of one who knows exactly what they're looking for. I saw a video online of a guy in London who was mud larking, which is basically sifting through mud and stones at the edge of the River Thames to find valuable objects. He fished out an ancient Roman coin that even when I watched the video again, I could not spot. That's what Frankie's shopping style looks like to me. Why does she pull out that top and not the one next to it that looks the same? The tattooed pink-haired woman behind the counter hasn't even bothered to ask if Frankie needs help. She recognizes a world authority when she sees one.

"Here." Frankie hands me a blue-and-gray argyle-patterned sweater vest. She has her own items slung over her other arm.

"I'm going to look like Archie," I say, doubtfully. "The geeky 1950s version, not the cool *Riverdale* one."

Frankie eyes me sternly. "I find your lack of faith disturbing."

"Okay, master," I say, and only half-jokingly, add, "Please don't force-choke me."

We depart to separate changing rooms, and I pull the vest over my blue polo shirt. Wow. Frankie really has an eye. My next winter staple sorted.

"I look goddamn adorable," I call out to her. "How about you?"

"Come and see," she replies.

Oh, man. She's outside striking a pose in a rose-pink dress with capped sleeves and pencil skirt, waist cinched with a black patent leather belt. She is the sexiest thing I've seen and it takes all my willpower not to drag her back into the changing room and lock the door.

"Does something for me?" she says with a smile, enjoying the fact my eyes are on stalks.

"Does something for *me*, that's for sure." I say. "Don't suppose—?"

"I'm just getting started," she says, immediately. "This is still my first wind."

I know when I'm beaten. We change, pay for our clothes, and hit the road. Nothing for it but for me to buckle up and enjoy the ride.

Two hours later and I really *am* beaten. Non-stop shopping on top of half a morning spent phoning Spanish hotels and I am collapsed on this particular store's velvet chaise longue pleading for mercy.

"Pfft," says Frankie. "I thought you were a hiking, running endurance athlete?"

"I didn't train for this," I say, waving my hand around at the store. "And I need food. I'm so light-headed, I'm starting to hallucinate. Pink poodle skirts are dancing around my head."

Frankie's rubbing her forefinger and thumb together. Right, she's playing a tiny violin. Normally, my competitive instinct would be sorely provoked by this affront, but right now, I'm too fucking tired to care. Wait, maybe that's my way out…

"I think I might have to call off our 'later' engagement." I say. "Need to crash for a siesta, instead."

"The hell you will," says Frankie, hands on hips. She purses her lips in annoyance, then says, "Oh, all right, let's go to lunch."

She reaches out a hand to pull me up off the chaise longue. I'm prepared for her strength, so I don't go flying into the nearest rack of vintage biker gear, all black leather and ripped denim. I wonder briefly if Brendan gets his outfits here, but assume he'd never do anything as unmanly as shop. Probably orders his T-shirts and jeans directly from Hell's Angels. They come wrapped in chains and the scalp of your enemy.

I need food. Now.

Frankie's face when we pull up outside her choice of café is pretty priceless.

"Well, this is ... interesting," she says, noting the assortment of animal figurines on the floral-bunting-and-fairy-light-draped front porch. "Why is that porcupine wearing a dress? Or should I say *how* is it wearing one?"

"Inside it's even more cute," I say. "And by cute, I mean terrifying."

"You've been here?"

"Once. With Mom. And all my brothers and sisters," I tell her. "It was a bun fight. Literally."

"Could the food be described as dainty?"

Frankie looks like she wants to turn around and find another place. No way I'm going to let her. I get out of the car.

"Just order two of everything," I say. "And quickly. My body has consumed all its fat and glucose stores and is now turning on my internal organs."

"No stamina," Frankie mutters, but she gets out and locks up the car.

Fortunately, the menu contains enough substance to satisfy us both. Reuben sandwich for me, grilled cheese for Frankie, and a chocolate milkshake each. The sandwiches come with a leafy green side salad. Frankie scrapes hers off onto my plate. My sister, Ava, lived for years on nothing but protein bars and air, and my brother Max still spurns all watery vegetables, such as cucumber, iceberg lettuce, and tomatoes, so I'm used to quirks around food. But I have to ask.

"Are there any vegetables you eat?"

"Carrot sticks," says Frankie. "Plain popcorn. Pickles. Potatoes in their only acceptable form, which is fries. Green beans if they're blanched to perfect al dente. It's a fine balance to get the correct consistency, which is why I don't often eat green beans."

"And fruit—?"

"Apples. Have to be fresh and crisp, not a hint of flouriness. Every so often, I'll eat a nectarine as long as it's not too ripe. *Very* occasionally, I'll eat a slice of watermelon if someone has removed the seeds."

She stares me down. "Got a problem with that?"

"Not a one," I say, truthfully. "Each to their own."

"Is there any food you won't eat?"

I have to think. "I tried a roasted grasshopper once. Wouldn't rush back for seconds."

Frankie looks like I just admitted to cannibalism.

"They're the protein of the future," I say, with a shrug.

"Don't care," she says. "If I catch you barbecuing a tarantula, there'll be no coming back from that."

"Noted," I confirm. "No bugs. I'm guessing no beaver, muskrat, or raccoon, either."

"No one eats those!" protests Frankie. "You're making it up, like you made up the loony thrasher bird!"

"My mom has an old copy of *The Joy of Cooking*, from the 1930s. Totally a recipe for beaver tail in there. Also bear and woodchuck."

"Who writes a book like that? Davy Crockett?!"

Frankie picks up her milkshake and scowls. "Now, I don't want to finish this. You've put me off."

"I'll make it up to you later," I say. "And by later I mean how fast can we get back to mine?"

"Half an hour ago, you were dying," says Frankie.

"I've perked up," I say. "All of me is now super perky."

I see her hesitate. Frankie's a cautious person, and she has to feel sure she's doing the right thing. I get it, I do. But I still really hope she chooses the getting naked with me thing.

"You owe me half a milkshake." Frankie lowers her voice. "But I'll settle for several orgasms."

"Deal." My face is one giant grin. "I'll grab the check."

Chapter Thirty-One

FRANKIE

It was only a matter of time before Danny commented on my eating habits. To be fair, most people comment immediately, and they only pretend to be curious when they're actually being a hundred percent judgmental. When I was a kid, I was always called "picky". Even my own pretty chill parents became frustrated, and I became frustrated right back because it seemed obvious to me that I wasn't trying to be difficult. I was trying to be clear about what I would and wouldn't eat, and if they'd only stick within my parameters, we wouldn't have any fights. It's not as if I ate only white food and was at risk of going blind through Vitamin A deficiency. I ate vegetables, and fruit – just a narrow range of them. Mom tried all the time to introduce new foods into my diet, and occasionally, I'd be okay with whatever it was. Mostly, I wasn't, and when I was little, I could never properly explain that it wasn't just the taste of certain foods that I objected to but also the texture. All I could do was spit stuff out, and then the whole family would get angry with me for being gross and abnormal.

And, of course, when you're "bigger", people judge you even more. I've learned how to ignore stares and whispered comments from fellow restaurant diners. Because I know full well that it's not me they're judging. They're projecting their own fears onto me, that have been instilled in them by the ridiculous amount of societal pressure to be a certain size. This pressure is so insidious that we've come to believe it's normal and correct. But it is patriarchal, capitalistic bullshit, that uses our fear of rejection to oppress and control. Women mostly but also men. The system sucks, people. Don't buy into it.

I have to admit, I've been surprised by how little Danny seems to care about what I weigh. When we first met at Nate and Shelby's wedding, I thought he was your typical vain L.A.-dweller, where nothing less than Hollywood-standard physical perfection is socially acceptable. I thought he'd choose who was on his arm as carefully as he'd curate every other aspect of his appearance. He is vain about his own looks, but he knows it, and he's funny about it. He hammed it up in front of the mirrors today, a born showman. But whenever he looks at me, I only ever see pleasure and appreciation in his eyes. To be honest, I'm not used to it, and there's part of me that doesn't fully trust that it's genuine. I hope it is, but I can't convince myself just yet.

I can sense Danny looking at me now. When I'm driving, I keep my eyes firmly on the road, plus I've been mentally ranting, so I haven't said a word since we left the freaky-animal café. Probably should rectify that. It's a little rude to demand multiple orgasms and then ignore your partner completely.

"So … when should we talk about the crush party?" I ask.

"Whenever you like," he replies. "How about in the rest periods between our upcoming energetic bouts of sex?"

"Amazingly, I'm not at my most mentally alert during those times," I say. "How about tomorrow morning? In the winery office?" I add because someone has to inject a note of professionalism.

"Sure," says Danny. "Boring but practical."

He's still looking at me. I don't think it's a simple adoring gaze.

"Something on your mind?" I enquire.

"Just realized that in our shopping frenzy, we never talked about how you feel about your Mom probably coming home early," he says.

"There's a very good reason we didn't talk about it," I say. "And that is: I don't want to."

"Okay." Danny doesn't sound convinced.

"Do you want to talk about your relationship with your dad right before we have sex?"

"Fair point well made," says Danny. "Consider the subject closed."

We're coming up to the turnoff to the workshop. If you didn't know it was there, you'd miss it, owing to it being overgrown and approximately the width of a deer track. I remember once Cam had settled in and was officially making barrels, Dad asked him if he wanted a sign put up, or a mailbox, but Cam was happy to hide out like a serial killer. We could park back at Flora Valley Wines and walk instead, but we'd be spotted immediately and it would be embarrassing having to come up with a patently false excuse for why we're hurrying away.

With a silent prayer for the Karmann Ghia's paintwork, I drive slowly down between bushes and low-hanging branches to the workshop. The original building is over a hundred years old, all that's left of an old lumber yard. Dad fixed it up and made it useful again, and Cam slept in it on a camp bed before he decided to stay and build his tiny house. I kept away from this place when I was a kid — mainly because my older brothers told me frightening stories about it. By the time I was old enough not to be spooked, Cam was living here and it felt weird to invade his privacy. I'm glad of Danny's presence in the space. Feels like a few ghosts have been exorcized.

I pull my car in beside the BMW. Soon as I turn off the engine, I'm struck by the silence in this clearing. Gradually, my ear attunes and it's not silent anymore. I hear bird calls, the rustling of leaves in a slight breeze, the creaking of branches. The mid-afternoon sun makes shifting leaf-patterns on the ground and walls. I don't think I could live this remotely all the time, but there's something to be said for a cabin in the woods. Especially if you want to get loud in the bedroom.

Danny unlocks the door and closes it behind me. Now that we're alone in here, I feel strangely self-conscious. After all that anticipation, I'm suddenly at a loss for how to proceed.

My hesitation must show because Danny's looking at me quizzically.

"We don't have to get down to it right away," he says. "We could watch a movie on my laptop, instead?"

"No, I want to," I say. "But could we take it slowly?"

Danny smiles. "Nothing I'd like better." And he follows me up to the bedroom.

We get undressed at leisure. Danny's been smart enough to leave the window blind down, to prevent the sun turning the room into a furnace. We stand facing each other, and the soft light filtering in through the gaps gives our naked bodies the dewy golden quality of a renaissance painting.

"You are incredibly gorgeous," says Danny. "The first time I ever laid eyes on you, my jaw dropped." He gives me a lopsided grin. "When you tore a strip off me at the wedding, I was simultaneously terrified and aroused. I'm glad you decided not to stab me with a cocktail skewer. I'm very glad you're here."

I move towards him, brush my fingertips across his chest, and then slowly down his ab muscles, feeling them tighten under my touch. Lil Danny is straining at the leash, but if I stroke him, too, going slow may no longer be an option. It's nice to know he's glad to see me, though. I trace my fingers around Danny's ab muscles again, enjoying the contrast of hard muscle and soft skin, and the sound of Danny's quickening breath. Enjoying the sensation of my own body loosening with desire, becoming soft and molten and ready. I'm close enough now to feel the warmth of Danny's body and smell the musk of his sweat. Danny's not much of a cologne guy, another surprise, so his scent is pure him, with a hint of the cedar body wash I found in his shower the other morning and may also have liberally used.

"It's Old Spice, isn't it?" murmurs Danny. "That you smell of?"

"Why, yes, it is," I say. "The original and best."

He bends his head to the crook of my neck. His mouth hovers above my skin, and a delicious shiver goes through me. I want him to kiss me all over. Every inch from head to toe until I'm vibrating with lust and on the brink of coming like a freight train.

I must have let out a small noise because Danny groans, too. "Can we lie on the bed now?" he says. "My knees are starting to shake."

"No stamina," I say, with a smile.

I position myself on the bed in my best pin-up pose, one knee up, one hand on the pillow behind my head. Modesty aside, I have sensational boobs and I arch my back to show them off to best advantage.

"We're still going slow, right?" Danny says. "Just … you know, checking, in case you've changed your mind?"

"Kiss me everywhere," is my instruction. "Head to toe. Or vice versa, not fussy. And yes, slowly…"

Danny gives Lil Danny a quick squeeze at the base to get him to behave, and with admirable athleticism, positions himself above me like he's about to do push-ups.

"I'll keep going until my arms give out," he says. "Can't promise how long that will be."

And he starts to kiss me, gently, unhurriedly. He kisses my forehead, my eyelids, my mouth (far too briefly), my chin. My neck, my throat, my shoulder blades, my breasts, my nipples (again, too briefly). Every place his warm mouth lands instantly becomes lava, and I begin to arch up to meet his kisses, as he blazes a trail down my body. My eyes are closed, so I can focus only on the sensation. Danny's kisses on the soft skin by my hip bones almost make me beg for mercy, but then he's off down my left leg, on the inside where it's most sensitive. He kisses the tops of my feet and then starts up on the inside of my right leg. And then I gasp, as his tongue finds my center, and steadily circles and flicks and strokes until I think I'll expire if I don't come right now. Suddenly, I'm desperate to feel him inside me, to fill me as I orgasm.

"Now!" is all I can say, and he'd better understand what I mean.

Glory, he does. Quickly wipes his mouth, grabs the condom, and rolls it on. My eyes are open now because I want to watch his every move, his muscles as they work, the urgency in his face, as he lowers himself over me again, and I guide him in.

"Ah, shit," he mutters. "Are you okay if I—?"

I'm beyond okay. Every one of Danny's strong thrusts sends me higher until I orgasm like a fighter jet breaking the sound barrier. Danny joins me up in wild blue yonder, and his orgasm sends electric pulses of pleasure through me that become one with my own, a series of rippling and tingling little aftershocks that take eons to subside. Force nine quake on the Richter scale. Everything destroyed. We're the only two people left on earth. Yes. It seems I've become mildly unhinged.

"We forgot to take it slow," I hear Danny murmur. His face is buried in my hair.

"That's because we suck at sticking to a plan," I murmur back.

Danny props himself up and looks down at me. His hair is all mussed up and his face is soft with post-sex peace. His eyes are faded denim blue, your favorite pair of jeans blue. I find myself falling into them, like I'm floating in the sky, falling, falling—

Shit. Danny and I react the same way at exactly the same time. A jolt, like we've suddenly smacked hard into the ground. We gaze at each other wide-eyed.

"Oof," says Danny.

He's still searching my face. I have no idea what he might see in it. My brain is desperately trying to re-boot.

"Uh, do you think…?"

Danny's braver than I am. Most of me wants to pull the covers over my head and pretend no one can see me. But there's a tiny part that absolutely needs to confront this.

"Could be," I say. "I wouldn't know. I've never felt it before."

"Really?" Danny's genuinely surprised. "Not even a high school crush?"

"Nope. No Daddy-issue attachments to college professors. No awkward attractions to work colleagues. No regrets that one-night stands were only one night. No distance-stalking through social media. Nada."

"Incredible."

Now Danny's amused, damn him. This is no laughing matter!

"I'm picky!" I say. "And private. And cautious…"

And terrified. Of giving my heart to someone who'll shatter it into a million pieces.

Danny's not smiling now.

"I'm far from perfect," he says, softly. "But when I commit, I give it my all. I can't guarantee I won't piss you off at times but I'll always do my best." He hesitates. "If you'll let me…?"

Such a simple question. Such a huge one. Because whatever answer I give will change everything. And there'll be no going back.

"I really *want* to let you but, no surprise, I have to think about it," I say. "And don't say anything more right now because I might have a panic attack. This is the scariest conversation I've had in my whole entire life."

"I hear you."

Danny's smile is kind, and my urge to hyperventilate starts to subside.

"Nate's cooking tonight," he says. "Chicken pot pie. Our mom's recipe."

"Biscuits or pastry on top?"

"Biscuits. Nate makes a fine light and fluffy biscuit."

"Hot damn," I say. "I'll race you to the shower."

Chapter Thirty-Two

DANNY

Unlike Frankie, I have been in love before. Or something that only felt like love because it didn't feel like this. I'm not making much sense, mainly due to the fact that someone appears to have let off fireworks in my brain. I'm trying to stay cool but inside I'm like that Kermit the Frog GIF where he's waving his arms around like a lunatic.

Frankie's in the shower, and I'm lying in bed wondering when it will be safe to tell her that I'm pretty sure I love her. Maybe she'll never want to hear it, and every time I start, she'll make the mouth-zipping motion? Maybe she's the kind of person who'll consider it a given, so there's no need to say it out loud.

I'm not that kind of person. I like to express myself freely and I like to hear that my affections are returned. Growing up, Dad was pretty sparing with the emotional declarations but Mom made up for that. Of course, that meant all of us Durant kids were fixated on pleasing Dad, because his compliments were so scarce. Poor Mom, who was unfailingly kind, loving, and supportive, must have felt like chopped liver at times.

Frankie's got the opposite problem. No issues with her dad that I've picked up on, but plenty with her mom. Seems the parent we feel least connected to is the one who occupies most of our brain space. Thanks, Freud.

It'll be a test for us two when Frankie's mom returns. Frankie's emotions will be running high, and I'll have to make sure I don't add to her load. Which will be tough for me because I'll want to have her all to myself. But Frankie's needs come first, so I'll have to keep any selfish tendencies in check.

The shower's still running, so I grab my phone and check my emails. Finally, one from the producer guy. Shit, *okay*, the first pitch meeting with Netflix went really well. No commitment yet but definitely a favorable response. He should know more in a week or so.

I won't get my hopes up. Well, I won't get them up any higher than they already are, which is almost certainly too high. So many unknowns, but – duh – that's how it is. Only a psychic can see into the future and even then, they're mostly full of bs. I had a reading once and they said I was going to have six kids and live on a farm. Might as well have taken my thirty bucks and set fire to it.

Footsteps on the stairs and Frankie appears, wrapped in a towel that she drops to the floor. She's naked and glowing all over, and I am suddenly hard as a rock.

"Come here." I intend to sound chill. I fail.

She raises an eyebrow. "I just had a shower."

"I can make it quick." So much for keeping selfish tendencies in check.

"That bad?" she says, with an amused, knowing smile. "Oh dear…"

She saunters over, and slowly peels back the covers. The urgency of my condition is exposed.

"My, my," she says. "Whatever can we do?"

Holy shit. She grabs a pillow and kneels on it beside the bed. Fair call, these wooden floors are as hard as I am. Oh – *fuck!* – she wraps her hand around the shaft, and then lowers her head, and her tongue circles and teases the tip before she takes me fully into her mouth and—

Excuse me a moment. I've lost all capacity for rational thought.

I emerge from a haze to find Frankie now sitting on the edge of the bed, smiling at me.

"No words," I say. "I'll return the favor soon as I can."

"Yes, you will," she says. "But now, you need to get your butt out of bed and into the shower. If I miss out on chicken pot pie, I won't be answerable for my actions."

The pie is sublime, but the atmosphere around the dinner table is … tense. Nate's jaw is set so tight it's a wonder he can open it to eat, and Shelby looks like she's been crying and might burst into tears again any second. Neither of them is saying a word. Frankie and I exchange more than one "uh-oh" look as we eat.

Finally, Frankie steps in. "Did Mom call?" she asks Shelby.

Shelby nods, several times, over-quickly.

Frankie winces, and says, "Guessing she wasn't happy."

Shelby shakes her head the same frantic way, and then emits a gulping sob and claps her hands over her face.

Nate puts down his fork. "Shel," he says, wearily, as if this has been going on for a while. "Stop. You can't afford to be this upset. It's not good for you or the baby."

"She was so mad at me," gulps Shelby. "Mom's never been mad at me in her life!"

Frankie purses her lips. My guess is that statement does not apply to all the Armstrong kids.

"Shel, Nate's right, you need to chill," says Frankie. "Mom will forgive you. She probably already has. She's probably already made a mixtape of whale music for the birth."

Frankie sees Nate's face. "I'm not kidding. Prepare yourself for the song of the humpback."

Now, Nate looks like he might cry. "She's not going to insist we have a water birth, is she?"

This day has not been fun for him. I won't mention how much fun *I've* been having. That would be cruel.

"Luckily, Mom isn't entirely averse to modern medicine," Frankie tells him. "She had pre-eclampsia when she was pregnant with me. Modern medicine saved her life and mine."

"I didn't know that," I say, surprised.

Frankie gives me a quick, tight smile. "Lots about me still to discover."

She's creating distance between us. Rational me knows it's because the subject of her mom sucks up all her bandwidth. Emotional me is hurt. I know she got more vulnerable today than she ever has, but I'd hoped she wouldn't retreat to safety quite so rapidly.

But then, I hate feeling rejected and I react to it more

strongly than I should do. So, I give emotional Danny the mental equivalent of a pacifier and hand control back to rational Danny. We talked about Frankie coming back to mine again after dinner, but now I think it'd be better if she stayed here with Shelby. Nate looks worn out, and it's in his nature to keep pushing until he collapses. Frankie can provide a buffer, and another shoulder for her sister to lean on.

"What episode of *Gilmore Girls* are you up to?" I say and am ridiculously pleased to see Frankie flash me a grateful smile.

"The one where Rory gets two birthday parties," she says. "Shel? You up for another binge?"

Shelby is still sniffling, but amazingly, seems to rally at the offer. "Can we make popcorn this time?" she says.

I see Nate sag with relief, poor bastard. Maybe he and I should head into town for some brother bonding over a beer?

"Bro," I say. "Want to kill an hour at The Silver Saddle?"

Nate's not much of a drinker, and I can see his initial instinct is to say no. But it's been a long day for him, hard on the heels of a broken night, and he could do with a change of scene.

"Sure," he says. "Why not?"

"Go on." Frankie makes a scoot gesture with her fingers. "I'll take care of the dishes."

"Thanks." Nate sounds slightly bewildered. He's not used to people taking charge and doing stuff for him.

I collect the plates and pile them next to the sink. Then I drop a quick kiss on Frankie's cheek and she smiles up at me.

"Don't get into a fight with Brendan," she says. "He'll ban us all. Again."

"We'll be good," I reply, with a grin. "Mostly." And I steer my brother out the door.

Chapter Thirty-Three

FRANKIE

I don't do well when I'm confronted by other people's raw emotions. Because I keep my own on such a tight leash, witnessing other people's running wild makes me super anxious. What would happen if mine got loose? Would I make a fool of myself, get hurt or rejected? I've never been eager to risk it.

Not even when I know I'm feeling something I've never felt before. There's a French term for love at first sight, *coup de foudre*, which literally means a lightning strike. I most definitely did not fall in love with Danny when I first saw him, but this afternoon, that's exactly how I felt – like I'd been struck by an outside force. It wasn't lust, because I already know how that feels. This was very different – more transcendent than primal. Like it flooded my whole being and lit it up from inside.

As you might guess, I found it terrifying. I shrank into myself, and only barely found the strength to be honest with Danny about my fears. It was a test, instinctive on my part, to see how he'd react. He passed it with flying colors. But my fears haven't gone away, and nothing else Danny can do or say is going to make them. It's up to me now.

I had a very mixed reaction when Danny invited Nate out to The Silver Saddle. I was grateful to him for not forcing me to choose between him and my sister. I was disappointed because I wanted to go back to his place – I mean, he owes me a serious sexual favor, right? And I was angry. With my mom, and my sister, for being openly emotional. And *myself* for finding that so stupidly hard to deal with. As a result, I've raided Nate and Shelby's fridge for beer to take the edge off and am now drinking IPA, eating popcorn, and watching yet another episode of a TV show I may be coming to hate. I'm starting to resent Rory's close relationship with her mother, and I'm envious of Lorelai's ability to be funny and articulate at the drop of a hat. Which is ridiculous. They're fictional characters and someone else writes Lorelai's lines.

I resent that, too. If *I* was fictional, I could read my own story and know what happens.

Think this had better be my last beer.

Shelby hasn't said a word since we sat down on the couch, but she's nibbling on popcorn and seems to be enjoying the show. She laughs when Lorelai jokes about pelting the nurses in the birthing suite with ice chips. The episode ends and Shelby hits pause because she needs to pee. But when she comes back, she doesn't touch the remote. She sits down on the couch and lets out a sigh.

I don't know whether to ask her how she's doing now or just let her be. I may have drunk one too many beers, but that doesn't mean I'm buzzed enough to cope with another emotional outburst.

I could always talk to her about Danny. Might be nice to share how I'm feeling with my sister.

Or maybe I could avoid all the tricky subjects and talk to her about the crush party? That right there is the coward's way out and I will take it.

"Danny and I are going to start planning the big crush event tomorrow morning," I say. "Any particular advice?"

Shelby gives me a startled look, like she'd forgotten I was there. I'll forgive her. She has a lot on her mind.

"No…" She frowns. "Just make sure Chiara's dad gets paid. He always wants to give us the cannoli, and I have to literally press the cash into his hands before he'll accept it. And make sure Iris has help. She might have wrestled a full-grown alligator but she's almost seventy and it's not good for her to be standing all day over the grill making sandwiches. Javi can usually find someone who'll meet Iris's exacting standards. Javi can also find bouncers to enforce the strictly no-alcohol rule. Ironic, I know, seeing we're pressing wine grapes, but there are kids around. Ted has a store of extra picnic blankets for people who've forgotten theirs. They're super posh ones that you can roll up and fasten with leather straps. People always try to steal them, so Javi's bouncers will have to do checks on the way out, too. Not that Ted would care, but we shouldn't set a precedent. And we'll have to ask Ted nicely to provide normal non-alcoholic drinks. Last year, they were adding things like sea buckthorn cordial and strawberry tree curd, and I think maybe we could just stick with ice and lemon. And if I'm not having a baby that day, don't let Nate do anything. Tether him to a hitching post if you have to. And don't let me think I can sit in a beanbag or we'll have to call the fire department to hoist me out. The dogs will have to be shut inside, which they'll hate, so we'll need to bribe them with treats and let them sleep on the couch, and someone – probably Cam – will have to supervise Ham and Luke so they don't get overfed or in their excitement accidentally eat someone's hand…"

She draws breath. "Apart from that, I can't think of anything."

"Sure now?"

I'm smiling, but she takes me seriously. "Okay… Well, we'll also need helpers to make sure people park in an orderly fashion. Farmer Johnston across the road always lends us his field, but if we don't have people in hi-vis vests directing traffic, it ends up like New York in rush hour, all fist-waving and yelling and honking. The noise freaks out Farmer Johnston's turkeys, so you add frantic gobbling to the cacophony. We'll need a medical tent for anyone who gets injured or dizzy or has a turkey phobia. Javi has a registered nurse friend who can help out. Porta Potties, but you probably had those on the list already. Don't let anyone sneak into the main house to use the bathroom because then the dogs will get out and steal everyone's sandwiches. Sunblock stand. Water. Smelling salts for when I inevitably have a fit of the vapors…"

This time, I'll assume she's finished. Otherwise, we could be here all night.

"Grapes are gaining color fast," I say.

"Mm," is Shelby's response.

"Your favorite time of the year." Can't accuse me of not making an effort.

My sister looks over at me. Her eyes are still reddened from crying, and there are shadows under them from stress and lack of sleep.

"Frankie, did you really hate being brought up here?"

Where did that come from?

"Not *all* of it," I say. "I have some fond memories for sure."

"But it was hard on you," Shelby persists. "Mom and Dad always so busy, us kids forced to do a lot of the work so Mom and Dad could make ends meet. Never having as much money as our friends. Never taking vacations to places like Disneyland, even though it's not that far. No PlayStation or even cable TV. No McDonalds or Ben and Jerry's or Krispy Kreme donuts. No shopping at the mall with your friends. It was tough, right?"

"Well, I guess I felt that at the time," I say. "But now I'm older, I think what I truly missed was Mom and Dad's attention. I mean, I don't even like McDonalds! The pickles are great but that special sauce is not special enough to tempt me."

My attempt at a joke falls flat. If possible, Shelby looks like sadder than before.

"Shel, what's the matter?" I say. "Why are you asking me all this now?"

Her eyes brim again, and I brace myself. I'm not sure I can handle more tears. But I see her breathe deeply, getting herself under control. I've said it before: my sister may be a little flaky but she doesn't lack courage. Whatever's bothering her must be serious.

"Frankie, I'm so worried," she says. "What if my baby

grows up the same way we did? What if Nate and I have to work such long hours that we never have time to spend as a family? What if it's years before the winery turns around, and we have to keep scraping by? We can't really afford to have this baby, let alone more and—"

She pauses, breathes some more. I wait.

"I'm afraid Nate and I won't make it," she says. "Mom told me she and Dad almost broke up at least once a month when times were hard, but they'd had five years before they started the winery for their love to deepen and strengthen. Nate and I have been together fifteen months. The baby wasn't planned; I'm sick and can't do my job properly; the winery still isn't profitable, and if it wasn't for you and Danny, we…"

Her voice catches, and she can't go on. She doesn't need to.

"Hey," I say, softly, and shuffle over so I can put my arm around her. She leans her head on my shoulder and lets out a long shuddery breath.

"We'll make it work," I tell her. "Me, Danny, you, Nate, Mom, Cam, Ava, Chiara, Jordan, Javi, Doug, even Ted. We're a team. We're the Ghostbusters. The Avengers. The Mighty Ducks."

I hear a small snort of laughter.

"Want to watch *The Mighty Ducks*?" I ask. "Only the first one, though, the other two suck."

"Yes, please," Shelby replies. "I'll go make us some more popcorn."

Chapter Thirty-Four

DANNY

"Don't," says Nate as soon as we're in the pick-up.

"Don't?"

"Don't tell me it's all going to be okay."

Ah, shit. Nate knows me too well.

So instead, I say, "I'm here for you, bro. For as long as you need me."

"Thanks," says Nate.

There's a flatness in his voice I've never heard before. Being the oldest Durant, Nate's always had an overblown sense of responsibility, and he can work himself to the point of exhaustion. He never gives up, though, not even when he's clinging on by his fingernails. But that's what I hear now in his voice. Nate sounds defeated.

I revise my plans for this evening. I thought we'd go out, have a couple of beers, shoot the shit, head home mildly buzzed, get a good night's sleep. Now, I feel like I'm being my worst, most shallow self. Nate doesn't need brews and banter. He needs … what?

An idea to call Ava pops into my head. She and Cam would be willing to do anything to help out. I reject it because they're still in the first flush of love, and I don't feel like Nate needs two starry-eyed love birds giving him advice. He needs someone who's been through the mill and out the other side. I don't know anyone like that except for my parents. And that is a hard no from me.

Shit, oh well. We're parked outside The Silver Saddle now. Guess the best I can do is lend an ear if Nate wants to talk, and drink in companionable silence if he doesn't.

Every time I push open the door to this bar, I expect a scene from a Western movie, where all the patrons fall silent and stare at the city slickers who've had the nerve to enter their joint. The fact this never happens always disappoints me, but then I am a sucker for attention. Though, let's face it, the only attention I'm really after is my father's.

Brendan nods at us, which is his equivalent of a hearty welcome. I could feel flattered but his mood tends to change on a dime, so I won't provoke him by being over-familiar. The place is surprisingly full, so the only seats for us are up at the bar. Nate and I take the stools furthest away from Brendan. No point in being closer. Brendan would take his sweet time serving us if we were literally an inch away from his face.

Amazingly, he comes over right away, takes one look at Nate and fetches the bourbon off the shelf. Pours us a shot each. Walks off without a word.

Nate stares at his for a moment, then downs it in one. I'm driving and his need is greater than mine, so I push my shot glass his way. He cricks his neck, like he knows he's going to regret it, downs it anyway.

"Might want to wait for those to kick in before you go again," is my advice.

Nate says nothing. He's staring at the wall behind the bar. There's a sign on it that says *Line dancers will be thrown out on their achy-breaky asses.* Brendan sure knows how to make people feel welcome.

I checked around as soon we came in to see if anyone we know is here. Chiara and Jordan, in particular. It's safe. Well, maybe not if Nate's mood gets any darker. Apart from Ava, us Durants are more lovers than fighters. But I've never seen my brother like this. I don't know whether to try to get him talking or let him drink himself into a stupor. Both those options seem equally risky right now.

"Beer?"

Brendan's back and talking to me. It's unnerving.

"Uh, maybe later," I say.

I don't have to explain that I need to watch out for my brother. Brendan picked up on Nate's mood soon as we entered, hence the bourbon.

"Bumps in the road?" he says to Nate.

Nate turns his head slowly and blinks at him. Not sure if the shots have taken effect or if he's stunned by the fact Brendan's engaging him in conversation.

After a beat, Nate says, "A few."

"Money or love?" says Brendan.

"All of the above," says Nate.

Brendan nods. A guy at the other end of the bar has started waving to get his attention. Obviously new in town.

"Conventional wisdom says you gotta roll with the punches," says Brendan. "But you can't do that when you're on the ropes. When everything's coming at you, it's hard to keep perspective. Even the smallest blows feel big."

Nate's shaking his head. "The blows are big. Nothing's small. I can't make my wife well. Can't make our baby's birth safe. Can't get the winery out of low gear. Can't stop worrying. Can't sleep. And if I can't cope now, how the fuck am I going to cope when we have a new baby?"

Out of the corner of my eye, I can see the guy at the other end of the bar stick two fingers in his mouth like he's about to whistle. I'm torn between listening to Brendan and witnessing this slow-motion car crash.

"Don't look so far ahead," Brendan's telling Nate. "Don't even take it a day at a time. Do one thing. Do another thing. That's it. That's all—"

Holy shit, the guy whistles. And my Western movie fantasy comes true; the whole bar goes silent.

Brendan tilts his head to one side. I have visions of the scene in *Terminator 2*, where the T-1000 morphs its arm into a kitchen knife and impales the foster dad in the kitchen.

"Excuse me," he says to us.

The whistling guy is young, maybe barely old enough to be in the bar. And he's cocky. Soon as Brendan turns his way, he opens his arms in the "about time" gesture. Bet I'm not the only one considering diving for cover.

Brendan walks to where the guy is waiting. Close up, Brendan's biceps look like melons, if melons were tanned and tattooed. His black T-shirt emphasizes the breadth of his chest and shoulders. With his blond, shaggy hair, he looks like he drinks blood out of the skulls of his enemies. If I were that young guy, I'd need a change of underwear. But Mr Cocky is either high or his parents did not set firm enough boundaries when he was growing up.

"What the fuck, man?" he says. "Can I get a beer or what?"

"You can get out," is Brendan's even reply.

"*What*? Are you fucking with me?"

"My bar, my rules," says Brendan.

Mr Cocky is bouncing up and down on the balls of his feet, clenching and unclenching his fists. He's fit and wiry, maybe does martial arts. Maybe has a very specific kind of death wish, who knows?

"He's not going to take a swing, is he?" Nate murmurs.

Why, yes, he is. Mr Cocky's fast, I'll give him that. And if the punch had landed, it would have hurt. But Brendan catches his fist in mid-air and now has the guy pinned on the bar, twisted around with his arm so far up his back, his shoulder must be about to dislocate. The whole room collectively flinches.

The guy squirms and struggles but he may as well be held in an iron vise. Brendan bends his head and whispers in the guy's ear and he goes suddenly limp. Brendan lets go of his arm and shoves him up off the bar. Mr Cocky hightails it without a backward glance.

The bar stays quiet a moment more. Then the conversation starts up again, pool balls go click. Someone feels confident enough to put money in the jukebox and Kacey Musgraves comes on. I realize I've been holding my breath and let it out in a whoosh. Turn back to Nate and find him looking less pinched and gray. Two shots of bourbon and the floor show have probably helped, but I'm glad to see it, nonetheless.

"Do one thing. Do another thing," he says. "Did Brendan actually tell me that?"

"It's not bad advice," I reply. "Can't hold a candle to 'Live, Laugh, Love', of course."

Nate almost smiles but then his face crumples. "I love Shelby," he says. "So much. It's why I'm so fucking frightened. Every hard thing I thought I'd faced seems so trivial now. If I've never really been tested, what if I don't have it in me to deal with this? What if I fuck it up and break everything?"

He has a point. Us Durants know how to work hard, and we know how to compete. But we've never had to deal with serious failure. With the collapse of our lives as we know them.

But that hasn't happened, and it might never happen. Nate should take his foot off his own neck and cut himself a break.

"I don't know *anyone* who's more capable than you," I tell him. "And maybe when you think of your problems, you should picture them looking like that cocky guy, and unleash your inner Brendan?"

Nate pauses. "What do you think he whispered to him?"

"Hope I'm never in a position to find out," I reply. "Which is why I'm going to ask extra nicely if we can have another round of drinks."

Chapter Thirty-Five

FRANKIE

I did *not* have a good night's sleep. Didn't get to bed too late, because Shelby was shattered, but I lay awake for ages trying to arrange the thoughts churning away in my brain into some kind of order. Trying to figure out my next steps – "Actions for Frankie", as if I was holding a meeting with myself.

Here's where I got to: I made a list of the most important subjects and divided each into my two typical assessment categories – what I *ought* to do, and what I *want* to do – to see whether there's any common ground.

Subject 1: Mom.

Situation: Cam's picking her up from the airport tomorrow afternoon and bringing her straight here.

What I *ought* to do: be happy to see her.

What I *want* to do: avoid her as much as I can. Her attention will be on Shelby, anyway, so it shouldn't be too difficult to stay out of her way.

Subject 2: Danny.

Situation: I might be in love with him.

What I *ought* to do: sit down with him and talk about what next. What happens after Shelby and Nate's baby is born and we need to go back home, him to L.A. and me to San Diego? Or wherever my law firm wants to post me?

What I *want* to do: have fun and a lot more sex with him and ignore the subject as long as humanly possible.

Subject 3: Me.

Situation: my emotional blender is on its highest setting. I could make a smoothie out of golf balls.

What I *ought* to do: confront my darkest fears, of being vulnerable, and rejected, and forced to compromise. Throw a bucket of water on them and hope they melt.

What I *want* to do: have even more sex with Danny, watch TV with Shelby, feed the pigs, get super busy organizing the crush party, and basically utilize every distraction technique I can think of.

So that's it. There is no common ground between what I ought to do and what I want to do. I'll have to pick a path. And soon.

Right now, however, I'm carrying a mug of coffee over to Danny in the winery office. He texted me to say he'd slept in and could I be an angel? I'm no angel but I can tote a beverage. Even one that could burn right through to the earth's core.

I open the office door to find Danny slumped over the desk, head resting on his arms.

"Hit the hard stuff last night, did you?"

He sits up and widens his eyes hugely, like he's trying to force them to stay open.

"I had two beers," he says. "I also had a brother who

needed to get a lot off his chest. This is an emotional hangover, not an alcohol one."

I set the steaming mug in front of him. He gazes at it reverentially and whispers, "Bless you." Hard to tell if he means me or the coffee. I wait until he's drunk it. Never get between a man and his caffeine.

Thanks to Nate, the office is nowhere near as messy as it used to be, but it's still cramped. Danny's sitting behind the desk, and I've positioned a chair in front. I brought a legal notepad and Danny has his laptop. There isn't room for both on the desk at the same time.

"We could work at the kitchen table?" Danny suggests.

"Things were still a little ... um, *tender* between Nate and Shelby this morning," I say. "I ate my breakfast on the back porch with the dogs to give them some space."

"Tender but improving?" says Danny.

I wonder what Nate offloaded on him last night. Much the same as Shelby offloaded on me, I'd imagine. With luck, they'll start sharing with each other now. I know exactly what Danny means about having an emotional hangover.

"Tender as in both stepping very carefully around each other," I say. "Hard to say if that's an improvement or not."

Danny gazes at me for a moment beyond my personal comfort.

"What?"

I sound abrupt but Danny doesn't take offense.

"I wonder what would have happened if you and I had met under different circumstances?" he says.

"Such as?"

He shrugs. "I lost a bet and signed up for Lindy Hop

lessons? You wanted to sell your car and needed the best broker in the country?"

"Uh huh." I refuse to encourage him.

Danny grins. "I mean, what would it have been like if we had met with no family around us? If we'd been free to go out and have fun, get to know each other without all this extra pressure."

"Maybe it's good that we are being tested?" I suggest. "If we can survive this, we can survive anything?"

It happens again. That jolt. That sudden shifting of the ground beneath us.

Danny and I stare at each other, our expressions, I'm guessing, identical. A mixture of alarm and anticipation and hope, like we're both clinging to a rope, preparing to swing for our lives across a raging crocodile-infested river.

"I want this so bad," he says. "But I also don't want to put any pressure on you."

Don't look down, Frankie. Don't let those crocodile fears psych you out.

"I want it, too," I tell him. "But … I need time to figure out some stuff."

"We've got time," he says. "So long as our families don't implode."

"If that happens, we could always go on a very long hike," I say. "Hide out in a cabin somewhere. You know, until the National Guard sounds the all clear."

"I like how you think." Danny grins. "I like *you*. More than anyone ever."

Damn it, he knows exactly how to win me over.

"I like you, too," I say. "A lot. Now, let's focus. We have shit to do."

"Don't suppose we can organize the crush another day?" he says.

"Sooner we get the plan done, sooner we're free to—"

"Don't say it," he warns. "If you say it, I'll have no choice but to ravish you right here on this very small desk."

"Ravish?" I raise an eyebrow. "My, my. Fancy."

"Damn," he says. "I'd hoped Lil Danny wouldn't understand that word, but it seems he has."

"Lil Danny would understand it if you spelled it out in semaphore."

Danny makes what I assume he thinks is an endearing puppy face. "Quickie on the filing cabinet?"

"No!" I say. "Work now. Ravish later. Threaten Lil Danny with a stapler if you have to."

"Ouch." Danny winces.

Then he takes a breath and fires up his laptop.

"Okay, hit me. What exactly have we let ourselves in for?"

Chapter Thirty-Six

DANNY

It's hard to focus on grilled sandwiches and Porta Potties when you can't stop thinking about a quickie on the filing cabinet. But I do owe Frankie a sex favor, and I'm pretty sure she'll expect better than wham bam on an aging set of metal drawers.

Uh-oh. She's giving me the look. The one that means she's asked me a question. That I didn't hear.

"Seriously?" She knows exactly why I didn't hear. "Not even the stapler threat worked?"

"I looked over at the filing cabinet," I plead. "What can I say?"

"You can say, 'Sure, Frankie, I'll liaise with Farmer Johnston about the parking.'"

"I will do that. Noting it down now."

"And you'll need to hunt out last year's signs and the store of hi-vis vests. And talk to Javi about volunteers who aren't scared of turkeys."

"Turkeys. Got it."

"And pick one turkey to be our ritual sacrifice. Ensures a good vintage."

"Ritual sac—"

Oh, ha, ha.

"Anything else?" I say, with dignity.

She checks her notepad. "Seeing you and Ted are best buds now, you could politely ask him to make the mocktails with normal ingredients, not ones sourced from berry trees and seaweed."

"I'll mention it," I say. "But it's possible he thinks those ingredients are normal."

Frankie pencils a tick and scans her list. "Done," she says. "Phew. I need to let off some steam."

Music to my ears.

But her next words are, "Let's go play pickleball."

She's messing with me again. Has to be.

"I can think of a lot more fun ways to let off steam," I suggest.

"Matches are short – thirty minutes max," she says. "Plus, the time to drive to the courts, and lunch after because I do not skip meals. We'll be gone for two hours tops."

Two *hours*. We could have a lot of sex in that time.

Frankie notes my pained expression, but instead of relenting, she raises her eyebrow and says, "Afraid I'll wipe the court with you?"

That's it. My competitive urge is triggered.

"I'll grab my gear and meet you by your car in twenty," I tell her.

Of course, while I'm hanging around by the Karmann Ghia,

who should roll up but Ava and Cam in the old Dodge, its cargo bed full of wine barrels.

Out they both get, Ava quickly, Cam the polar opposite of quickly. He's wearing the summer version of his usual backwoodsman outfit – old jeans and a faded checked cotton shirt, sleeves rolled up to expose his manly forearms. Ava's in a black athletic tank top and cropped leggings. I, on the other hand, am wearing running shorts and a T-shirt that says, "Big Dink Energy".

"Cute," says Ava. "What's a dink?"

"About to find out," I reply. "Frankie's challenged me to a pickleball match."

Ava's eyes light up. "Can I come?"

"*No!*" I say. "You're supposed to be taking it easy! Besides, you can't play pickleball with three people."

At least I hope you can't.

Doug's turned up to help Cam unload the truck. Each barrel must weigh a good ninety pounds but Cam wraps his big ol' manly arms around one and lifts it off like it's nothing. When he's cleared a space, he hops onto the cargo bed, squats and hefts each remaining barrel, hands them across the tailgate to equally strong-as-an-ox Doug, who sets them on the ground. I feel like I'm witnessing a bunch of health and safety laws getting violated, and I'm also vowing never again to skip leg day at the gym.

"Frankie!" Ava spots her before I do. "Can I come play pickleball with you?"

Frankie is in the cutest outfit, a short pink strappy dress and matching sneakers. God, I adore her.

"Not this time," she says to Ava. "I have to teach your brother how to lose."

Ava high fives her. I'm outnumbered and outgunned.

"Are you going with Cam to pick up Mom tomorrow?" Frankie asks Ava.

"Squeeze in between them on the Dodge's cozy bench seat, you mean?" Ava replies.

They exchange a look that I'm not sure how to interpret.

Then Ava grins. "Enjoy your pickleball. Don't mind it if Danny sulks. He's always been a terrible sulker."

"Insult jar!" I insist.

"Not an insult if it's true!" Ava yells over her shoulder, as she hops off to go watch Cam and Doug compete for the title of world's strongest man. They'll probably be ripping phone books in half next.

Frankie's expression is thoughtful, but when she notices I'm looking at her, she smiles.

"Ready?" she says.

"Not even a little bit."

"Perfect. Let's go."

I'll spare you the details, but Frankie kicks my ass. Pickleball isn't hard, but there's definitely an art to it that she's mastered and I comprehensively have not. We play three games and in each one she cleans me up in record time. It's more of a drubbing than I'd ever had playing Izzy and Max at tennis. But do I sulk? No, sir, I do not! I am a most gracious loser. Because, of course, I want Ava to have a second entry in the insult jar. If I can't win at pickleball, at least I can win at petty revenge.

We grab sandwiches and sodas from a place that we select

for its outdoor seating because we smell like sweat and, in my case, defeat. I remember what Frankie looked like coming out of the shower yesterday, her bare skin all rosy and glowing, and the supportive gusset of my running shorts proves no match for Lil Danny at full salute. Luckily, the table provides adequate concealment.

"Have you considered that you might be a sex maniac?" says Frankie.

Not adequate enough, it seems. Though she is sitting right next to me.

"It's not my fault!" I protest. "I'm up against hormones and pheromones and primal mating instincts and the irresistible magnetism of Old Spice!"

"It is a sexy scent, isn't it?" says Frankie, smugly.

"And you!" I add. "You and your cute little dress, and your big blue eyes, and the melted cheese on your bottom lip – what's a red-blooded guy to do?"

Frankie gazes at me with her big blue eyes, as she lifts the string of melted cheese off her bottom lip with one finger and pushes said finger all the way, very slowly, into her mouth. Lil Danny is on the brink of an incident, and I did not bring a change of clothes.

"This is cruel and inhuman punishment," I say. "First a pickleball thrashing, now a sex act with cheese. Can we leave now? Do I have to beg?"

"You're so cute when you're desperate." Frankie bats her eyelashes at me. "Yes, we can leave now."

She glances at my shorts. "But you might want to hold your pickleball paddle over that. Spare our fellow diners' blushes."

It's hard to walk casually when you're holding a paddle

over your groin. I remind myself that the day's humiliations are almost at an end, and long hours of pleasure await as the afternoon stretches on to evening.

My phone buzzes. It's a text from Nate.

Ava and Cam staying for dinner.

Fuck. I forgot. It's my night to cook.

"Uh, Frankie," I say, as she's about to unlock the car. "Can we go via the grocery store?"

She gives me a look. "Okay, but if Lil Danny gets overexcited in the dairy aisle, I'll make you both hitch a ride home."

Chapter Thirty-Seven

FRANKIE

I guess it's hard to be subtle about your horniness when you've got a body part that goes off like a smoke alarm whenever there's even a hint of heat in the air. Women get perky nipples and maybe a little flushed in the face, but apart from that everything happens on the inside. You can be walking around a grocery store finding the ingredients for *pasta all'arrabbiata* and nobody there will be able to tell from looking at you that you're in a fever of lust. It's so bad, I'm thinking about slipping Danny's hand under my skirt for a quick finger bang by the frozen desserts. But that wouldn't be fair on him. He's suffered enough today – pickleball plus an abrupt curtailing of our afternoon fun-time because he forgot he was tonight's chef. You can't take a rain check on dinner when you're the one cooking it. On top of that, Ava and Cam are joining us. Poor Danny. He's holding that bottle of tomato passata like it weighs ten tons.

"Will you eat this?" he says.

"When sparingly applied to the pasta," I reply. "And not accompanied by mushrooms, anchovies, capers, or olives."

"Chili all right?"

He's so sweet. I kiss him on the cheek. "Chili is fine if it's in flake or powder form," I say. "But I will spend hours picking actual chili peppers out of any dish."

"Got it." He screws up his mouth. "Sorry. Nate reminded me when I dropped him home last night, but by then my brain was fried."

"Don't apologize," I tell him. "Focus, so we can get out of here."

By the time we pull up outside Danny's, it's five minutes to three. Dinner's expected at seven-thirty. Okay, so we could swoop in at the last minute, puffed and still sweaty, and ensure everyone knows exactly what we've been up to. Or we could allow, say, thirty minutes for showers and getting dressed, five minutes to drive, and an hour for cooking plus polite pre-dinner conversation. Which would leave us ninety minutes, give or take. I'm a planner, what can I say?

Good thing about both of you being in a fever of lust is that you don't need to waste time on chat. Soon as the front door is closed, Danny and I are in a clinch, hands shoving away clothing, kissing like we've been starved of each other for years. My whole body is humming, desperate for him to be inside me, to touch me in every good place. I can feel his erection straining inside his shorts, pressing against me, so close, yet so far. My knees are starting to jellify. I need us to get horizontal fast.

But Danny starts moving backwards and because I'm basically surgically attached, I go with him. He half topples, half sinks onto one of the wooden chairs, and pulls me down so that I'm straddling his lap.

"Sorry," he breathes. "Knees were giving out."

"Don't be sorry," I say. "Get inside me."

"Can't," he says. "Condoms upstairs."

"I am not moving," I tell him. "So let's do this…"

Gently, I ease his erection from his shorts so that it's standing proud. Quick as I can, I slip off my own panties and straddle his lap again. I press my center against his hardness, and start to move, up and down and around. Danny groans.

"Frankie, I—"

"Shh," I hiss, urgently. "I'm so close…"

And I'm there. My orgasm is quick and explosive. No surprise, it's been building since the frozen dessert section. I move against Danny, slower and slower, until it recedes, and rest my forehead against his chest. I become aware that his heart is thumping and whole body is trembling. Took a lot of self-control on his part not to come along with me. For which I'm grateful. Be embarrassing to have to explain how my pickleball dress looked like I had an incident with a jar of mayo.

I lift my head. Danny's head is tilted backwards, his eyes are shut and his whole face is screwed up in concentration. Probably still reciting his times tables.

"You okay?" I say.

He screws his face up even tighter. That'd be a no, then. I could help him out the way I did before, but I'm too happy sitting here, and even with cushioning, this wooden flooring is very hard on the knees. I could use my hand but I'd need a …

how shall we say? … receptacle. Otherwise, this'll be like Old Faithful in Yellowstone.

I check around. Answer is right in front of me. Danny's "Big Dink Energy" T-shirt is loose, and soft, and already kind of stinky. Perfect. Ideally, I'd put lube or moisturizer on my hand but I don't think this will take long.

With one hand, I poise the T-shirt in readiness, and with the other take hold of his erection. He groans again, screws his eyes shut even harder, like he's in pain. Poor boy. Help is on the way.

I'm only a few strokes in, when he grabs my hand with both of his and makes a sprint for the finish line. The T-shirt does its job. Except I forgot that now he'll have to take it off, which could prove messy. Oh well. That's why showers were invented. And cedar body wash.

"Urghh." Danny's peering down at his T-shirt bunched-up in my hand. "Is that what I think it is?"

"Couldn't reach the dish towel," I say. "Lift up your arms. I'll be careful."

There's a tiny bit of leakage but could be worse. I dump the shirt on the floor. Danny can wash it later. Or burn it, whatever.

His face is relaxed and soft now, and he's smiling at me with wry affection.

"On the way back here, I had visions of us taking our time in the comfort of my bed," he says. "We could have done this in your car by the roadside."

"Nope." I shake my head. "Not enough room."

Danny's no longer so amused. "That's a very definitive answer."

I give him a steady look. "Do we want to list every one of our previous sexual encounters? Or would we prefer to draw a line under them and move on?"

He's struggling not to make the sulky-boy face. "Move on," he agrees, grudgingly. And immediately adds, "But if you were to list them, how many would there be?"

"Fifty-nine," I say.

"*What?*" Danny's aghast. "Seriously?"

"No!' I smack him lightly on his bare chest. "It was a stupid answer to a stupid question!"

"You're mean," he says. "But I'm glad you were lying. *My* list only totals fifty-five."

I fix him with my best courtroom glare, until he gives in and grins. "Messing with you," he says. "My list is actually only—"

"Shut up or there'll be no encore."

"And it doesn't include any time I didn't get past second base—"

"Shut up now." My voice has that sing-song warning lilt to it.

"Or any time I—"

"Right, that's it." I hop off his lap, scoop my panties up off the floor. "I'm having a shower. And after that, I will think about going back to bed with you."

"I could join you in the shower?" he calls out after me. "Too soon?"

My answer is short and involves my middle finger. I can hear him laughing as I slam the bathroom door behind me. Then I lean against the door myself and indulge in a silly, goofy smile. I am happier than I've ever been in my life. It's wonderful, and it's terrifying, but I'll do my best to ignore that part.

When I come back out into the living area, Danny's nowhere to be seen. His T-shirt is gone from the floor, so maybe he's hosing it down outside. Then I hear a creak above me, footsteps on the bedroom floor. I'm naked and wrapped in a towel, conveniently packaged, if you like. I hope Danny is ready and waiting. I am most certainly primed for round two.

"Hey." Danny's lying on the bed, one arm crooked behind his head, a pose that heightens the definition of his chest and ab muscles. He's lean and fit, and his skin is tanned golden all over, apart from a cute paler area in the middle that's shaped like a pair of running shorts. Lil Danny has revived in the interim. And he's condomed up. Big Danny's not only ready, he's raring to go.

I drop my towel, and Danny grips the base of his erection. His eyes darken with desire, and my insides turn entirely liquid.

"If it's okay with you, I'd like you to fuck me senseless," I say. "We've got forty-five minutes."

Danny sits up and opens his arms. "Then get your gorgeous ass over here right now."

Chapter Thirty-Eight

DANNY

I've had quite the workout today, though the less said about the pickleball games the better. The last forty-five minutes was a non-stop sexual world championship bout, with the final score for that round: Frankie, two orgasms, and me, one, but worth the wait. We shower together but only because we're running late, no time for hanky-panky. I pull on a change of clothes and we hop, still damp, into the Karmann Ghia and screech around to Nate and Shelby's. Frankie dashes upstairs to change and I take a deep breath, set my expression to relaxed casual, and tote the groceries into the kitchen to be greeted by Nate and Shelby, Cam and Ava.

"Where's 'Big Dink Energy'?" says Ava.

"Dinked out," I say, dumping the bag on the counter. "I lost all three games in record time."

"And you're admitting it?" says Ava.

I spread my hands. "What can I tell you? I accepted a total trouncing with grace and dignity. Frankie will back me up."

"Well, well." Ava doesn't seem bothered at all. "Another name in the jar for me."

"I can't believe there are only three names in here so far," says Nate, who's gone to fetch said jar. "And that only two of them are Ava's."

"Early days," says Ava as she drops her name in. "I predict a late run by Danny will take home the punishment prize."

"Oh, you do?" I say.

She smirks at me. "You're so easily provoked."

I could defend myself, but that would prove she's provoked me, damn her. Time to focus on cooking. Pasta, tomato, chili flakes, oil, a green salad that Frankie won't touch, and French beans I intend to cook just right, so she *will* eat them.

Just at that moment, Frankie enters the kitchen, looking fresh as a literal daisy in her yellow pants with a cropped white top. She says hello to the others and sidles up beside me, slips her arm around my waist. I drop a kiss on her hair.

"Beer, Frankie?" says Cam.

I sense Frankie's reluctance to leave my side. But she gives my waist a last squeeze, and heads for the table.

"Sure," she says to Cam. "Thanks."

My back's to the table, and I need to focus because soggy pasta is not good, so the chat comes to me in snippets. Cam is talking to Shelby about grapes, and the conversation turns to testing and other subjects beyond my ken. I catch a mention of the crush, but Frankie's just reassuring Shelby that it's all under control. And then, Shelby asks Cam about her mom's arrival tomorrow. I tune in because I know how much this bothers Frankie, and I want to be there for her if she needs me.

"Picking her up at two," Cam says. "Be back here around four, if traffic's not too heavy. Don't have to swing by her place. She's got what she needs in her suitcase."

"So she's staying here? In the house? Until the birth?" I hear the edge in Frankie's voice.

"We've got room." Shelby sounds anxiously apologetic. "And it's a long drive to Mom's house from here. She can't go back and forth every day."

"Why does she need to be here every day?" says Frankie. "That's why you invited me, isn't it? Or is it that now Mom's back, I'm of no more use?"

I leave off trimming beans and turn round. Frankie's expression is full Angry Bird, and Shelby looks again on the verge of tears.

Nate steps in. "Frankie, we want you here, too. You and Danny, both. Please don't make a thing about this."

"*Me*?" Frankie's hands are on the table, like she's about to launch herself upward. "*I'm* the one who risked losing my job to come here! *I'm* the one who's left her home and her friends! Why shouldn't I make a 'thing' about it? Why is what *Mom* wants more important than what *I* want?"

Shit. I have to take pasta off the stove. In that moment, Frankie shoves back her chair and storms out. Ava flashes me a sympathetic glance, as I'm stuck here, dumping pasta in a colander. Nate looks gray and weary again, and Shelby, tearful. Even Cam looks on edge, and he usually looks like he's off drinking margaritas in a beach in his mind.

Pasta's drained. Fuck the sauce, it can wait. I start to walk out, to go check on Frankie, but Cam gets up and blocks my way.

"I'll go," he says. "Frankie and I have some talking to do."

I'm torn. It should be me who comforts Frankie, who hears her out. Plus, I'm scared Cam will fuck it up, make it worse, and Frankie will leave for good. I can't chase her all the way to San Diego. Can't leave Nate in the lurch.

Cam reads my mind. "It's okay. Frankie's not a quitter."

Being scared makes me angry, but it's not fair to take it out on Cam. All of a sudden, I feel Ava's hand on my arm. Her expression is affectionate and kind.

"Come on, I'll help you with the rest of dinner," she says. "Pasta's not great when it's cold."

I look at Nate, and though he's trying hard to keep it together, I see the plea in his eyes. Cam's waiting for me to decide. He's not going to ride roughshod over my wishes. These are good people I'm surrounded by. I should trust them.

"Okay," I say, abruptly, and hope I'm not making a huge mistake.

Cam starts for the stairs. I let Ava hook her arm in mine and lead me back to the kitchen.

Chapter Thirty-Nine

FRANKIE

I know I'm overreacting. No one needs to tell me! But the sheer unfairness of it all just gets to me. It's like when I was a kid, everyone worshiped Mom. In their eyes, she could do no wrong. She was the serene, flame-haired goddess and I was the chubby little ball of anger. The difficult Armstrong kid. The picky eater. The annoying baby sister who always wanted to tag along. The one everyone was too busy to spend time with.

It hurt then and it doesn't take much for me to feel that hurt now. And though I know I should shake it off and not make my sister's life harder, I can't. Not right away. So, I'll sit here in the room that reminds me of my childhood until I've worked this out of my system. The way I'm feeling right now, that could very well take another twenty-six years.

There's a soft knock on the bedroom door, and my heart leaps. Danny. Coming to see if I'm okay. I rush to open the door, desperate for comfort, desperate to see the one person who puts me first.

It's Cam. I'm so furious with disappointment that I could hit him. Not that he'd notice; it'd be like a flea smacking an elephant. Even though my expression must be pure molten rage, he doesn't flinch, which only makes me angrier. How dare he be calm? How dare he not be Danny?

"Can we talk?" he says.

"No!"

I try to slam the door but, of course, he takes hold of it, and my strength is no match for his.

"I owe you an apology," he says. "It's about a decade overdue."

My brain takes a moment to process what he just said, because it's the last thing I expected to hear. Curiosity does battle with anger, and after a short scuffle, wins out.

"An apology for what?"

"Can I come in?" he says.

"Fine," I say, ungraciously, and let go of the door.

Cam enters my childhood bedroom, which suddenly feels twice as small. I sit cross-legged at the head of the bed and hug a pillow to me. He pulls out the wooden chair I used to sit on to do my homework. I'm worried it'll crumple like matchwood beneath him, but he tests its sturdiness before sitting down. I forget Cam knows all there is to know about wood. He's a master cooper now, one of the world's elite barrel makers. He built the whole house that Danny's been staying in.

I realize I've known Cam for twelve years, nearly half my life, but I don't really know who he is. To me, he's the big guy, the ex-army veteran that Dad brought home one day. He looked like a homeless person, and barely said a word. Despite that, Mom and Dad let him stay in the workshop, which I found very weird. I was used to people coming in and out of our house all the time, because Mom and Dad were so hospitable. But Cam I was wary of, for reasons I couldn't work out when I was fourteen. Looking back, I think I instinctively knew my parents treated Cam differently from anyone else who worked in the winery. That Mom, especially, paid him more attention than most. I saw her and Cam develop a bond that I knew she and I didn't have, and the way I dealt with that was to shut them both out. To build a wall between us, of anger and distrust and hurt. I don't know who Cam is because I've never wanted to get close enough to him to find out. That's why I've got no clue what he wants to apologize for.

Talking doesn't come easy to Cam, so he always takes his time before beginning. While I wait, I look closely at him, noticing him properly for the first time. His face is much more handsome than I'd realized. Despite being six-feet-five, Cam has the ability to blur into the background. You get the impression of quiet bulk and shaggy blond-brown hair. But his features are strong and regular and bring to mind a Michelangelo statue. His eyes are dark brown, and despite his low-key demeanor, there are laughter lines in the corners. I can see why Ava fell for him. Maybe I can see why Mom did, too…

"I took your mom from you when you needed her," says Cam.

That's one heck of a beginning. I hold my breath, hug the pillow tighter.

"I was hanging on to life by my fingernails, and that made me selfish. I could use the excuse that I didn't know what I was doing because my head was so screwed up with PTSD, but that'd be a lie. I came to depend on your mom, and I didn't want to let her go. Even when I knew she had other people who needed her time and love. You, in particular."

I can see a faint flush under his outdoor tan. Cam swallows. This is hard for him. Not sure yet if I feel sympathy or not.

"Your brothers had left home by then," he goes on. "They were independent. Shelby was busy learning the ropes from your dad. You were in that in-between stage, not quite a kid, not yet a grown-up. That's when a girl really needs her mom, and I took her from you. And I'm so very sorry, Frankie. I am."

Goddamn it. I feel like I'm going to cry. I hate crying. I hate Cam for being here and saying all this. Why now? Why couldn't he have said this years ago?

Corner of Cam's mouth gives a wry upward twitch. "They say better late than never, but that's a crock."

Did I say my thoughts out loud?

"I took way too long to summon the courage for a good, hard look at myself," he says. "And if it hadn't been for Ava, I might still be hiding from the world. Being selfish. Asking for more than I was prepared to give in return."

He looks me in the eye, and I see a muscle flex in his jaw, as if he's already anticipated my next question.

"Did you and Mom…?"

"We were never lovers," he says, immediately. "But I did try to kiss her once. She put me straight right away."

Cam takes a deep breath. "I'm not asking for your forgiveness, Frankie," he says. "Not sure I deserve that. I just wanted you to know that you never did anything wrong. You were forced to compete for your mom's attention with a guy who knew how to play the emotional blackmail game like a pro. I'm not that guy anymore, but I've gotta accept that I was then. And deal with the consequences."

Okay. Or not okay, I can't tell. A small part of me knew all this already. I sensed it when it was happening, but I was too young to put a name to it. Too young to be brave enough to ask questions and demand answers. Too young not to believe that it was my fault my mom stopped loving me.

Better late than never? I'll have to sit with that for a while. Sit with everything Cam's told me.

I hug the pillow, rest my chin on it and turn my gaze inwards. Hear the little wooden chair creak as Cam gets up. I sense him hesitate, and screw my eyes shut, willing him to go away without another word. I've had enough.

He treads softly to the door and closes it behind him. I wait until I'm sure he's gone before I let myself burst into tears.

Chapter Forty

DANNY

I might have put too much chili in the pasta sauce. Or not enough. Can't tell. Can't taste it. Ava made the salad and blanched the French beans. Everyone who's left is eating and making appreciative noises. I'm eating, too, but on autopilot. All my attention is focused on what's happening upstairs. Cam has been up there approximately four thousand years and I've died and been reborn way too many times over.

Thank fuck, I hear him on the stairs. Can he not walk at the speed of a normal human? We all look up the instant he enters the kitchen, so I'm not the only one who's been on tenterhooks. I search his face, trying to work out how it went with Frankie, but Cam seems his usual reserved self. Though he does sit down a little heavily and Ava does reach her arm around to give him a quick hug. She and Cam gaze briefly at each other, and whatever he communicates is enough for Ava to smile at him and give him another comforting squeeze. Cool, great, awesome. *Tell me what happened!*

Finally, Cam turns my way. "I'd give her a few moments," he says. "Let her work through it."

"Work through what?" He's making me insane. "What did you say to her?"

"Something I ought to have said years back."

Honestly, I'm going to stab him with this fork. Cam's eyes drop to where I hold said utensil in a death grip, and he nods, slowly.

"Uh, I apologized for monopolizing her mom's attention when she was growing up," he says. "I was a selfish asshole back then."

Okay. Thank you. Was that so fucking hard?

"So was I," says Shelby, glumly and unexpectedly. "Except in my case, it was Dad's attention. I should have seen that Frankie was being left out, but she was always such a private kid; it was hard to tell what was going on with her. I could have asked, though, and I didn't. I owe her an apology, too."

Nate blows out a breath. "Yeah, well, we all have regrets. Mine are old friends. They like to have a good long chat with me around three in the morning."

"I've had to learn not to fight mine," says Ava. "They're like Arnold Schwarzenegger. If you don't give in and accept them, they just keep coming back."

I don't know whether it's the stress, but I feel like I've been beamed into a parallel universe. Us Durants never show weakness in front of each other! Nate spilling his guts to me at The Silver Saddle was the first time he's ever confided in me to such an extent. And Ava? Accepting she has regrets? Who is this person sitting here and what has she done with my sister?

"I don't have any regrets," I say. "Not major ones, anyway!"

Both Nate and Ava stare at me, each with a small, knowing smile. Now that expression I'm used to, and my defenses immediately go up.

"Yes, you do," says Nate.

"Oh, really?"

"Sure." Ava piles on in. "For one, you regret not having a good relationship with Dad."

That hits me square in the guts. I am so close to saying, *Fuck you*. But years of sparring with my siblings have honed my determination not to give an inch. Instead, I say, "You're wrong."

"I'm not judging you, Danny," says Ava. "I'm really not."

Her expression is open and sincere and I don't believe her for a second.

"I kept barriers up between me and Dad for years, because I thought I needed to protect myself," she says. "From his ridiculously high expectations and his disappointment when I failed to reach them."

Possibly unconsciously, she reaches for Cam's hand, and he engulfs it in his giant manly mitt.

"But I put up those barriers, not Dad," says Ava. "And they stopped me from letting me accept that he really did love me, expectations or not."

I remember, at the end of last year, a dinner at Mom and Dad's that got pretty emotional. Dad told us that he loved us and was proud of us. Have to confess, I didn't believe he meant me. What Ava's saying might be true for her, but I know Dad is disappointed in me. He's said so often enough.

"Dad's not great at showing love," says Nate. "Yeah, I know, understatement of the year. But do you think you might want to give him a chance? For both your sakes?"

Give Dad a chance to show he loves me. Sounds so reasonable, doesn't it? But – and this is true for Frankie, too – her mom and my dad were adults when they parented us. Sure, they might have been doing their best, but they must have been aware that they had choices. They chose to treat us the way they did, and I didn't see why we should be the ones who need to do the heavy lifting to rebuild our relationships. If they want us to love and be close to them, then they should be the ones to make the first move.

I won't say any of this to Nate and Ava. It'll only buy a fight, and I'm not in the mood.

"I should check on Frankie," I say, getting up from the table. "Leave the dishes. I'll do them later."

"I'll do them," says Nate, but he says it to my back. I'm through with this conversation.

Upstairs, of course, I realize that I've never been in Frankie's room and have no idea which one it is. I wander the hallway, past closed door after closed door. Right at the end, I spy one sporting a faded hand-written sign that reads, "Don't even think about it". Bingo. I listen outside. Can't hear anyone in there. I try a tentative knock. No answer.

"Hey," I call softly. "It's me."

Still no answer. "I was about to come up but Cam insisted on speaking to you first," I say. "And he's bigger than me."

It's not the time for jokes, but I'm embarrassed now that I didn't tell Cam to wait. I should have gone to Frankie first. I should have been the one who comforted her. I feel like I let her down. Regrets – okay, so I *do* have a few.

The door opens to crack to reveal half of Frankie's face. It looks a little tear-stained. "I'm over talking for today," she says. "Just so you know."

"Me, too," I agree. "Talking sucks."

More of Frankie's face appears. "You can come and lie on the bed with me if you want. But no fooling around. For one thing, I'm wrung out, and for another, it's too creepy-weird to have sex in my childhood bedroom."

"Lying on the bed with you sounds like heaven," I say, sincerely. "Lead me to it."

After all us Durant kids left home, Mom redecorated our rooms. Removed our sports and popstar posters, packed away our old toys, repainted the walls. Bought new bed linen and covered the beds with more pillows than anyone who's not a multi-headed Hydra needs. Someone who didn't know my mom might accuse her of a lack of sentimentality but she did it *because* she's sentimental. If she didn't have to look at constant reminders, she wouldn't miss us so much. She stored all our stuff in boxes in the attic for us to take back whenever we wanted. Not sure I'll ever want my Queens of the Stone Age poster again, but nice to know it's there if I have a sudden hankering for psychedelic skulls.

Frankie has a Warhol Marilyn print and a Pink poster on her walls. Her bed is a double, with a crocheted coverlet. There are Powerpuff girl stickers on her desk. I'm swamped by a huge wave of affection, swiftly followed by a need to protect young Frankie from all the hurt she felt when she was living here.

Frankie's already lying on the bed. I slip off my sneakers and join her. The old bed sags in the middle under our combined weight, and we slide closer together.

"Sorry I wasn't here for you," I say. "I should have been."

"Cam looks like a gentle giant," she says, "but he knows how to get his way."

There's an edge to her voice, so I leave the subject there. It's remarkably relaxing, lying here next to Frankie, staring at the ceiling. No one here but us.

"Want to go go-karting tomorrow?" I say, after a while. "It's Saturday."

"Is it? I've lost track of the days."

"We don't have to. Don't have to do anything."

There's a pause. "Is it true you're extremely competitive on the track?"

"Is a bear Catholic?"

Frankie's shoulders shake with silent laughter.

"We could go to a karaoke bar afterwards," she suggests.

"Or"—I'm full of bright ideas—"we could go beer tasting and *then* go to a karaoke bar?"

"You want to get lit." It's not a question.

"Blazed," I confirm. "Comprehensively shickered."

"Cool," says Frankie. "It's a date."

Chapter Forty-One

FRANKIE

Danny leaves sometime after I fall asleep fully clothed on my bed. I wake early because I'm uncomfortable, skip the shower because I had two yesterday, put on a new set of clothes, pack a day bag, and creep downstairs. On the kitchen table, I leave a note for Shelby to let her know I'll be out all day and most of the night, so she shouldn't wait up. I add, "Don't worry, I'm good", which is not quite a lie. I'm certainly better than I was, but I'm not yet up to facing Mom and Cam, which is why I said yes to a date with Danny. Though it might seem rude for me not to be there to greet Mom, it's Shelby who's the main reason she's come back. I know, I know – I'm making excuses, but last night was a lot, and I've always needed time to sit with my feelings and work through them. I've no doubt Cam will tell Mom everything that he told me on the ride back from the airport, so she should understand. And, honestly, it's not my problem if she doesn't. Sounds harsh, but I've got enough overheated emotions of my own to handle. I don't need to deal with my mom's, too.

It's a beautiful morning, and though I'm eager to get going, I take a moment to put the top down in my car. Danny and I have agreed to meet at the go-kart track at eleven, then we'll grab lunch at the craft beer place. There's a karaoke bar in Martinburg, so dinner in town, then hit the bar. Somewhere along the line we'll have to figure out what to do with our cars as neither of us can afford to get a DUI. But that's a problem for later. Right now, I'm happily driving with the wind in my hair – well, my hair's under a scarf, but you get the picture. My plan is to get breakfast at Iris's Cracker Café in Verity, then cruise to the go-kart track to meet Danny, possibly via some more vintage clothing shops. My day bag has a selection of outfits that will take me from beer tasting to an evening's bad drunken singing. But there's always room for one more perfect vintage item.

Iris's café opens early, and on a Saturday its clientele will change throughout the day. The morning crowd is made of Verity locals getting coffee and breakfast, plus the odd trucker who makes a special detour for Iris's legendary baking. From eleven on, you'll get the summer tourists and out-of-town visitors, who come to wander Verity's quaint, old-fashioned main street. Now that e-bikes are plentiful, you'll see gaggles of weekend-only cyclists wobbling along, on their way through to the wineries. Verity's pizza and ice-cream parlor does great business during the summer, even though its pizza should be considered a national crime by Italian justice. I park outside the computer repair store, called, naturally, Byte Me, secure the convertible top and lock up. Verity's quaintness has fooled many an unwary visitor into thinking it's a crime-free paradise.

I've known Iris for fifteen years, from when she first set up the café. Dad, of course, charmed her from the start, and despite her reputation for gruffness, Iris has had a soft spot for all our family ever since. The Cracker Café is notorious for the stuffed alligator on the wall, which Iris may or may not have killed with her bare hands back in her Florida days. It probably sassed her or made some ridiculous demand when ordering food. With Iris's menu, what you see is what you get, and if you don't want it that way, you know where the door is. Occasionally, a Californian liberal will complain about the name of the café being racist. You'd think Iris would show them the door, too, but she never does. She sits them down, brings them coffee and a slice of pie, and tells them about the generations of her Florida forebears who herded cattle on horseback using only dogs and buckskin whips, hence the term "cracker". None of your show-off fancy lassos. Her best story is when an entire herd was killed by a massive swarm of mosquitoes. The liberal Californians go away better informed and intent on buying the biggest bottle of mosquito repellent from the local pharmacy. A win-win for small business.

"Frankie, honey," says Iris. "Take a seat and I'll bring you your usual."

No need to double check if I want it; I always do. I take a seat by the window, and in short order, Iris brings me out scrambled eggs, well done, on whole wheat with a side of bacon, orange juice (no stringy bits), and black coffee.

When I'm done, Iris comes to clear the table. "Now, how's that sister of yours?" she says. "She doing okay?"

"Yup, she's hanging in there."

I silently hope that a whole crowd of customers will come in to distract her, but no dice.

"And I hear your mom is coming back today?"

Of course, she has.

"Mom wanted to be sure she was here for the birth," I say. "Baby might come early."

Iris is in her late sixties and looks like she's spent every waking minute of her life outdoors. She's lean and tanned, her face lined like a satellite map of a mountain range. Her iron-gray hair is tied up into a tight bun, and she has on her usual uniform of blue jeans and a cotton button-down shirt, both items so faded she might have been wearing them since her teens. I know Shelby was worried about Iris being on her feet all day at the crush, but I suspect that Iris will still be standing when the world has crumbled into dust.

"I'll box up some key lime pie for you to take home," she says. "It's Shelby and your mom's favorite."

"Mine, too," I want to say, but I bite my tongue. Iris isn't to know that she touched on a tender subject. I also won't mention that the pie will never make it home because no key lime filling survives hours in a hot car. Danny and I will have to do the right thing and eat it so it doesn't go to waste.

Iris bustles off just as my phone rings. I expect it to be Danny, but it's Nate. I reject the call and a minute later up pops a text.

Can you please call me ASAP?

No, damn it, I can't! I know exactly why he wants to talk. Shelby's been upset by my note, and normally, I wouldn't want to upset her, not in her condition. But I also refuse to be emotionally blackmailed into being at home to greet Mom.

I almost call him back, but instead, I call Danny.

"Are you in the car?" I can hear the background rumble.

"Yup. Heading to the track. Thought I might get there early, get in a practice lap."

"Oh, you did, did you?"

"Insanely competitive, remember?"

"Nate wants me to call him," I tell Danny. "I left a note to say I wouldn't be back until late, and Shelby's deputized him to force me to come home in time to see my mom. I feel bad about it, but I just can't handle that right now."

"Yeah, he phoned me, too, but I was on another call. He didn't leave a message."

"He'll keep calling until I give in," I say. "Okay, I'm going to switch off my phone. It's the only way to get some peace today, and I'm *determined* to enjoy myself."

"Okay, sure," says Danny. "I'll switch mine off, too. I often do over the weekend, especially when I'm out hiking. If someone gets pissed that they can't reach me whenever they want, I don't want to deal with them, anyway."

"Thanks for being in my corner," I say.

"Always," says Danny. "See you soon."

I end the call and switch off my phone. I feel both guilty and liberated. I'll be there for breakfast tomorrow, and Mom and I can talk then. But right now, I'm going to have a me-and-Danny day, and I'm going to enjoy every minute of it.

Chapter Forty-Two

DANNY

I understand where Frankie's coming from. All the same, I'm a little concerned that Nate's tried to get hold of both of us, so I leave my phone on until I pull up in the parking lot of the go-kart track. For a second, I think about calling him, but that would feel like betraying my promise to Frankie. So, I double check that there's no message and switch off my phone.

The go-kart track is indoors, a twisting circuit with enough challenge for experienced drivers but not so hard that amateurs can't enjoy it. I scan their promo blurb – hot dang, the karts go up to forty-five miles per hour. I book a race slot for me and Frankie, and a practice one for me, and get handed a helmet and given a place to wait until it's my turn. These karts look like a cross between a racing pedal car and a hovercraft. The drivers out on the track right now are a family group that resemble mine but are in no way as competitive. That sister just let her brother pass without weaving slowly in front of him to make him insane. Incredible.

I catch a whiff of Old Spice before I see her. Frankie sits down beside me.

"You're early," I say. "I've got a practice lap coming up in five minutes."

"That's why I'm early," she says, with a smile. "I'm going to study your style. Take notes."

I smile, indulgently. This will be pickleball revenge. She will eat my dust.

I get the signal that it's my turn. Kiss Frankie before I pull on my helmet. Strapped into the kart, I await the green light and then scorch it until my fifteen minutes is up. I hop out, expecting a round of applause, but the track staff aren't paid enough to care, so I'll have to settle for unbridled awe from Frankie…

…who says, "Not bad. Your line was off on a couple of corners."

"Excuse me? My line was perfect."

"Uh huh," is her maddening reply.

In my mind, I hear Ava taunting me with her "sore loser" chant. I'm going to get us some soda and take some calming breaths while I'm at it.

Soon enough, it's our turn. Frankie looks cute in a helmet. We get the safety briefing, then we're strapped in and ready to go. We coast to the start and wait for the green light. And we're off!

Goddamn it, she's ahead! How is that even possible? Did she bribe someone to give her the fastest kart? I put my foot to the floor and start gaining ground. Next corner she goes wide, I'm undertaking.

I sit on her tail the whole goddamn way. Cannot get past. She zips from side to side like a speed skater and corners like a pro. Our fifteen minutes are up. I … have lost.

This race. I've lost this race. No way she will beat me in the next. Which means I can be gracious in defeat.

"Nice work," I say, and can't help adding, "Almost like you've done this before."

"Not go-karting," says Frankie. "But before the Karmann Ghia, I owned a Nissan Skyline R33 and used to take it to the track for hot laps on a Friday night."

I stare at her for a good half minute. "Why am I only hearing about this now?"

"Because we've been too busy having sex to talk about our past lives in any detail?"

"What model R33?" So help me, I'm a car salesman.

"1994 GTS25 Type S," she replies. "Could never even hope to afford a GT-R."

"You're going to win the next race too, aren't you?" I say.

She wins the next race. I'm never go-karting with her again.

"Pizza and beer?" she says, after we've handed back our helmets.

"Sure," I say, sourly. "Why not? I can drown my sorrows."

Frankie pats me on the arm. "Cheer up. I most definitely cannot sing, so your time will come."

"When you say you can't sing," I ask, as we walk to our cars. "Does that mean you can't hold a tune at all, or that you narrowly missed out on a place at the world's top opera conservatory? You can see what I might want to check."

"Guess you'll find out tonight," says Frankie, with a grin.

The craft beer brewery does pizza – artisan, of course. Frankie's booked us a tasting for two thirty, so we've got time to sit outside, relax and enjoy the sun, or in my case, lick my wounds. I have to admit, I did not expect to lose and it smarts more than it should. I'm not a toddler in the playground; I'm a grown man. It occurs to me that I'm over-sensitive to failure the same way I am to rejection because to me, failing reminds me of all the times I've faced Dad's disapproval. His disappointment that I'd fallen short, yet again. Everyone who beats me at anything becomes an avatar for my father, which isn't fair on them – or me. I don't need to keep carrying that psychological burden, but it's a hard one to shift.

By the time we're ushered to the tasting, I've already had three beers and am pretty buzzed. The bearded guy with the tattoo sleeve presents us each with a long wooden board with round indents along it for the sampler glasses. For each beer he pours, he talks about bouquet, and color, and clarity, and mouth feel, and hoppiness, and whether it's sweet-toasty-nutty-grassy-citrusy-floral until my head is spinning. Though that might be the alcohol. Frankie listens attentively, holds each glass up to the light, and smells and tastes with the utmost care and seriousness. I'm just happy to drink and watch her work. There's not going to be a quiz at the end, so why worry?

"What's your favorite so far?" asks the brewer.

Okay, so a short quiz.

"This one." I raise the glass I'm currently holding. "It's very ... drinkable."

Frankie's laughing at me. "This has gone right over your head, hasn't it?"

And, indeed, to it. I am officially tanked.

Frankie rolls her eyes affectionately, and begins a short, intense conversation with the brewer. I understand not one word, but it results in Frankie being given a card for a brewing supplies store, so guess it was also about beer. She thanks the guy, takes my arm in quite a firm grip and leads me away.

"I hope they'll be okay with you leaving your car here," she says. "Because you're in no condition to drive."

This is undeniably true. "We can swing back tomorrow and pick it up."

"Do you want to head into Martinburg now?" says Frankie. "Or find a hay barn where you can sleep it off?"

I draw her into my arms to kiss her, because as we all know, there's nothing more appealing than a drunken fumble. Surprisingly, she tolerates my advances and we neck a little in the brewery parking lot before she pushes me away.

"Take a nap in the car," she says. "Get your second wind. We have singing to do."

"Singing!" I launch into "Sweet Child o' Mine". People are staring. Let them.

"Get in the car!" Frankie steers me into the passenger seat. "And stay there! I need to pee. I'll be back soon. Don't move!"

I have no intention of moving. But as I wait, the worry that's been grumbling away since this morning penetrates my beer-fog to nag in earnest. I really should make sure that Nate's okay. My phone's in my pocket. No sign of Frankie so I pull it out and switch it back on. Check my messages. Fuck. Fuck, fuck, *fuck!*

"What?" Frankie's back and she's seen my face.

"Shelby's in hospital," I tell her. "They might have to do an emergency cesarean."

Frankie grabs her own phone out of her bag and boots it up. Goes very still.

"Karaoke is on hold," she says. "We're driving straight to Martinburg General."

I've got half an hour to sober up.

Chapter Forty-Three

FRANKIE

I will not blame myself for this. It is not my fault this happened to Shelby on the one day I decided to take for myself. According to Danny, who's been on the phone to Ava while I drive, after I'd left this morning, Shelby woke up with a vicious pounding headache and immediately vomited all over the bedroom floor. Nate bundled her into the pickup and took her straight to hospital. Now, they've got her in a ward under surveillance and it looks like she won't be coming out until after the baby's born. It's very common for mothers with preeclampsia to have an emergency birth if there are complications. That's exactly what happened with me. I was born when Mom was thirty-six weeks pregnant.

Danny's not said anything but I know he feels guilty that he wasn't around when his brother needed him. Soft top's up on my car, so he's rolled down the window, hoping the fresh air will sober him up faster. He wasn't that drunk, so he should be fine by the time we get to the hospital. Which will be in about six minutes.

"Dumb question," he says. "But are you okay?"

"I don't want to talk about it."

I don't. I'm angry and scared and struggling not to feel like I'm somehow to blame. That my emotional outburst last night caused Shelby so much stress that this was the result. I'm struggling not to turn my anger against other people, which is a bad tendency I have when I'm really wound up. I snapped at Danny, and I shouldn't have. He's probably my only friend and ally in this whole awful situation and I do not want to push him away.

"Sorry," I say.

"Don't be," he replies. "It *was* a dumb question."

"I'm glad you're here," I tell him.

"Ditto." He gives my shoulder a squeeze, and then he says, "Um…"

"What?" I try really hard not to snap again, but my patience is at an all-time low.

"I'm terrified of needles," he says. "Like, pass out when I see them type terrified. When Dad was in hospital, I had to ask the rest of the family to run interference, give me a warning any time it looked like a nurse was going to whip one out."

Not what I expected. "How do you cope with blood tests?"

"Avoid them at all costs," he says. "Childhood vaccinations were enough of a nightmare."

"So do you want me to help out today?" I ask. "Tell you when you need to clap your hands over your eyes?"

"Ava will do that," Danny says. "And when Cam arrives at the hospital, I can hide behind him. I just wanted you to know in case you suddenly noticed I was acting weird."

"Okay…"

I sound distracted because I am. When Cam arrives at the hospital, he'll have Mom with him. In my panic, I'd completely forgotten. I'll get to see her today after all. Thanks, Worse.

We're here.

Martinburg General is a small hospital, but well appointed, mainly because it's in a high socio-economic area where everyone has full health insurance. Our family scraped to afford a basic plan because the financial consequences of not having it would be way worse. But when Dad got cancer, we'd have been screwed without generous donations from friends and extended family, and even our winery clients. Which sucked, but it also proved how much Dad was loved. Shelby's covered now because Nate's parents' wedding gift was a comprehensive health plan, premiums paid for the foreseeable. Sounds coldly practical but let's face it, it's of way more use than a matching set of cookware.

I park, and switch off the engine, and find I can't move. Everything about me feels stupidly heavy.

"Heads high," says Danny, gently. "We're here now. No point in beating ourselves up with what-ifs."

A rush of gratitude spurs me to pull him to me and kiss him as hard as I can. He tastes like beer, which is excellent. But much as I'd prefer it, we can't sit here kissing all day.

"How much do I need a breath mint?" he asks, when I release him.

"Personally, I love eau de IPA," I say. "But we should probably both grab some Tic Tacs from the hospital store."

"Ready?" Danny's observed that I'm still hesitant.

"Nope. But let's do it, anyway."

Visiting hours are up to eight at night here. I know, because towards the end of his life, I spent as much time as I could with Dad. I remember hating seeing that it was almost eight and knowing I'd have to leave. When I say I spent as much time as I could, it should have been more. I'd just started with my law firm and hadn't yet proved myself so valuable that I could take a whole lot of compassionate leave. Plus, as I might have mentioned, I don't do well around collective grief. My most treasured memories are the brief moments when Dad and I were alone. If he was sleeping, I'd rest my head on the edge of his bed and just be with him. I—

Goddamn it, I'm bawling.

"Come here." Danny folds me into his arms and lets me soak his shirt with my tears. "It's all going to be okay, you know. Shelby and the baby will be fine."

He doesn't know that for sure but I don't care. It's what I need to hear. I fumble for a tissue in my bag and wipe my face. Bet I look a mess.

"You look gorgeous," says Danny the mind-reader, with a smile. "You are the most gorgeous woman I know, and I could not adore you more."

"I am so glad you're here with me," I tell him.

Reception tells us where Shelby is. Her condition is stable, apparently, no need yet for an induction or emergency cesarean. She won't be leaving until the baby's safely out, but they have no major concerns. The relief makes me weak at the knees. Good thing Danny's arm is round my waist.

Danny and I grab a box of mints, and head towards Shelby's ward. Halfway down the first corridor, we see Ava coming towards us.

"Cam and Lee are almost here," she says. "I'm going to meet them."

Ava gives me a look that's shrewd but kind. "If you need to go outside and scream at any time, let me know and I'll join you."

"Thanks." I manage a smile. It's good to know I have Ava in my corner, too.

"And our mom and dad are here already," she says to Danny. "So, you're also welcome to join the screaming party."

"Jesus," says Danny. "Shelby better be in one of the big rooms."

"Yes, she is." Ava grins. "Dad saw to that."

"Of course he did."

Danny sighs. Ava pats him on the arm. Speeds off down the corridor like a black-clad Exocet missile.

"You know, they have a plastic surgery ward here," says Danny. "We could get new faces, new identities, and live out the rest of our lives on a beach in Mexico."

"I like my face," I say. "I like yours, too."

"Guess we'd better show them, then," he says.

We walk hand in hand down to Shelby's room and push open the door.

Shelby's in bed, Nate next to her, Mr and Mrs Durant over by the wall. Danny's hand clutches mine tighter, and I squeeze back once, and let go.

"Frankeeee!"'

Soon as she sees me, my sister opens her arms, and I rush to her and hug her gently. I start to apologize but she shushes me immediately.

"I'm the one who should be sorry," she says. "You were having a lovely day and I ruined it."

I risk a quick glance at Nate. He looks as worn and wrung out as an old dish rag but he manages to lift the corner of his mouth. I've been half expecting him to scold me for switching off my phone, but I realize he's had bigger things to worry about than a temporarily incommunicado sister-in-law.

Danny greets his parents, receives a hug from his mom and a handshake from his dad. Danny beckons me over.

"Mom, Dad," he says. "This is my girlfriend, Frankie, Shelby's younger sister. You met her at Nate and Shelby's wedding."

Danny's mom, Ginny, is a super pretty blonde who looks a lot like him. She smiles warmly at me, and gives me a hug, too.

"Lovely to see you again, Frankie," she says. "Mitchell, isn't it sweet that our family has another connection to the Armstrongs?"

Danny's dad, Mitchell, looks as if nothing could please him less, but as far as I can tell, that's his default facial setting. He opens his mouth but whatever he's about to say is interrupted by the entrance of three more people: Ava, Cam … and Mom.

Showtime.

Chapter Forty-Four

DANNY

Frankie slips her hand in mine again as her mom walks in the door. Lee Armstrong looks washed out, as you would if you'd flown halfway across the world to be met with the news that your pregnant daughter's been rushed to hospital. She's still stunningly beautiful, though, slender and graceful like a dancer, with long red hair that's not been dyed because you can see faint streaks of gray. Frankie's grip on my hand tightens. I squeeze back, reassuringly, but I'm not sure she notices. Her eyes are fixed on her mom.

Who has eyes only for Shelby. Lee Armstrong ignores us all and heads straight for the bed. Nate fetches her a chair, and she sinks into it with barely a glance his way.

"Oh, my dear." She takes Shelby's hand in both of hers, and gazes intently at her daughter. "You're better. I can see that now. I'm so relieved."

Shelby smiles. "Hello, Witchy Mom. Yes, I'm better. But I'll have to get used to being bed-bound."

"May I?" Lee hovers her hand over Shelby's pregnancy

bump. Shelby nods and Lee gently lowers her palm and rests it on the bump, closes her eyes and breathes in, deeply.

Frankie clutches my hand again. Can't tell whether she's concerned about what her mom might pick up, or whether she's annoyed that her mom's being weird in front of everyone. I glance at my own parents. Mom is wide-eyed, but Dad is peering, fascinated. It occurs to me that for all his rationalism, he's a complete sucker for woo. When he had his heart problems, he researched every crazy alternative treatment out there. We were lucky he didn't book a one-way flight to freaking Peru.

Nate is too focused on Shelby to notice, but I catch Ava's eye and she grins. Her finger makes a circling motion by her temple to indicate the presence of looniness in the room. She's got her other arm hooked firmly in Cam's, and I sense a gesture of possessiveness. The big man's watching what's going on at the bed, but who can tell what he's thinking.

Lee opens her eyes and smiles beatifically. "I can't wait to meet this little one out in the world," she says. "They're a treasure."

Finally, she acknowledges the treasure's father-to-be. "Nate, dear. What a time you've had."

"Glad you made it, Lee," he says, politely. He has his poker face on, which means he's working hard to stay in control, poor bastard.

"And Ginny and Mitchell." Lee turns to bestow a smile on my parents. "Isn't this incredible? Our first grandchild."

My mom is the kindest and most courteous person I know, so of course she says, "It's wonderful." But I get the strong impression that she'd prefer it if her co-grandma wasn't dominating the room's attention quite so much.

"Frankie, my dear."

Oh, shit. Lee's smile is as warm as ever, but she greeted my parents before her own daughter.

"Hey, Mom." Frankie sounds relaxed, but her grip on my hand is cutting the circulation from my fingers.

"You and I must make time for a proper catch-up," says Lee. "We have a lot to talk about."

"Sure." Frankie crushes my hand so hard, I wince.

"And Danny."

Last, but not least, I hope. I put my best charming face forward.

"So generous of you to come all this way to help out."

"Very glad I did." I make a point of smiling at Frankie. "Wouldn't have got to know *this* treasure if I hadn't."

Lee looks genuinely pleased, but I can feel Frankie bristling beside me. I understand. My dad has that effect on me. Good thing he's been relegated to the background here.

"Mom, you must be exhausted," says Shelby. "Go home and rest. Come and see me tomorrow."

I sense at least half the room silently willing Lee to agree. Honestly, she seems like a sincerely warm and kind person, but there's no denying that when she's around, it's like royalty is present. Everyone defers to her, whether she realizes that or not.

Lee stands, bends over and kisses Shelby's forehead, like she's a little kid. Well, I suppose she *is* Lee's kid, so that's fair. Once a mom, always a mom.

She drops her hand on Nate's shoulder and looks over at Cam. "May I trouble you for a ride home?" she asks him.

Cam turns to Ava. "I'll drop Lee off and meet you back at ours."

"That you will."

Ava says it lightly but the firm undertone does not go unnoticed. Nate and I exchange a glance. Ava's establishing the ground rules, and it will not go well for Cam if he ignores them.

Cam's smarter than he looks, because he says, "I'll swing by The Silver Saddle and bring home dinner."

Ava's smugness is a sight to behold.

Lee gives Shelby a last hug, and everyone else a smile. When she's gone, Cam following on behind, Frankie finally lets go of my hand. Which is good because the ends of my fingers are starting to turn black.

"Could someone get Nate some food?" Shelby asks. "I don't think he's eaten all day."

"Shel, I'm fine," he protests, embarrassed.

"Oh, I completely forgot!" Mom reaches into her tote bag and pulls out a snaplock container. "I brought cookies!"

'Huzzah!" says Ava. "Let me at 'em!"

"You need *protein* for real energy, Ava," says Dad. "Not empty calories and a glucose spike."

"That is so true, Dad," says Ava, who already has the lid off. "But this has been a tough old day, and we need cookies."

She hands them round, and everyone but Dad and Shelby takes more than one. They're chocolate and salted caramel, and they disappear in a flash. Ava's right. There are times only cookies will do.

Nate's color starts to come back. I can't even imagine what he's been going through emotionally.

"Bro, can we bring you dinner?" I ask. "There's a Denny's next door."

"Nate's going to come home with us and we'll feed him there," says Mom.

Nate gives me and Frankie an apologetic look. "Thought I might crash at Mom and Dad's for a couple of nights. Be closer to Shelby. Would that be okay with you?"

"Tell us what you need," I say, without hesitating. "Frankie and I will hold the fort."

"Thank you." Shelby blows us a kiss.

"Time to go." Frankie walks to the bed and gives her sister a hug. "Bye, Shel. Take care. Obey all medical directives."

"I will. I promise." Shelby smiles. "You two should go back to your date that I so rudely interrupted."

Frankie raises a wry eyebrow at me, and says, "Maybe a quiet dinner for two?"

I'm filled with affection for her. I thought she'd want to crash into bed for an early night, but she's chosen to spend a little longer with me.

"Sounds perfect," I tell her.

It's only after we've said our final goodbyes and are walking back to the parking lot that I realize why Frankie might not want to rush back home. With Shelby and Nate gone, it's only her and her mom at the house. No buffer between them at all.

I'm okay with Frankie using me as an excuse to stay away as long as she can. Means she might spend more nights with me in the tiny house. If you look hard enough, there's always an upside, isn't there?

Chapter Forty-Five

FRANKIE

Danny must think I hate my mom. I don't – that's the problem. I look at the easy, loving relationship she has with my sister and I want it so bad, I become furious. I want Mom to respond to me the way she responded to Shelby's baby, who isn't even born yet, whereas I've been in the world twenty-six years and counting. What do I have to do – who do I have to *be* – in order to get Mom to see me?

My pent-up emotions power me across the hospital parking lot, but when I reach my car and have to stop, I can't prevent a sobbing sigh from escaping. Danny's right there, and he pulls me into his arms.

"I know," he says, softly. "I know. It's been a day…"

I rest my cheek on his chest. He feels firm, steady, reassuring. Part of me wants to stay here in his arms forever, and another part wants to teleport us both to his bedroom, so I can work off all this emotion with a scandalous amount of sex.

"What do you feel like now?" Danny says. "Quiet dinner out? Burgers back at mine?"

"My brain's stopped functioning," I tell him. "You decide."

He's quiet for a moment, pondering.

"I think I'd like to take you to dinner. Somewhere nice," he says. "Not Denny's, in other words, though their cake batter shake with sprinkles is revoltingly great."

"I'd like that, too. I bought a dress with me to change into but I've run out of energy." I lift my head from his chest and look up into his warm, kind blue eyes. "Do you want to drive my car?"

His face lights up instantly. "Hell yes! Hand me those keys."

Of course, he has to push the driver's seat back about six inches. I look on as he checks out the instrumentation and adjusts the mirrors, with as much seriousness as if he's setting up a race car. With a pang, I realize that Danny doesn't just like cars, he loves them. They're his passion and his world, and that's what I want to be. I want to be more important to him than anything.

This might be my pent-up emotion talking, so I won't say it out loud. Not yet. But I'll start planning. Figure out what needs to be done to make Danny and I viable.

"Oh man, I love this car." Danny's grinning from ear to ear. "Ever got it up to top speed?"

"No!" I laugh. "And don't you dare try! You'll break it!"

"Impossible. It's German," he says, but thankfully sticks to the thirty-five-mile speed limit.

He parks in the center of town and leads me to a cozy-looking place with yellow-framed windows and a lot of greenery. We haven't booked, but Danny charms the maître-d' into giving us two seats at the bar. I'm always a little anxious in a new restaurant, just in case there's nothing on the menu I can eat. So, I'm relieved to see this menu is pretty simple, only a few ingredients in every dish, and at least one dish where all those ingredients are palatable to me.

"I'm guessing you've been here before," I say to Danny. "You knew it would be okay for me."

"With my mom and dad," he confirms. "Dad won't eat anywhere unless all the produce is forensically certified as fresh, local and organic. This place is one of the few he'll dine out at."

The waiter takes our orders. We decide to risk a glass of wine each. Figure we've earned it.

"Do you think your dad is happy he's going to be a grandfather?" I ask.

"Interesting question." Danny chews on his bottom lip. "Dad's never been great at accepting his own mortality, so I'm not sure how he feels about being promoted to Grandad. Or 'Sir' as he called his own grandfather."

I hoot with laughter. "*Sir*?? You are kidding me?"

"No indeed," says Danny, with a grin. "Explains a lot, doesn't it?"

"Wow." I have a sudden thought. "I wonder what my mom will want to be called? Seems bizarre to think of her as a grandma."

"Yep, your mom is a stunning woman," says Danny. "Doesn't look her age at all."

I glare at him. "Don't *you* start! Bad enough to have Cam fawning all over her still."

"Did you think he was?" Danny raises his eyebrows. "I'd

say Cam's survival instincts are better honed than that. Mine certainly would be if I were in a relationship with Ava."

He winces. "That came out very wrong, but you know what I mean."

"Cam drove all the way to the airport to pick her up and bring her back. That's a four-hour round trip," I point out. "She must have other friends she could have called on. She could even have taken the bus. But as usual, Mom clicked her fingers and Cam came running."

Our wine glasses arrive, and I take a big swig of mine. Danny's watching me, his expression earnest and a little wary.

"Cam told me how he apologized to you the other night," he says. "Will you ever forgive him?"

It's a totally reasonable question, but it pushes my anger buttons hard. "Why should I?"

Danny shrugs. He's being conciliatory, and the provoked irrational part of me resents it.

"Are you ever going to forgive your dad?" I clap back.

Fortunately, the waiter chooses that moment to present us with our entrees. It's enough to circuit-break my anger and let me regain my self-control.

"I'm really sorry, Danny," I say. "I have a bad habit of lashing out when I'm feeling stuff I don't want to feel."

"Well, that's too bad," he says, lightly. "Because, of course, I expect you to be as perfect as I am. Executing everything in life with flawless excellence and flair."

"You're a dick." I say it with a smile.

He toasts me with his wine glass. "So I've been told."

"Thank you for today," I add. "For everything." I hope he knows how much I mean it.

Danny takes a moment before responding.

"I know this has been an emotional day, and I don't want to add any more into the mix." His eyes dip a little shyly, before he looks right at me again. "But I would honestly do anything for you, Frankie. You only have to ask."

I only have to ask… Such a generous, wonderful offer, from a generous, wonderful man.

Trouble is, before I ask, I have to know exactly what it is I want.

Chapter Forty-Six

DANNY

Frankie was trying to bait me when she asked if I'd ever forgive Dad, but she had a point. I haven't been brave enough to face him and tell him how I feel. Not once, not ever. I've done exactly what Ava said she'd done: build barriers between Dad and me. And for exactly the same reason: to protect myself. I keep my distance because I hate how bad he can make me feel. And I tell myself that's his fault. I tell myself that he's a shitty father and pile all the responsibility on his shoulders. Do I really want to have that kind of relationship with him for the rest of his life?

I'm driving the Karmann Ghia back to my place. Five minutes in, Frankie falls asleep, and her blonde head's now resting lightly on my shoulder. If this wasn't a stick shift, I'd put my arm around her. As it is, I do my best to keep the gear changes smooth, so I don't rock her head too much. Needless to say, I'm not going to test out the Karmann Ghia's top speed. The dial promises 150mph. Another day, small, blue German car. Another day.

Kiss My Glass

My BMW is still parked outside the craft beer place. Maybe tomorrow, I'll ask Frankie to drive me there and we can meet up again at the hospital. After that, I might phone Mom, find out what she and Dad are doing, see if I can entice Dad out for an organic, fair trade, non-alcoholic, sugar-free beverage somewhere.

We pull up outside my wooden shack. Frankie wakes with a start, gazes at me a little wildly.

"What time is it?" she says.

"Eleven-fifteen." I smile at her sleep-rumpled face. "We can hit the hay platonic-style if you'd prefer?"

She seems to be weighing it up. "Can I have sex without actually moving?"

"Happy to experiment." I lean in and kiss her gently. "Come on, sleepyhead. Time for bed."

As it turns out, spooning while lying on our sides is the answer. I can caress Frankie's breasts and put my other hand to even better use lower down her body, while moving inside her slowly and leisurely all the way to a not-so-slow-and-leisurely climax. By the time I've dealt with the condom, Frankie is fast asleep, still lying on her side, a small, happy smile on her face. I forgot to lower the blind this morning and there's moonlight pouring through the window, giving Frankie's bare skin a luminous, almost pearlescent sheen. She looks angelic, and a wave of affection for her rushes through me, shortly followed by a tsunami of terror. I have to get my insecurity under control, or there's no hope for us. And I want there to be an us. I want it badly. I settle down to sleep, and hope courage magically comes to me in my dreams.

I wake up with the jolt that's your brain's tough-love way

of telling you you've overslept. Frankie's side of the bed is empty and I can't hear the shower, or any other noise downstairs. I check my phone. It's nearly ten am, and there's a text from Frankie.

Been summoned. Having breakfast with Mom. Cu later?

I text back.

Whenever ur free.

And add a bunch of love heart emojis because that's the kind of romantic sap I am.

Lil Danny is his usual eager morning self, but I'd better get moving. I can hardly crash Frankie's Sunday morning breakfast with her mom, so I guess there's nothing for it but to make good on last night's vow to talk to my dad. But before I do anything, there must be coffee. Can barely put my pants on straight without it.

Three cups later, and I'm still finding ways to procrastinate. I read my emails and DMs but there's nothing interesting, unless I actually am the lucky recipient of ten million dollars left to me in a stranger's will. I scroll through my feeds and click on every cute dog video. I call Nate. He's feeling better now Shelby's in safe hands and Mom is feeding him. He's going to spend the day at the hospital making sure Shelby doesn't try to abscond through sheer boredom. Ava's bringing them both a decent lunch. I think about calling Ava but what the heck would we talk about? Ditto Izzy and Max, who will also think it's super weird that I'm calling them out of the blue. I send Frankie another text with coffee cup emojis and more love hearts, which is pretty much the complete rundown of my morning so far. And that's it. I'm out of excuses.

Mom hates texts, so I call her. She immediately invites me

round for lunch. I say yes right before I remember I have no car. I peer outside and Frankie's is still there. Seems she chose to walk to meet her mom, probably because it takes longer. I text her.

cn I borrow ur car for 3 hrs? Lunch w my mom & dad.

She texts back.

sure but DO NOT BREAK IT!! Also u owe me.

I text her back the ROFL face, more love hearts and an eggplant emoji because I'm horny as well as romantic. I wait but she doesn't text back. Guess sexting isn't as much fun when your mom's sitting right next to you.

I shower and dress. Time to go. *Deep breath, Danny. You've got this.*

On the way, I swing by the craft beer place, to explain why my car is still in their lot. No problem, says the tattooed guy. Pick it up whenever. I buy a mixed half-dozen because it's only polite. It'll be a gift for Frankie. Who knows, after spending a morning with her mom, she may need to drink all six in quick succession. I hope she's doing okay, but I figure I've texted her enough love heart emojis for one day.

It's the perfect summer Sunday, clear blue sky, hot but not too hot. The kind of Sunday I always hated when I was growing up because unlike my friends, I wouldn't get to laze around, go swimming and sunbathe on the riverbank, or the beach when we were all old enough to drive. I'd be sweating on the soccer field, or in training, or watching my siblings compete. Some of that resentment comes back to me now as I cruise down the tree-lined driveway to our family home. I push it aside, because it'll only get in the way. If I want a productive talk with my dad, my opening line shouldn't be to call him a controlling asshole.

"Danny, dear."

My mom is always glad to see me, and I'm always glad to see her. My siblings are adamant that I'm Mom's favorite, and it's true, we do have a very close bond. Trouble is, that only highlights the lack of closeness between me and Dad.

He's come out to greet me, which is new. I shake his hand, and we follow Mom through the house to where lunch is waiting for us outside on the patio that overlooks the large back garden. Sounds weird given my parents' wealth that we don't have a swimming pool. My guess is that unless Dad could build a full size Olympic one for us to train in, he didn't see the point. Mom likely vetoed that suggestion and settled for pretty plants and an ornamental bird bath instead. We do have a tennis court, though, I'll just throw that in there.

As usual, Mom has prepared a feast. A platter of grilled vegetables, sliced heirloom tomatoes, fresh-baked focaccia, a range of dressings and sauces on the side, and sliced bavette steak for me because I'm a growing boy and need my protein. As usual, Mom leads the conversation, starting with today's update on Shelby, and moving on to Izzy and Max, who both have summer jobs, but are planning to be here for the crush so they can meet their new niece or nephew and, in my opinion, confuse the wee mite no end with their identical faces.

Dad, as usual, says nothing and eats very little despite the effort Mom's gone to. And as usual, I find this irritating, and my intent to have a productive conversation is fading by the minute. Would it kill him to be polite once in a while?

Then, finally, he speaks to me. But what he says is, "Are you serious about the Armstrong girl?"

"Yes, Dad, I am." *The Armstrong girl?* Frankie would love that.

"And how do you propose to make the relationship work? I gather she lives in San Diego."

He makes it sound like she lives in a cardboard box beneath an overpass. I work on controlling my breathing without making it obvious.

"We haven't got to that stage, Dad. We don't want to rush things."

Dad nods. "Good to hear that. You have a track record of being impulsive."

I bite back my first response. If I get defensive, it'll be rapidly downhill from here. Instead, I treat this as an opportunity to engage.

"Making quick decisions isn't necessarily being impulsive," I say. "I do actually weigh up the pros and cons beforehand."

"But you still err on the side of risk," says Dad.

It's not a question. He's decided that's the whole truth and no evidence I can offer will sway him. I give up. I won't end this conversation rudely out of respect for Mom. But I'll end it.

"You know best, Dad," I say, as neutrally as I can. "Mom, thanks for lunch, it was delicious as always, but I'd better be going. Got a lot to do."

"Oh, so soon?" says Mom. "I made a dessert!"

Damn it. Mom's so kind, and she goes to so much effort, I feel like a real churl. But if I stay, I'll fight with Dad and that would only make her feel worse.

All I can do is say, "Thanks, Mom. Save it for Nate."

Dad's out of his seat now, waiting to shake my hand, because that's the rule. Durant men shake hands. I could refuse to take it but that really *would* be churlish. I give the minimum viable handshake, and – yeah, all right, to make a point – I kiss Mom on the cheek, and say, only to her, "I'll see you soon."

And I walk off feeling about as bad as it's possible to feel. I came, I saw, I failed to conquer my defensiveness when it comes to anything my dad says about me. I sincerely hope Frankie's had a better day than I have so far.

Chapter Forty-Seven

FRANKIE

I really hope Danny's having a fun lunch with his parents. I'm currently hanging out with Ham and Luke, so you can guess how well breakfast with my mom went this morning. It was my fault. I went into it like a siege engine, covered in armor and ready to lob flaming missiles. Mom took one look at me, made her usual sad face, and sighed, "Oh, Frankie." It went downhill from there.

We didn't fight because Mom never fights. She asked me polite questions and I gave polite answers. Very short polite answers. I ate toast and eggs, and she ate some seed mixture that she'd created from what she found in Shelby's pantry. I had a glass of pulp-free orange juice, and she had herbal tea. We had a brief (polite) tussle over who'd do the dishes. I let her win and left the house. Thought about going back to Danny's and screaming at the top of my lungs, but I knew I'd miss him too much and do weird stuff like pick up his shirts and bury my face in them to inhale his scent. So, I went to see Ham and

Luke, stealing some lettuce from the vegetable garden on my way. They grunted happy greetings and made short work of the lettuce. They let me scratch them behind their wire-brush ears and waddled off again.

And now, I'm stuck here. Danny has my car, and it's four miles into town, too far to walk on a hot summer's day. So, it's either hole up in my bedroom or go to Danny's and sniff shirts. Funnest Sunday ever.

I hear a distant but familiar rumble heading up the drive. Great, that's all I need. Cam, definitely, and Ava, possibly. If I stay by the pigs, no one will know I'm here. Unless…

As I feared. Here's Cam. With a bunch of food scraps for Ham and Luke. He spots me, lifts his chin in greeting. I do likewise. He ambles up and chucks the scraps to the pigs who fall upon them oinking and grunting in a way that implies the last time they had food was five months ago rather than five minutes.

Cam grins, and then turns to stare at me – meaningfully, damn him.

"What?" I am *not* in the mood.

"Here to take your mom to the hospital," he says.

Am I supposed to comment?

"Ava's already there," he says. "She took Nate and Shelby lunch, so Shel didn't have to eat hospital food. Bought enough for all of us, including you. If you want to come with us?"

"Sit between you and my mom in the Dodge?" Ava already said no thanks to an offer like this, and I don't blame her.

"It's roomy enough," is Cam's misguided opinion. "But I guess you have your own car."

"Nope," I admit. "Danny borrowed it."

Cam frowns. "Where's his car?"

"We're currently in a very complicated car-location situation!" I say. "Okay?!"

"Okay," says Cam, and after a beat, "Come with us?"

Jesus. I do want to see Shelby. And right now, there's no other way for me to get to her. Danny won't be back for a couple of hours.

I huff out a breath. "Alright," I say. "But I am not sitting in the middle!"

Dumb decision because, of course, that means Mom's right next to Cam. And I can't enjoy the scenery out the window because I'm paranoid that as soon as I turn my head, she'll put her hand on his knee. I stare fixedly at the two of them, frowning like an Angry Bird.

Eventually, Mom turns, and with a small smile, says, "Frankie, dear, I feel like a beetle being scorched under a magnifying glass."

I mutter something that could be taken as an apology and begin to stare fixedly out the window instead. After a minute or so, I hear strange, muffled snuffling sounds. I turn to see and ... oh, shit ... Mom is *crying*.

Cam notices at the same time, and his eyes widen. "Want me to pull over?" he says to her.

Mom shakes her head and starts wiping her face with her hands. I fetch tissues from my bag, and Mom takes them with a little half-laugh, half-sob. Cam's eyes are flitting anxiously between Mom and the road, and I'm staring with my mouth open. I do not recall the last time I saw my mom cry. She always appears so goddam serene!

Mom blows her nose, sob-laughs again. "It's nothing, I'm being foolish," she says. "Ignore me."

"You never cry," I say. "So, there must be something wrong."

Mom looks down at the damp, shredded mess of tissue in her hands. Her long red hair hides her face.

"I'm so tired of feeling like a failure," she says. "I try my best, but I can't seem ever to be present when I'm really needed. Physically…" She hesitates. "And emotionally, too."

"Lee—" Cam begins, but Mom cuts him off.

"No, don't defend me," she says, with unusual heat. "Because what you're about to say isn't true. I was never truly there for you, even when I appeared to be. Half my mind was always elsewhere, either occupied with the thousand other tasks I had still to do, or away in some neverland of my own imagination. You thought I gave you all my attention and I gave you barely any of it. I listened enough to make the right noises in return. I made it as easy for myself as I could."

Cam looks genuinely shocked, but before he can respond, Mom turns to me. "Frankie, that's why I was such a terrible mother to you. I couldn't give you the time and energy you needed, because I simply didn't have it. From the moment you were born, I was exhausted. Worse, I resented the fact that you weren't as easy as your brothers and sister, and I don't think I did a good job of hiding that at all."

Tears are falling freely down her cheeks, but she doesn't seem to notice. She reaches out and cups my face.

"You poor little thing," she says. "You deserved so much better, and I am so, *so* sorry."

I can't breathe. No, really, I cannot breathe. My chest is too tight, and I can't get air.

We're shaken around as the Dodge bumps to a sudden stop on the grassy verge. Cam leans across Mom.

"Frankie, do what I say. Raise up your arms."

The unexpected authority in Cam's tone makes my body obey, even before his words register.

"Good," he says. "Now lower them. Okay, now raise them again…"

That's it. The breath I've been holding comes out in a whoosh.

"Good work," says Cam. "Now, breathe in again, slowly, while you count to four. Hold it for four – that's it. Out again for four."

He makes me repeat the cycle until it's obvious my breathing has settled.

"Thanks," I manage to say.

Cam gives me a quick, crooked smile and sinks back into the driver's seat. Takes a deep breath of his own. He took up quite a bit of space leaning across Mom, but now I can see her clearly. We stare at each other. Her face is tear-stained and her expression is – I'm not sure – despairing? Pleading? Both?

"It's okay," I tell her, because it is. It really is. Because now I know why we had the relationship we did, and it wasn't all my fault.

I open my arms, and she falls into them, cries on my shoulder. It feels like she's the child and I'm the parent, as I pat her back and shush her. It feels good. I am suddenly weirdly, ridiculously happy.

Cam meets my eye, and gestures with a tilt of his head to ask if we should drive on. I'm grateful to him and should probably apologize for being cranky with him all these years. I settle for a smile, and he puts the Dodge in gear and pulls out again onto the road.

Chapter Forty-Eight

DANNY

I'm barely in the door when I get a text from Frankie to say she's at the hospital, and Shelby and Nate have news. So, I hop in her car again, and head on back to Martinburg. When I arrive, I see I'm not the only one who's been summoned. When I said I'd see Mom soon, I didn't think it would be later this afternoon, but here she is and so is Dad. Cool, great. This is turning out to be a super awesome day.

Shelby's room is now as packed as a New York subway car in rush hour. Ava is clearing away the remains of a shared lunch, and there's a general jostling as enough chairs are found for everyone. I can't get a seat near Frankie, but I sure as heck make sure I'm not sitting close to Dad.

"Update for the newcomers," says Nate, who looks a hundred times brighter. "Shelby's going to have a planned cesarean on Friday. Baby will be on the cusp of being considered premature so we should prepare ourselves for the baby to spend time in the neonatal unit."

He reaches out and squeezes Shelby's hand, and they share a resigned smile.

"Not the birth we would have chosen, but honestly, as long as Shelby and the baby get through this without incident, we no longer give a fuck."

"Nate!" protests Mom.

"Sorry, Mom," says Nate. "It's been a rough few days. Or weeks. I've lost track."

"Let the boy swear, Ginny," says Dad. "There's scientific evidence to say it minimizes pain."

Nate laughs. "Thanks, Dad."

Damn it. Why can't Dad be kind to me like that? I hate them both right now, and I don't want to feel like that. It sucks.

I look over at Frankie, sitting next to her mom on the other side of the room. I manage to catch her eye, and she smiles. She looks both happy and tired. I want to rush to her and take her in my arms, but I have to settle for smiling back at her. I'll catch her when we all leave, though I have such a need to be with her right now, I don't know how I can stand to wait.

After an excruciatingly long half an hour or so of chat, Cam and Ava say their goodbyes, and then, thank god, so do Mom and Dad. There's room for me now to sit next to Frankie. Her mom greets me with a kiss on the cheek and a warm smile. She also looks tired but happy. I can only assume things went better than expected this morning. Glad one of us had a successful parental experience.

"Ready to go?" I ask, trying my best not to sound overly eager.

"We should go pick up your car on the way back," says

Frankie. She frowns. "Oh, but mine only seats two, and both Mom and I need a ride."

"I'll take Lee," says Nate, quickly. "I want to go home. Staying at Mom and Dad's was great, but—" He makes a face.

"But you have nightmares about being smothered under a tsunami of small decorative pillows?" I suggest.

"I should not be ungrateful," admits Nate. "But I miss our bed. I even miss the cats."

"Of course you do," says Shelby. "And the cats miss you!"

"Shel, if I died during the night," says Nate, "they'd have my corpse half-eaten by morning."

"That's not true!" says Shelby. "Well, maybe just a little nibble…"

This is all very domestic and charming, but I'm itching to leave and be with Frankie. Her mom must sense my impatience because she gives me a smile.

"I'm content to wait here until Nate's ready to go," she says to me and Frankie. "You two should scoot."

But Frankie seems reluctant, and I'm not sure how to take that.

Her mom says to her, "How about I cook us all dinner tonight? I could make macaroni and cheese, your favorite?"

"No peas in it, right?" says Frankie. "Or disgusting slimy tomato slices?"

"Plain and simple," her mom assures her.

They're still holding hands. Lee gives Frankie's hand a squeeze and lets it go.

"Have a fun afternoon, sweetheart," she says. "I'll see you back home at six."

The two of them hug, tightly, and I experience a sudden

stab of jealousy. Frankie's obviously made up with her mom, and I'm glad for her. But at the same time, having a difficult relationship with a parent was something we had in common. Now we don't, and I feel the gap. And I don't want any more gaps to appear in our relationship.

Yeah, I know, I'm being selfish. I should not make this about me. But for the first time, I realize exactly how important it is for me to be with Frankie. It's no exaggeration to say that I really don't think I can live without her.

I hold the door open for Frankie, and as she walks through, I instinctively and somewhat possessively put my arm around her. She gives me a surprised, amused look but doesn't object. We walk out of the hospital without speaking, and when we arrive at her car, I hand her the keys.

"I didn't break it," I say.

"Good to hear," she replies.

We get into the car and she re-adjusts the driver's seat and rear-view mirror. She seems only partially present, and my anxiety starts my heart pounding. My brain knows I'm being a huge baby, but these feelings are strong. I've been sensitive to rejection all my life and that's not something you get over in a day.

"Good breakfast with your Mom, then?"

I didn't mean to sound snippy but that's how it comes out.

As it happens, Frankie doesn't seem to notice.

"Breakfast was terrible," she says, then smiles fondly. "But after that, things definitely improved."

I wait for her to elaborate, but she doesn't. Just smiles at the road. I know that if I speak again, I'll sound like a sulky boy, so I do myself a favor and keep quiet. Put my poker face on and sulk inwardly for the whole half hour drive to the craft beer place.

There's a free spot next to my car, so Frankie pulls into it. Keeps her engine running while I get out. I wait for her to say something, until it becomes obvious that I'll have to speak first.

"Meet you back at mine?" I ask.

"Actually, I might go home," she says. "Hang out with Mom a bit more, if that's okay?"

Fuck. But I can hardly complain without sounding like a selfish asshole. I compromise with a small guilt trip instead.

"There's a six-pack of beer in the trunk," I tell her. "To say thanks for lending me your car."

Frankie's eyes widen. "Oh, shit," she says. "I forgot all about Iris's pie!"

Not a clue what she's talking about, Though, come to think about it, there was a takeout box in the trunk already when I loaded up the beer.

"Ugh," she says. "That pie is going to be rank." She shrugs. "Oh, well. Ham and Luke will eat it. They love Iris's scraps."

She puts the car in gear. "Bye," she says, with a wave. "See you at dinner!"

The parking lot is gravel and I'm left literally in the dust. I am this close to heading back into the craft beer place and drinking myself under a hand-adzed wooden table. But then I'd have to leave my car here yet again, and it's already outstayed its welcome. I have no choice but to head back to my tiny, empty house, and be by my sad lonesome self for the rest of this shitty old day.

Chapter Forty-Nine

FRANKIE

Now, I know exactly what people mean by the phrase "floating on air". I feel light as a balloon, bobbing high above the trees. I'm usually such a practical grounded person that I've no idea how I'm supposed to react. So I don't. I let the feeling wash through me and go with its flow.

I thought I'd be more resistant to Mom's appeal for forgiveness. I thought it would take me ages to trust her. But as soon as she apologized, the pain in my heart and all my doubts vanished like they'd never existed. Weird, but I'll take it.

I drove Danny to his car in a kind of happy daze, and though I could see he was disappointed that I chose not to go to his place, he'll forgive me. It's only one afternoon. Tomorrow, the working week starts again and he and I will have to push on with organizing the crush. And Mom will want to spend her time helping Nate prepare for the new baby. Mom's an artist, and there's nothing she'll love more than to decorate the baby's room. I foresee a lot of dolphin murals and crystals in that child's future.

Back home, I hold the takeout box well out in front of me and turn my head away as I dump Iris's pie in the pig pen. I do not want to see how gross it is. Ham and Luke squeal with delight and I leave them to it. Shove the gross box in the trash – ugh – and decide I need a shower.

After a thorough scrub-down, I put on my prettiest vintage sundress, candy pink with big white polka dots. It has a stiff skirt over a bunch of cotton petticoats so it's not super practical for everyday wear, but too bad. I'm feeling happy and it's a happy dress. I bounce downstairs to wait for Mom and Nate.

Don't have to wait long. Mom is surprised to see me, but happy, too.

"What a gorgeous dress, Frankie," she says, giving me a kiss. "I still have no idea where you got your fashion sense from. There's certainly none in the rest of our family."

It's true. Mom always looks great but that's because she's a beautiful, slender redhead. Her choice of clothing is much like Shelby's – jeans, old shirts, even older cowboy boots. If Mom could live in her artist's overalls, she probably would. My brothers also favor practicality over style, though Tyler will occasionally go crazy with a pair of bright-colored Adidas Gazelles and contrasting socks. I'm the only one of us who was ever interested in dressing up. Freud probably had something to say about that, but I do not care to hear it.

"Anyone for a beer or a glass of wine?" says Nate. "Sun's not quite over the yardarm, but what the hell."

"Sure!" I say. "Beer for me."

"Danny not around?" Nate asks, and I have a small pang of guilt.

"Um, no," I reply. "I'll text him to come over, shall I?"

I fire off a quick text, and look up to find Mom staring at me, mildly quizzical. The guilt pang returns, and I feel a need to explain myself.

"I wanted to hang out with you this afternoon," I tell Mom. "Figured we'd both be super busy next week."

"That's lovely of you," she says. "I appreciate it."

I sense a dreaded "but" hanging in the air. Seems it's only in my imagination, though, as Mom doesn't say another word. Nate hands her a glass of red wine, and me a beer. He's also poured himself a generous glass of red, which he raises up in a toast.

"Here's to all of us," he says. "May we keep a hold on our sanity, and … nope, that's it."

"To our sanity!" Mom and I chorus and laugh.

I check my phone, but Danny hasn't responded. I suppose he didn't need to; he's probably on his way. I set my phone aside, and drink and chat with Nate and Mom, until Mom says, "I should get started with making dinner."

Well-brought-up Nate says, "How can I help?" But Mom shakes her head. "You sit there," she says. "I'm only cooking for four, not a ravening horde."

"Mom used to cater for the harvest and crush all by herself," I tell Nate. "Us kids were in charge of table setting and doing the dishes afterwards. You can imagine how smoothly that went. No arguments at all."

Nate grins. "We had a dishwasher but Mom always insisted we hand wash her cast iron pots, and her good china, and the silverware. If Ava was on drying duty, she'd minutely inspect every item and drop it back in the sink if there was even a speck of food on it. Danny came *this* close to stabbing her with a fish knife once. I had to wrestle it off him."

Another pang. This time an anxious one. Where *is* Danny? He should be here by now.

At that exact moment, Nate's phone buzzes with a text. He reads it, sends a quick text back.

"Only three of us for dinner, Lee," he tells Mom. "Danny's got some business deal going down."

"On a Sunday evening?" I say, more harshly than I intended.

Nate shrugs. "The world of car traders is foreign to me. No idea what hours they keep."

"You could take him some leftovers, Frankie?" Mom says. "After we've eaten?"

My first response is that Danny doesn't deserve them. He should *be* here! But that's me being childish and I'm not entirely sure why. I suspect it's because I resent him taking a little shine off a day that I'd decided was perfect. That's not his fault in the slightest. I need to suck it up and deal.

Mom serves up dinner. It's delicious. We all have seconds. Well, I don't have seconds of the salad, but I didn't have firsts of it, either. There's still a good big portion of mac 'n' cheese left. Damn it. I will take it over to Danny.

"I'll cover it in foil, so it stays warm," says Mom. Shelby's right, she is a witch.

Standing outside Danny's door, wearing my pink polka-dot dress and holding a casserole dish, I realize I am a living McCall's magazine advertisement. I feel like I ought to walk inside and make Danny a martini.

He must have heard my car pull up, but then again, he

might still be on the phone. It's okay, I'll wait. It's a beautiful warm evening. Birds I cannot identify are still chirping loudly in the trees.

Danny opens his door, phone in his hand. Looks surprised to see me, and not necessarily in a good way.

"I bring food," I say. "And greetings from the 1950s."

Finally, he smiles. I am stupidly relieved.

"That is fucking adorable," he says. "Come inside. I'm still on a call but shouldn't be too much longer. You can fetch my pipe and slippers while you're waiting."

He unmutes his call. "Sorry," he says to whoever. "You were saying?"

I set the dish on the kitchen counter. Danny's pacing the small living area, nodding and saying, "Uh huh" and "Sure", so I can't tell for the life of me what the conversation is about. Danny normally has a pretty high energy level but it's dialed all the way up to eleven right now. This is not an ordinary phone call.

A weird anxiety starts to bug me. I really missed having Danny there at dinner, and it occurs to me that I brushed him off this afternoon without a proper explanation. I created a distance between us too casually, without giving it proper thought, and his absence at dinner brought it home to me that I don't want any distance between us. But that's all I can feel right now. I'm on the outside of this clearly important conversation, and I'm afraid something seismic is about to happen. A shift that could change everything. Maybe I've got a touch of Mom's witchiness? Or maybe I'm just paranoid? I really wish Danny would end this call soon and put me out of my misery.

He ends the call. Stands there, staring at his blank phone.

"You sell a Lamborghini this time?" I have to make a joke. I'm dying here.

Danny turns to me, blinks a couple of times, like he's trying to reboot his brain.

"That … was the producer I told you about…"

A look of utter incredulity comes over his face.

"Holy shit, Frankie!" he says. "I'm going to be on TV!"

Chapter Fifty

DANNY

Frankie looks like she's shocked to her core but trying desperately to pretend she's okay. I'm not sure what I expected her reaction to be. I'm not even sure I know what *my* reaction is. I guess it's like winning a huge lottery prize. You buy a ticket, never expecting to win, but there's always that tiny bit of hope. Then – boom – you're rich! And everything changes!

Oh, fuck. Guess I know why Frankie looks like that. Everything's changed, and not for the better as far as Frankie's concerned. She doesn't want to be part of this new life.

It was bad enough today when I thought I'd lost her to her mom. But that was temporary childish sulks and this is very real. My excitement gives way to a panicky dread.

"I can pull out," I tell her. "They've only agreed to film a pilot, so—"

"Don't be stupid," says Frankie, roughly. "This is amazing. You'll be great on TV."

I walk towards her, and see her flinch, like she can't bear for me to touch her. She might as well have slapped me across the face for the way it hurts.

"Frankie." I'm pleading and I don't care. "This is not as important to me as you are. It is *not*. Can you please believe me?"

Her mouth is trembling, like she's doing her utmost not to cry. Or yell.

"But it *is* important," she says. "It's a huge, big deal. It's not something you should give up just like that." She snaps her fingers. "You'd regret it for the rest of your life."

She blows out a ragged breath, turns her head away. I sense it's vital that I keep my mouth shut right now. Besides, I've no clue what to say.

When she turns to look at me again, her expression is calm. Too calm.

"I brought you my mom's mac 'n' cheese," she says. "You should eat it before it gets cold."

"Fuck the mac 'n' cheese, Frankie." I am very far from calm. "Can we talk about this? *Please*?"

"No," she says, instantly. I see her mouth tremble again, just for a second, and then she throws up her hands, as if warding me off. "I'm sorry, Danny. I can't. Not right now. Tomorrow, maybe…"

And before I can do or say anything to stop her, Frankie dashes out the door and slams it behind her.

Fuck. Ten minutes ago, I left like the luckiest guy on earth. Now, it looks as if every good thing in my life has to come with a price.

I try to tell myself that Frankie just needs time to process, and that she hasn't made any kind of decision yet. But my brain's having none of it. All I can feel is an overwhelming sense of, yet again, having failed. I can hear my dad telling me how disappointed he is that my shallow, ego-driven pursuit of minor celebrity has cost me something real and special. Yep, those would be my dad's exact words: "shallow and ego-driven" and the absolute kicker "minor" celebrity. Mom would be kinder but she'd still sigh in that way that shows she'd hoped for better from me.

Shit, Danny. Get a grip. If you convince yourself the worst is going to happen, it probably will. Get through tonight and things will look better in the morning. In the meantime, eat the fucking mac 'n' cheese.

I eat the fucking mac 'n' cheese. Straight out of the casserole dish. It's delicious and I resent every bite because Frankie's not here with me, wearing that goddamn adorable dress. I wanted her to take off that goddamn adorable dress and stand in front of me looking goddamn adorably naked. I very much wanted us to do what I'm picturing right now, and I wish I'd bought beer for myself as well as Frankie, because getting blazed into a stupor seems to be the only way for me to stop thinking about her.

I could text her. To let her know that I'm thinking about her…

As if reading my mind, my phone pings, and I grab it, hoping like hell it's a text from Frankie to says she's changed her mind and is coming right back over.

It's an email from my producer guy, subject line: *We did it!* I sit and stare at those words, and let their meaning sink in.

Yeah, we did, damn it. And Frankie's right: it *is* important. It *is* a big deal, and I should be proud that I made it happen.

This will be my show, where I get a chance to share my expertise with the world. It will not be shallow or ego-driven. Okay, maybe a little ego-driven, but in a good way. I'll get to talk about my passion, and what I really care about.

Thing is, I really care about Frankie, too. And it goddamn unadorably sucks that I might not be able to have both.

Chapter Fifty-One

FRANKIE

I wait in the darkness of the trees at the end of the path until I feel composed enough to go back in the house, and face Nate and my mom. Mom will pick up immediately if things are off with me, so I need to make sure I give nothing away. Luckily, I haven't cried, so I won't look red-eyed and tear-stained. And I've come up with a plausible cover story for why I'm back so quickly: Danny was indeed working on a deal, and so I decided to leave him to it.

As it happens, all my prep is unnecessary. Mom has already gone up to bed, and Nate is too preoccupied to pay me much attention. I sit down to watch TV but soon as I switch it on, up comes an ad for a cooking show featuring a handsome, young blond guy. I switch it right off again and head upstairs to lie on my bed, still in my stiff-skirted dress because I can't be bothered taking it off.

I deserve to feel uncomfortable after how I behaved. I should never have run out on Danny like that. No matter how much his news threw me, I should have sucked it up and celebrated with him. Instead, I ruined it by being selfish. By focusing on how it made me feel.

Which was terrified. That one piece of news triggered all my fears and anxieties, and they came rushing over me in a giant horrific wave.

All I could think about was the publicity Danny and his new show would get. The media attention, the photos. All that scrutiny, of everything about him and his life. Because there I'd be for all to see. The fat girlfriend. The one who doesn't deserve a handsome guy like that. The one from the wrong side of the tracks, who went to community college. A total outsider in the world of the wealthy. She's nobody and nothing, and she's overweight to boot. Why *her* when rich, handsome Danny Durant could have his pick? He should be embarrassed by her.

I could hear all the cruel comments, every single one. The kind I read too many times online about other women. Okay, so I'm no stranger to unkind comments on the dating apps, but in this situation, comments about me will also be about Danny. And no matter how much he seems to care about me, he'll also now have a public image, and he might start to care about how his choice in girlfriend reflects on that.

Speculation, not facts, Frankie. Do you really believe Danny would care that much about his image? Or is this you employing your usual tactic of finding excuses to back away, so you don't get hurt? He said the TV show wasn't as important to him as you, so why can't you trust that he means it? You can't see into the future. No matter how convincing a picture you paint, you can't know what it will really be like. The only way you'll know what happens is to witness it — either from a distance or right there beside Danny.

That's your choice, isn't it, Frankie, my girl? Back away or be there…

I could text him. Say sorry. Promise that we will talk tomorrow.

But then he'll call me and we'll have to talk right now, and I'm just not ready. My thoughts aren't straight. My thoughts are, in fact, like cooked spaghetti that's been left too long in the colander and become one giant congealed knot. Tangled up in there is more than fear of becoming a target for trolls. There's the fear of leaving behind my old, safe, familiar life and starting a whole new one in a strange place. The fear of leaping too quickly into a commitment and finding I've made a mistake. The fear of losing my independence and identity. And all that's fighting with the fact that I care about Danny. I care very much. I hate the idea of not having him in my life.

Back away or be there — that's my choice. Better make it soon, because Danny and I don't have much more time together. Shelby and Nate's baby is coming on Friday, whether we're ready or not.

Chapter Fifty-Two

DANNY

I think about skipping breakfast with Nate, Frankie, and her mom, so I can spend more time getting my thoughts in order. But I'm here to help Nate and he needs me now more than ever. So, I square my shoulders and stroll into the kitchen as nonchalantly as I can. I needn't have worried. Nate's the only one there.

"You okay?" he says, with a frown.

"Yes. Why?" I reply, immediately on the defensive.

"You're walking weirdly," he says. "Been practicing your Lindy Hop moves in between peddling jalopies?"

"I am not walking weirdly!" I protest. "This is a perfectly normal casual saunter!"

"Uh-huh," says Nate, with a skeptical lift of his eyebrows.

Before I can saunter over to give him a dead arm, Frankie's mom comes in through the back door. I catch the sound of enthusiastic kibble-crunching from the porch. She's fed the dogs.

"Danny, good morning," she says, with a smile. "Did your business calls go well?"

"Thank you, Lee, they did," I say, with dignity and a side-eye glare at Nate. "And thank you for dinner. It was much appreciated."

"My pleasure." Lee still looks a little weary. "What would you both like for breakfast?"

"I'll make breakfast, Mom."

It's Frankie. Looking sweet and fresh in a peach-colored cotton blouse and cropped jeans. I want to be with her so badly, I only just manage to stop myself pulling her into my arms. I settle for a hopeful smile, and to my huge relief, she gives me a quick smile back. It's only a fraction of what I want, but right now, I'll take what I can get.

"Pancakes alright?" she asks us.

Nate and I vote with a resounding yes.

"Mom?" Frankie double-checks and I remember that Lee's not a fan of refined flour and sugar.

"Why not?" she says. "Thank you, sweetheart."

Frankie gives her mom the same quick smile she gave me. Not that I'm comparing or anything. No, sir.

"I'll make coffee," I say. No need to consult. I'm the only one who'll drink it.

Of course, I also want the excuse to be close to Frankie. She's busy assembling all the ingredients for pancakes, and I don't like to interrupt her because despite eating all the mac 'n' cheese last night, I'm hungry. I grab the ground coffee and do my thing over by the sink. Try to time my move to the stove to coincide with hers, without being too obvious about it.

"If that thing explodes, you'll be the one wiping pancake mix off the ceiling," Frankie says.

It's not a declaration of undying affection, but as I said, I'll take what I can get.

"This thing has made it through snow, rain, heat, and gloom of night." I give the coffeepot lid an affectionate pat. "Nothing will stay it from its appointed round."

Frankie's response is to flip a pancake. She's focused, and I, for one, am going to back away and let her get on with it. I'm starving, and luckily, still young enough to metabolize a towering stack of carbs.

Lee and Nate are seated at the table, chatting quietly. Nate's phone pings. Normally, he wouldn't have it with him at the table, but these are exceptional times. He reads the message with a frown, and I can see Lee's face grow taut with worry.

Nate sees that, too, when he looks up, and makes an apologetic face.

"Cam," he explains. "He and Javi have been out checking the vines and they feel strongly that we need to harvest as soon as possible. Like, tonight."

"How can they be so sure?" I ask.

"They can't," says Nate. "But then, no one can be, not a hundred percent. Yesterday's test came back with a pretty ideal balance of sugars, pH and acidity, but there's no rain forecast and Shel's keen to give the grapes more hang time. The risk then is that the tannins won't have the same opportunity to develop, which means the wine won't age as well. But Flora Valley wines have always prioritized drinkability over aging, so I guess it makes sense…"

"What does *your* instinct tell you?" says Lee.

Nate shakes his head. "Honestly? My brain is too fried right now. I trust Cam and Javi's judgement, but I trust Shelby's too." He shrugs. "I don't know."

"Shel wants to put off the harvest until after the baby." Frankie offers her opinion from the stove. "Whereas I think it would be way better for everyone if she didn't try to oversee it with a newborn. Especially a newborn that might have to be in the neonatal ward."

There follows the kind of pause that always comes after someone has hit the nail right on the head.

"I'll text Cam," says Nate. "And I'll break it gently to Shelby when I see her today."

"I'll back you up," says Lee. She lets out a breath. "And I suppose I'd better start preparing food for the harvest crew."

"Let me help with that," I say, and when Lee looks surprised, add, "I'm a handy cook."

"He is," confirms Nate, and to me, says, "You realize it'll be an all-night harvest?"

"I can go all night, bro, don't you worry." I wink and enjoy his pained expression.

The coffee pot announces that it's ready with a strangled hiss of steam. I go to take it off the stove and catch Frankie's eye.

"Good thing I made a heap of pancakes," she says. "We're going to need all the energy we can get. Harvesting is hard work."

"I'm kind of looking forward to it," I say, quietly, so only she can hear. "Picking grapes next to you under the moonlight."

Frankie tries to give me a stern look but a smile escapes,

nonetheless. "You're the world's most ridiculous optimist, you know that?"

"Guilty as charged," I say with a grin, and raise my mug of coffee to her in a toast.

"Are you going to tell them?" she says, even more quietly. "About the TV show?"

"Later," I say. "There's more than enough going on for us all right now. I can wait."

Frankie stares at me. This time, her expression stays serious. "I am working on it," she says. "I can't give you anything more than that right now."

A part of me wants to plead with her to at least give me a hint about where her thoughts are at. I don't need to know specifics, just a general sense that – you know – everything's going to be okay. But rational me knows that would be counterproductive. I'll need to be patient about a lot of things, it seems.

"You can give me pancakes," I tell her. "And you can definitely give me more than Nate."

"I heard that!" Nate calls from the table. "Do not give him more pancakes than me, Frankie!"

Frankie laughs and shakes her head. "You can both come and get your own pancakes! *After* I've served up mine and Mom's!"

She hooshes me with her hand. "Scoot. Your turn will come."

And because I am a ridiculous optimist, I choose to interpret that in the most positive way.

Chapter Fifty-Three

FRANKIE

Javi has us all lined up like we're soldiers about to go on a route march. Which is how we'll feel after a long night of hand picking. Not every vineyard harvests at night, but when the days are hot and long, the cool of night is easier on workers, and better for the grapes. Dad always preferred it, and Shelby and Nate have kept up the practice. We get bright lights brought in, and work our way down the vines, snipping off bunches and placing them carefully in baskets. When the baskets are full, we lug them down to empty them in the bigger containers at the end of the vines. When those are full, one of Javi's team takes them away on a tractor and loads them onto the truck that'll transport them to the winery. The grapes spend time in their skins before they're crushed – the next big day on our calendar. But let's get this one over with first.

I remember the last time I picked grapes for Dad. Shelby and I were the only Armstrong kids on the crew. Our older brothers, Jackson and Tyler, had other commitments, namely full-time jobs in different states. I envied them. I was about to start community college, and I remember cursing the fact that the year didn't begin before harvest. I'm no shirker, so I put my back into the picking, but I resented every minute of it.

Looking back, I wish I'd chosen better. Dad and Mom always made harvest a fun time, with a lot of laughter, spurred on by Dad's bad jokes and his irrepressible positivity. He was probably worrying how the hell we'd pay all the workers who weren't family, but he never let on. And Mom was always right there, feeding us tasty snacks, keeping us hydrated. She'd cook up a feast for the after-harvest breakfast. Javi always recruited people who were great to be around. I could have enjoyed myself, but I chose not to. What a pain in the ass I was back then. Sorry, fam.

Tonight, I'm here with Cam, Doug, Javi's team, and Danny. Nate's been put under house arrest, as Danny calls it. Shelby may have a cesarean planned but babies notoriously do not give a shit what your plans are, so Nate has to stay home, just in case. Mom's been given a reprieve, too. She and Danny shopped for the food, but seeing how tired Mom still was, Danny gave Javi a call, and his wife, Valentina, has taken charge of our kitchen. If you think Javi runs the harvest like a military operation, you should see Valentina in action. Like a whirlwind with knives. Mom and Nate are hiding out in the rest of the house. Even Ava is too scared to pop in and see how it's going.

Javi's finished his pep talk, which is basically a list of what not to do or else. Like I said, Javi isn't a big guy but you'd never cross him. We start to make our way down the vines, and I feel strangely pleased when I realize I know exactly what I'm doing. After an eight-year break, I thought I'd be rusty, but it's all coming back. The feel of the grape bunches in my hand, silky and heavy. The clean snip of the shears. The satisfaction of removing any rotten fruit or insects before I place the bunches in the basket. The musty smell of ripe grapes, earth and leaves, and the bite of cooler air on my face as the night settles in. The sky above is clear and every time I glance at it, more stars have appeared, like someone's up there shaking cosmic salt.

We work one side of the vine rows each. I'm back to back with Cam, whose slow, steady pace is exactly right for this job. Over the other side of me is Danny. The vines are too tall for us to see over the top, but we catch glimpses of each other through the leaves. Mostly, I see Danny frowning with concentration. Probably because he's back to back with Javi, who has eagle eyes, and Danny does not want to make a mistake.

I should let him focus, but instead, I hiss through the gap, "Are you getting the hang of it?"

"Shit!" I make him jump, and his hand holding the shears darts forward. Luckily, not too far, or I might have been stabbed through the heart.

"Uh, I think so," he says, when he recovers. "These purply round things are grapes, right?"

"Funny." I see his teeth flash white in a grin. "Are you remembering to pick out the bad ones?"

"The bad ones? What did they do? Mug an old lady?"

"Wow, you're on fire tonight," I say. "Thought my dad told the worst jokes, but yours are right up there."

"I will treasure that compliment," says Danny. "How bad, exactly, were your dad's jokes?"

Javi, who has lynx ears as well as eagle eyes, turns around, grinning. "What did the grape say when it was squashed?"

The night is so quiet that everyone hears him.

"Nothing!" replies a chorus that includes me. "It just gave out a little whine!"

"That", says Danny, bemused, "is truly terrible."

A few rows over, Doug joins in with, "What did the green grape say to the purple grape?"

"I'm scared to guess!" calls Danny.

"Stop holding your breath!" comes the chorus.

"Okay, so I've died and gone to joke hell," says Danny.

"Why did the grape go out with a pineapple?" This is my contribution.

"IT COULDN'T FIND A DATE!"

"Please make it stop," Danny mock-whimpers.

"Right." Javi claps his hands. "*Todos*. Back to work. We're making Danny cry."

We all get back to work. But I'm acutely aware of Danny on the other side of the vines from me, and it's all I can do not to keep talking to him. Ironic, I know, considering I'm the one who refused to have a conversation with him yesterday. It's as if being here again, working in the vines, has brought what's important to me into sudden sharp focus, and I want to tell Danny all about it. I want to tell him that I've realized that my choices in life might have been actually counter to what I needed. I chose distance and independence, and while it was good for me to learn how to stand on my own two feet, I missed out on eight years of connection, to my home, my family, and my community. Connection to this place, and these people all around me. I want to tell him that maybe, just maybe, it's time for me to come back home.

And that, of course, clashes with the other thing I want – which is Danny. I cannot let my life be ruled by my fears. I can't keep running away from things just because I think it'll make me feel safe. It never does make me feel safe, because wherever I go, there I am, and all my fears and anxieties are right there along with me. I want to see if Danny and I can make a future together, but his life, his business, his brand-new career on TV, they're all in L.A. He can't leave and I won't ask him to. It would be hugely unfair to put that kind of pressure on him.

Argh! I have so much I want to talk to him about! But of course, I couldn't have chosen a worse time to feel chatty. Unless I want the whole harvest crew to share their opinions with us. Which, amazingly, I don't.

Danny starts humming a song. Can't tell what it is. But Javi obviously knows because he joins in. Oh, right. It's "Patience" by Guns N' Roses. Either Danny is psychic or the universe is sending me another message, this time via the medium of a gritty hard rock band in acoustic ballad mode.

Now pretty much everyone's joined in. I turn to check if Cam is also quietly humming away, only to find him staring back at me, with a quizzical look.

"Not a GNR fan?" I ask him.

"Can't hold a tune," he says. "That gene passed me by."

"Same. I can dance, but do not ask me to sing."

Cam stares a moment longer. "Are we … okay? You and me?"

I realize he and I haven't really spoken since his apology.

And that I also never thanked him properly for helping me through my panic attack on that truck ride with Mom. I've had a lot going on, but still. *Do better, Frankie.*

"We're good, Cam," I say. "I'm sorry it took so long for us to get there."

"Me, too," he says.

Neither of us being a super huggy person, we just nod at each other and get back to work. But I'm smiling. It feels good to be friends with Cam. Even if all we ever do again is nod at each other when we pass by, it'll be a friendly nod.

"Psst!" It's Danny.

"What?"

"Hear that?"

I listen. All I can hear is quiet shuffling and snipping. Wait, is that a distant hoot?

"It's a great horned owl, I'm pretty sure," says Danny. "Beautiful birds."

His voice has a hint of awe in it. He genuinely does love our feathered friends. Which is really kind of cool.

Damn it. I don't care if this is a terrible time. If I don't say something to him, I'm going to burst like an overripe grape.

"Danny," I say, very quietly. "I want to make you and me work so badly, but I don't know how."

For a moment, there's no response. Then I hear, also very quietly, "I can't shout '*Yes!*' out loud, can I? Because then everyone will want to know our business."

"They totally will."

"And we don't want anyone to know until we've figured this out, right?"

"Definitely."

"And we will figure it out because I love you and you love me, right?"

"..."

"Frankie?"

"Yes," I say. "Yes, Danny, I love you. I love you so, *so* much!"

Guess I forgot to be quiet.

"*¡Estupendo!*" Javi claps his hands and shouts, "Love is in the air for Danny and Frankie, everyone!"

There's a chorus of cheers and congratulations, until Javi claps again. It echoes like a gunshot, and everyone immediately shuts up.

"*¡Ya basta!* Enough!" orders Javi. "Back to work!"

A moment later, I hear a quiet voice through the vines. "Love you, too, Frankie. All the way to that big ol' moon and back."

And I work the rest of the night in a smiling, rose-tinted, blissful, love-filled daze.

Chapter Fifty-Four

DANNY

All I want to do is get Frankie alone, and not for the reason you might expect, given it's me. I want to hear her say she loves me again, and possibly a hundred more times just to make sure. I want to tell her the same, at least a hundred times, and let her know that I'd do whatever it takes for us to be together. Even give up the TV show, if that's what she wants. I'm pretty sure she'd never ask that of me, but I'd do it in a heartbeat if it was going to be any kind of barrier. I'd even move to San Diego – it's not that far from L.A. Three hours' drive max. And San Diego has the Air and Space Museum. Who doesn't love an educational science experience?

I want to tell her all this, and so much more, but we're surrounded by people, all packed in tight around Shelby and Nate's big kitchen table. Javi's wife, Valentina, has put on a post-harvest breakfast spread that would fell an army of elephants, and she's given us all the clear message that if we don't eat every bite, we'll feel her wrath. And I thought Javi was scary.

Despite it only being five thirty in the morning, Nate, Lee, and Ava have all come to join us. And, of course, the whole harvest crew immediately blabs to them about Frankie and me being officially *enamorado*.

Ava's reaction is, "Amazing. I never thought Danny would fall for a woman with an actual brain."

"Insult!" I point an accusing finger. "Name in the jar, Ava!"

Before anyone can protest, I fetch it and present it to her along with a slip of paper and a pen.

"How many have I got in here now?" she asks. "Three to your one! Oh dear. Danny can't even win at insults."

"That's four!" I insist. "I am going to have so much fun picking your punishment."

"You know I'll get my own back," says Ava, with an evil grin. "One day, when you least expect it…" She mimes giving me a snake bite arm burn.

"*¡Cállate!*" says Valentina, in a voice that will not be disobeyed. "Your mouths are for eating, not childish bickering!"

I sit back down next to Frankie, whose shoulders are shaking with silent laughter.

"I let Ava get to me again, didn't I?" I murmur to her.

"It's like she doesn't even have to try," agrees Frankie. "It's okay. I have siblings, too. If Jackson was here, I'd probably have already thrown an empanada at him."

"I love you," I say, quietly. "When can we talk?"

"After breakfast," she says. "But I might need a quick nap beforehand."

"We can nap together?" I suggest. "Though perhaps 'nap' isn't the word I'm thinking of…"

Frankie elbows me in the ribs.

My "Ouch!" receives another glare from Valentina. I settle down, drink the coffee that's tasty but nowhere near as potent as Shelby's. Mind you, anything more potent and you'd never sleep again.

Finally, breakfast is over. Frankie's mom and Nate offer to help Valentina clear up but she waves them away. All the harvest crew are drifting out the door now, yawning but still chatting away. Cam wraps his arm around Ava, and they're gone, too.

"You two should get some rest," Frankie's mom says to us. "Would you like some of my herbal tea to help you wind down?"

"No, that's okay, Mom," says Frankie, hastily. "I couldn't honestly eat or drink a thing more."

Nate's phone pings. "Shelby," he says with a smile. "Demanding to know how the harvest went and, more importantly, that I bring her some of Valentina's leftovers."

He calls her. "Hey, gorgeous, how are you?"

My older brother has what I call resting granite face, stern and reserved like our dad's. But as he wanders out of the room, talking to Shelby, his face is alive, lit up by love and affection. It suits him. I kind of wish I could see that expression on my dad's face, too, when he talks to me…

I feel a hand slip into mine. "Want to go?" says Frankie.

I'm about to say, "How fast can we walk?" when my phone starts ringing.

"It's my mom," I tell Frankie. "I'd better take it. In case something's wrong."

"Of course," she says.

"Mom? Everything okay?"

"Everything's fine, dear," Mom assures me. "Are you free to come round this afternoon? I think your father would like to talk to you about…"

She pauses and my mind churns through a million possibilities, not one of which sounds like a fun time.

"About *what*, Mom?"

"Well, perhaps I shouldn't say anything more," is her reply. "I'll leave that up to your father."

Jesus. Is he going to finally disown me? Okay, I am not facing this alone.

"Mom, I'll bring Frankie with me."

I feel the burn of Frankie's glare, but I'm a desperate man. I'll make it up to her later.

"Oh! Yes, that would be lovely," says my surprised but ever-gracious mom. "Shall we say three o'clock?"

"Three it is. See you then, Mom." I end the call.

"What did you just do, Danny?" Frankie's voice is low and threatening.

"Dad wants to talk," I tell her. "I don't know about what but I can't imagine it's anything good. Sorry for roping you in but I could really do with the support."

She nods her understanding. "Okay. Then I'm definitely going to need a nap, or I'll be super cranky."

"And by 'nap', you mean…?"

"I mean if Lil Danny wakes me up before I'm ready, I won't be answerable for my actions."

"Got it," I say on behalf of Lil Danny and also my now shrunken balls. "Let's go get some rest."

Kiss My Glass

I set my alarm for one o'clock in the afternoon, to give us time to get ready before we hit the road. With Frankie lying naked beside me, I expect not to sleep at all but as soon as my head hits the pillow, I'm out, until the alarm jangles us both awake. Frankie has her just-woken-up face on, so I don't suggest a quickie. We both shower and dress, and then it's time to go.

Soon as I shut the car door, I let out a sigh. "I had better plans for this afternoon, you know?"

Frankie gives my knee a squeeze. "I know."

I lean over and we kiss, and I seriously consider ditching my parents, but Frankie breaks us apart.

"Sooner we get there, sooner we can get back here" are her words of wisdom.

We hit the road, and far too soon are at my family home. It's the first time Frankie has been here, and I'm a little anxious at what her reaction will be.

As it happens, it's not what I expect. "This is nice," she says, as we pull up outside the house. "I'd imagined something way more insufferably swanky. But it looks really homey."

She turns to me. "You being rich makes me uncomfortable. Stupid, I know, but there it is."

"Technically, I'm only moderately well-off," I say. "Like I said, Dad's made it clear to all of us that there'll be no handouts, ever."

Frankie frowns, like she's only now processing that information. "Not even if you were about to go bankrupt?"

I shake my head. "Not even then."

"Huh," says Frankie. "Your dad's kind of a hard ass, isn't he?"

"And on that note," I say. "It's time to find out what His Hard Ass-ship has to say to me."

Mom greets Frankie with a kiss on the cheek and a genuinely pleased smile. Mom likes Frankie. I'm glad at least one of my parents approves.

"I thought we'd have afternoon tea in the garden," Mom says. "Come through. Mitchell is there already."

Dad is seated but rises as we approach. Takes Frankie's outstretched hand and gives it a firm shake. No smile, but then we weren't expecting miracles.

"I trust the harvest went well, Miss Armstrong," he says, as we all take our seats.

"Very well, sir," says Frankie politely.

She is way more composed than I am. I'm dying to grab my father and demand he tell me what's on his mind. But that would be extremely counterproductive. No Durant likes being backed into a corner. Besides, seems Dad hasn't finished interrogating Frankie.

"And once the baby is born, how long do you intend to stay? I assume you've not taken indefinite leave from your job?"

"I haven't," says Frankie. "But I'm not sure I'll return to my law firm." She hesitates ever so slightly. "I'm considering moving to L.A. to be with Danny."

"You are?" I can feel my eyes bugging out of my head. "Seriously? You'd leave San Diego?"

Her amazing blue eyes are clear and sincere. "I don't want a long-distance romance," she says. "And I think I can get a job there pretty easily. But, if it's okay with you"—the slight hesitation is there again—"I'd like to set a deadline of a year. Because I think what I really want is to come back here. Come back home."

I can't stop staring at her, so I have no idea how my parents are reacting to all this.

"What about the TV show?" I have to ask. If we were in a room instead of outdoors, this would be the elephant.

She shrugs likes she's annoyed with herself. "I just got all hung up thinking about what the trolls will say. You know, about your chubby, gold-digging girlfriend…"

Okay. Now I understand.

"Fuck those people, Frankie," I say, with all the intensity I can muster. I hear my mom suck in a breath but I do not care. "Anyone who talks like that is either a moron or fucked up and evil, and whatever they are, they don't deserve a second of our attention. And besides, I…"

She notes my sudden pause and looks at me with deep suspicion. Which in this case is entirely justified.

"What did you do, Danny?"

"Um… I might have sent the production team a photo of you and me that I took when we went vintage clothes shopping…"

Her gaze could fry an egg. But it's too late now.

"I … uh … thought it was a great photo of me, and you just happened to be in it. And they … uh … they loved it. Loved you and your look. Wondered if you'd consider an audition for—"

"Absolutely not."

"That's what I told them you'd probably say."

"That's what you told them, is it?" Frankie says.

I am that egg. I can smell my extremities sizzling.

"Well, I … uh … wasn't sure, but…"

Thank the lord, the corner of her mouth is twitching. Of course, she might be about to go for my jugular, but I really hope she's finding this funny.

"You're impossible," she says. "Absolutely impossible."

Dad clears his throat. Fair enough. He and Mom have been shut out of this conversation.

"May I ask?" Dad begins. "What is this TV show you're talking about?"

Here we go. I brace for battle.

"Mine," I tell him. "I'll be fronting a reality show about selling classic cars. It's been picked up by Netflix."

"Goodness, Danny!" exclaims Mom. "How wonderful!"

Dad looks as if "wonderful" is the last thing he'd call it.

"Television can be a fickle business with no guarantee of financial reward," he says. "You might even lose money. It sounds to me like a highly risky venture, especially as you have no experience in this area at all."

I expected this kind of response, but I still can feel my whole body getting hot and angry. I need to stay calm, breathe, and not let him get to me.

"Yes, Dad, there's a risk," I say. "There's also a risk I might be hit by a bus tomorrow, or choke to death on a peanut. No decision in life comes without risk, and I've done pretty well so far not playing it too safe. I know you'll never acknowledge that, but it's the truth."

Dad stares at me. Normally, his poker-face is impenetrable,

but right now, I see regret, and what looks like shame. I have the urge to rub my eyes, in case I'm hallucinating.

"Danny, I invited you here to apologize," he says. "And I've ended up falling immediately back into old habits. That was wrong of me."

Apologize? This is definitely a hallucination. No other explanation for it.

"I *do* have your best interests at heart," he goes on. "I want all my children to be safe and well and prosperous. My children and my grandchildren," he adds, with a faint hint of surprise. "I've come to realize, however, that I have no right to dictate your life's path, or to criticize you for making choices that I would not. I've not supported you as I should have, Danny. And for that I'm very sorry."

Holy… I have no words. I'd better find some.

"Thanks, Dad. That means a lot."

He nods. I nod. This could go on for a while.

"Coffee?" says Mom, brightly, before things become super awkward. "I've baked a dark chocolate cake. It's almost sugar-free."

Dad smiles at her. Shit, that's my smile. I've always thought I looked exactly like Mom.

"Ginny, you're a miracle," Dad says.

And then he puts his hand on my shoulder!

"I am a very lucky man."

Chapter Fifty-Five

FRANKIE

I am not a morning person, but waking up next to the man I love feels pretty great. I'm on my side and Danny is spooned against me, fast asleep except for Lil Danny, who's as perky as if he's starring in a breakfast cereal commercial. Which is amazing, considering how many workouts he got last night.

In between, we talked about our plans. I've decided to ask my firm if they can post me to their Reseda office. It's not a bad commute from Santa Monica, according to Danny. I've also decided to keep my house in San Diego. It's the first house I've owned and I'm sentimental about it. I'll rent it out and ask my neighbor to keep an eye on it. That means I'll have to find a rental close to Danny. I could move in with him, but we think it's smarter if we take it slowly. However, I totally intend to take a short-term lease, because neither of us are that patient. I wonder how Danny will feel about me setting up my beer brewing equipment in his garage.

As I reach for my phone to read the time, Danny stirs and

mutters something like, "And that's my final offer." I nudge him because it's past seven, and we have shit to do. It's only a few short days until Shelby's cesarean, and we have to tie up all the details of the crush before then. Danny grunts and scowls, so I put my hand around Lil Danny. It's like one of those videos where an owner places a treat in front of their sleeping cat's or dog's nose and films their reactions as they finally realize it's not a dream and wake with a start.

"Whoa! Wazzup?"

Danny's all wild-eyed and messy-haired.

"We're up." I let go of Lil Danny. "It's after seven and we need our orders from Nate."

"Can we have sex first?" he says.

"No!" I protest. "I'm already at risk of a UTI!"

He starts trailing kisses down my neck and brushes his thumb over my nipples. Ridiculous how his slightest touch can make me instantly damp and insane with lust. Guess I can always buy some cranberry juice.

He focuses entirely on my pleasure, and I come fast and hard. With a shout, Danny joins me, and we collapse into a sweaty mess.

"I love you." Danny's voice is muffled against my chest.

"I love you, too," I reply. "But you still have to get your ass out of bed."

At breakfast, Nate looks stressed. Even when we assure him everything is under control. Which it is, because Danny and I are an awesome team.

By Thursday evening, even though Shelby's her usual, cheerful self, Nate's a wreck. Mom makes him some kind of herbal tea that zonks him out. And then it's Friday morning, the big day, and we're all anxious as cats in a rocking chair factory. Except Mom, of course. I must ask her what's in that tea.

Nate heads off on his own in the pickup. Mom, Danny and I will go in his car.

"No more coffee, Danny!" I insist. "You'll get pulled over for a drug test and you will fail."

"I'm fine," he says, his feet tapping a jig on the floor. "Totally-totally-*totally*-fine—"

"I'll drive." I snatch the keys.

Everyone's at the hospital. Danny's mom and dad, Ava and Cam, Chiara and Jordan, me, Mom, and Danny. Only Nate is allowed in with Shelby. The maternity ward has a family waiting room and it's a good thing no one else is scheduled to give birth this morning because we fill the whole damn place.

"Who wants coffee?" says Ava and starts taking orders.

"None for Danny," I say swiftly, ignoring his scowl. "His heart will explode."

Ava grins. "I'll get him what my dad and your mom are having. Basically, compost in a pot."

"Yum yum," says Danny, sourly, but he goes to help Ava fetch the drinks.

His mom has brought cookies again, and Chiara hands around a box of her dad's cannoli. We're all making small talk and nobody's listening to anyone because we're all vibrating with nerves. This whole room is humming like a hive of anxious bees.

Shelby's cesarean was booked for nine, and it should take no more than an hour. Forty-five minutes in and we're all checking our phones and watches. An hour goes past. An hour ten. Danny's dad is getting restless. He stands up, and I see both Ava and Danny readying to intervene if he starts throwing his weight about.

The door to the waiting room is opened. A nice-looking male nurse smiles in.

"Congratulations," he says. "It's a strong, healthy girl. Six pounds, no need for incubation. Baby and Mom are doing very well. We'll keep them here for another three or four days, then they can go home."

"When can we see them?" Danny's dad, of course.

"Whenever Mom feels ready," says the nurse. "I'd give her at least an hour or so."

Mom. Shelby is a mom. I'm an aunt!

"Holy shit, I'm an uncle," Danny says to me.

We hug each other. Everyone hugs everyone. Danny's dad is the biggest hugger of them all. Danny's mom is tearful, and so is my mom. And Jordan. And *Chiara*. She has an actual heart, who knew?

Danny calls his sister, Izzy, and there is screaming down the phone. He calls Izzy's twin, Max. No screaming, but a lot of happy banter. Ava calls our brother Jackson, who deafens her with a whoop, and I leave a text message for our other brother, Tyler, who I know is in class, teaching. I get a row of thumbs-up emojis immediately in reply. He'd been waiting.

Then, as if on cue, we all sit down again and release a collective whoosh.

"My knees are shaking," says Ava. Cam puts his arm around her and kisses her temple. He's got a huge smile on his face.

"Alright, bets on a name," says Danny, who's also grinning from ear to ear. "I pick Chloe."

"Absolutely not," says Chiara. "I guarantee it'll be Billy. After her dad."

"Oh," gasps Mom. I rush over because she honestly looks like she might faint.

"I'm alright," she tells me. "I just... I didn't see that coming." Mom smiles at Chiara. "Seems I have to hand my witch crown over to you."

Incredibly, Chiara blushes. "I don't know for sure..."

"Oh, yes," says Mom. "There's no doubt."

She's tearful again. And now, I'm crying, damn it.

Jordan hands me a tissue box. "I've already used most of them," she says. "Sorry."

I blow my nose and wipe my face. Give Mom a last hug. Sit back down next to Danny, who wraps his arms round me and holds me tight.

"I love you, Frankie Armstrong," he murmurs. "We're going to spoil that kid rotten, aren't we?"

"I love you, too, Danny Durant," I reply. "We'll be the greatest aunt and uncle a girl can have."

Epilogue

FRANKIE

"My feet are dying! They have frostbite! Why didn't anyone tell me stomping grapes would be this hard? Or this cold?"

"You've been at it for five minutes, Danny!" I laugh. "I used to do it for an hour at a time! When I was only a kid."

"I will have my revenge when we go hiking next weekend," he pants. "Just you wait."

"I'll walk at my own pace, thank you," I remind him. "Besides, don't you want to stop and listen to the birds?"

"Can I stop and listen to the birds now?"

"Nope. You've got another ten minutes to go. Suck it up or be forever branded a giant weenie."

"My legs will be stained red for *weeks*."

"Yes, they will. Badge of honor."

"Isn't this great?" sounds a cheerful voice from the next bin along. Jordan's in tiny shorts and a tinier crop top, and there's a small crowd of men watching her, to which she is oblivious. "I love stomping. Best cardio workout ever."

Jordan has been a regular stomper since she was ten years old. And the only person we know who never gets tired and never complains.

Unlike Chiara, who has never once volunteered and never will. She's sitting with Ted on one of his posh picnic blankets, the both of them beautifully dressed, limbs elegantly arranged. She raises her glass to us. They no doubt sneaked in some champagne. No point in giving her the finger. She does not care.

It's a record crowd at the crush, and we've only had one turkey incident, so I consider that a win. Iris is in her happy place making sandwiches, and the local farmers and Chiara's dad have brought so much food, we'll be sending everyone home with giant doggy bags. I'll keep some aside for Ham and Luke, of course. They're under the watchful eyes of Cam and Ava. Cam is happy to be out of the fray, Ava not so much, but she had the most names in the insult jar, and pig-minding is the punishment Danny chose. Cam and Ava'll join us later, when we feed the stomping crew.

Nate wanders up with Shelby. He has a small bundle in his arms. Little Billy is still in that puckered newborn phase, but to all of us, she is the most beautiful baby in the known universe. And she's a redhead. Not such a surprise given it runs in both families. Izzy and Max arrived last night, thrilled to welcome another member of the redhead club. The twins are both helping Iris make sandwiches, causing more than one person to do a double take.

"Just think," says Nate to Shelby. "Only this time last year, I asked you to marry me. And *now* look at us."

They both smile fondly at the bundle, who doesn't notice owing to being fast asleep.

"Save me, Billy!' Danny reaches out a hand. "I'm too young to die!"

"He's got that natural dramatic ability," Nate remarks to Shelby. "It should transfer well to the small screen."

"How are you doing, Frankie?" my sister asks. "First time stomping for a while!"

"Like riding a bike," I tell her. "By which I mean pedaling it barefoot down a slippery glacier in the sub-Antarctic."

"Take a break!" Shelby insists. "There are plenty of volunteers!"

"I know. I enlisted them."

"You did," says Shelby. "Thank you." She pauses. "I'll miss you when you go to L.A."

I cease stomping and lean on the edge of the bin. "It's not as far away as San Diego, you know."

"I know, but still…"

"We'll be here as often as we can," I promise her. "We take our aunt and uncle-ing duties very seriously."

"You'll have to compete with the grandparent mafia," warns Nate. "You'd think Shelby had given birth to a minor deity rather than a baby."

I spy the three grandparents on another one of Ted's posh blankets. They seem to be getting on famously, though it's hard to tell with Danny's dad.

"Thanksgiving's going to be a riot, isn't it?" I say to no one in particular. "And I'm not even going to think about Christmas."

"Can I stop now?" says Danny. "You have!"

"I paid my stomping dues long ago," I tell him. "But yes, you can stop now."

"Thank you."

Danny climbs out of the bin, slowly, like he's aged fifty years. Hobbles up to my bin and kisses me. Smiles fondly at baby Billy, who's still asleep. Nate and Shelby wander off again towards the grandparents. Must have sensed them getting restless.

"What's the best way to get cleaned up?" Danny asks.

"Hose," I reply, brutally.

"Or—?" Danny lowers his voice and raises a suggestive eyebrow. "We could take a shower together? I could do that thing you like?"

I kiss him, and smile. "If you do that thing and the other thing, you have a deal. And we need to be back for dinner."

"Done," says Danny. "Now, let me help you out of there while you can still walk."

Sign up for Catherine's newsletter and get a FREE bonus epilogue!

Sleigh You Love Me:
A Flora Valley Christmas Story
🖤 🐑 🌲 🐑 🖤

www.catherinejrobertson.com

Acknowledgments

Thank you to Gaia Banks at Sheil Land Associates for championing me at every turn. And to Wendy, Shar, Trudy and Cheryl, the SPA Girls, for monthly pats on the back and kicks up the ~~bum~~ rear end. You keep me going.

The author and One More Chapter would like to thank everyone who contributed to the publication of this story...

Analytics
James Brackin
Abigail Fryer

Audio
Fionnuala Barrett
Ciara Briggs

Contracts
Laura Amos
Laura Evans

Design
Lucy Bennett
Fiona Greenway
Liane Payne
Dean Russell

Digital Sales
Lydia Grainge
Hannah Lismore
Emily Scorer

Editorial
Kara Daniel
Arsalan Isa
Charlotte Ledger
Federica Leonardis
Ajebowale Roberts
Jennie Rothwell
Caroline Scott-Bowden

Harper360
Emily Gerbner
Jean Marie Kelly
emma sullivan
Sophia Wilhelm

International Sales
Peter Borcsok
Ruth Burrow
Colleen Simpson

Marketing & Publicity
Chloe Cummings
Emma Petfield

Operations
Melissa Okusanya
Hannah Stamp

Production
Denis Manson
Simon Moore
Francesca Tuzzeo

Rights
Helena Font Brillas
Ashton Mucha
Zoe Shine
Aisling Smythe

Trade Marketing
Ben Hurd
Eleanor Slater

The HarperCollins Distribution Team

The HarperCollins Finance & Royalties Team

The HarperCollins Legal Team

The HarperCollins Technology Team

UK Sales
Isabel Coburn
Jay Cochrane
Sabina Lewis
Holly Martin
Harriet Williams
Leah Woods

eCommerce
Laura Carpenter
Madeline ODonovan
Charlotte Stevens
Christina Storey
Jo Surman
Rachel Ward

And every other essential link in the chain from delivery drivers to booksellers to librarians and beyond!

Whoever invented love at first sight should have left instructions for what to do when it only strikes one of you...

...is all Ava Durant can think as she watches the man of her dreams from across the room at her brother's wedding. Handyman Cam Hollander takes the "strong, silent type" label to new extremes and getting more than four words at a time out of him is Ava's primary life goal. But when Ava's health takes a hit it's Cam who unexpectedly steps in to nurse her.

Available now in paperback and eBook!

***Could the guy she loves to hate turn out to be
her perfect pairing?***

If Shelby Armstrong wants to keep her late father's beloved Flora Valley Wines in business, she'll have to listen to Nathan Durant's advice. But given the fact that Shelby is all heart and Nate is nothing but tough love, bringing the winery back to life quickly becomes a battle of wills. And yet, Shelby and Nate aren't incompatible in *every* way.

But as is always the case when it comes to love and money, things quickly get complicated…

Available now in paperback and eBook!

ONE MORE CHAPTER

YOUR NUMBER ONE STOP FOR PAGETURNING BOOKS

One More Chapter is an award-winning global division of HarperCollins.

Sign up to our newsletter to get our latest eBook deals and stay up to date with our weekly Book Club!
[Subscribe here.](#)

Meet the team at
www.onemorechapter.com

Follow us!
- @OneMoreChapter_
- @OneMoreChapter
- @onemorechapterhc

Do you write unputdownable fiction?
We love to hear from new voices.
Find out how to submit your novel at
www.onemorechapter.com/submissions